Fate Forever and Always

Danielle Lynn

DANIELLE LYNN BOOKS

Fate forever and Always

Copyright © 2024 by Danielle Lynn

This book is a work of fiction. Any references to events, places, or people are entirely fictional. Some names, characters, places, and events are the products of the author's imagination, and any resemblance to any place or person, living or deceased, is entirely coincidental unless otherwise referenced.

All rights reserved.

No part of this book may be used, including but not limited to the training of or use by artificial intelligence, or reproduced in any form or by any electronic or mechanical means, including information storage and retrieval systems, without written permission from the author, except for the use of brief quotations in a book review.

Book Cover by K.B. Barrett Designs

Editing by E.F Watson

Print ISBN- 979-8-9894147-2-7

Content Warnings

Although my books are on the lighter side, this book and the next will deal with some hard topics. To avoid spoiling a few of the smaller plot lines in this book for those who don't have issues with content, I have listed them on my website, which you can see by scanning the QR code. If you prefer, you can also flip to the back of the book right after the acknowledgments if you need them. (Just beware of spoilers on the last pages, you wouldn't want to see those by mistake.)

Be sure to protect your mental health first. A happy and safe reading experience for you is my priority.

Important Information!

This is book two in a series. Although it is an interconnected stand-alone and can be read independently, you may want to read Fate Will Bring You Home first to get a feel for the relationships and friendships you will see in this book. Seeing their beginnings is always my favorite part. Either way, I hope you enjoy it!

*To the person who wasted too much time in the wrong relationship,
you are worthy of love, care, and happiness.
This one is for you.*

Playlist

**Here are some songs that I listened to while writing this book.
They either stuck out or inspired me.
(NO particular order, but I would love to hear which songs you
thought inspired what parts.)**

The Smallest Man Who Ever Lived- Taylor Swift

I Hope- Gabby Barrett

Narcissist- Lauren Spenser Smith

Can I Be Him- James Arthur

I'll Break My Heart Again-Mimi Web

Rewrite the Stars- Michael Gerow

No Matter What- Jamie Miller

You Were Good to Me- Jeremy Zucker & Chelsea Cutler

Crowded Room- Conor Maynard

Tough- Lewis Capaldi

Hold You 'Til We're Older-Jamie Miller

Leave Me in the Dark-Alexander Stewart

I Think I Fell In Love With My Best Friend- The Change

Falling In Love With My Best Friend- Tyler Ward

I Can't Fall in Love Without You- Zara Larsson

Scared to Be Lonely- Martin Garrix & Dua Lipa

Kiss Me- Ed Sheeran

Mercy- Shawn Mendes

She's the One- Brantley Gilbert

Marry Me- Train

Make You Feel My Love- Adele

Find this playlist on Spotify by scanning the QR code in the About the Author section.

Nick

Prologue

Eighteen Years Old

I think my brain just short-circuited. My best friend just had her tongue down my throat. I was doing everything I could to avoid staring at her like an idiot. I settled for nervously glancing at her, then back at my hands that were awkwardly hovering near her face. Honestly, it kind of sucked. It felt like I was kissing my sister, and judging by the look on her face, I'm not sure if I ruined everything and she liked it or if she felt the same way.

Aubrey looked at me with wide eyes as I pulled away and righted myself back into the driver's seat of my car, clearing my throat.

"That was…"

"Awful," Aubrey finished for me in an almost laugh. "That was horrible, right? Please tell me you didn't enjoy that. I would die if you found any pleasure in that at all, and if you did, I would totally make fun of you for the rest of our lives."

I couldn't help but laugh. "Thank God. That was probably the worst kiss I've ever had."

She slapped me on the shoulder. "Hey, don't hurt a girl's feelings now." She was smiling just as big as I was. I was thanking my lucky stars above that this kiss wouldn't change anything between us and that no awkward feelings were happening.

"Okay, maybe it wasn't the worst. Can I say it was very awkward and had little to no feeling behind it? I felt like I was kissing my sister." I laughed again.

"That's better," Aubrey smiled.

Aubrey has been my best friend since I moved here, and everyone has always assumed we would end up together. However, after that kiss, I was now very confident our relationship wouldn't go beyond friendship.

She looked out the front window and gestured forward. "Take me home, Prince Charming. Let's not speak of this ever again, okay? Plus, my dad would kill you for corrupting his sweet, perfect, seventeen-year-old daughter," she smiled. "We don't even have to tell Callie if you don't want to."

My stomach dropped at the mention of Callie's name. Callie is our other best friend. She is the complete opposite of Aubrey in every way possible, yet they've somehow always been best friends. They are the perfect balance of sweetness and utter craziness.

Most people assume that I'm gay since I have two best friends who are both female. I don't date around much like most of the guys in my school, and I am also the drama club president. It's stereotypical of people to make that assumption, but I understand. I also don't give a shit what people think.

We are off to Callie's mom's restaurant for the prom after-party with some of our friend group. Callie and her date went in his car, so we are meeting them there. Aubrey and I have been hearing how perfect we would be together for the past three years, so tonight we tried it.

If I am completely honest, I immediately knew I had kissed the wrong best friend. The night would have been entirely different if Callie and I had kissed. I'm sure of it. Instead of the sibling-like kiss I got. I imagine Callie and me having a sweet, sensual kiss. The kind that would leave us wanting more.

I've had a massive crush on Callie since I first met her when I was fifteen. Although I've kept my mouth shut about it, I'm pretty sure Aubrey knows, and I'm pretty sure that's what that kiss was all about. That was Aubrey's way of trying to help convince me to tell Callie how I genuinely feel about her. Aubrey was never really a romantic option for me if I'm being realistic, but it was a last-minute thought for us since everyone and their mother has always brought it up at every chance they got. She will never admit that's what it was, but I know my best friend better than she thinks. I honestly hope she was serious about not telling Callie, though.

The prom was a few weeks ago, and I haven't stopped thinking about Callie since. Kissing Aubrey made me come to realize just how different I feel about Callie. Granted, I care about them both more than probably anyone in my life besides my grandma, but all this thinking about Callie has made me realize my heart wants more than a friendship with her. I was finally ready to tell her how I really felt.

Callie was showing me a few songs that she was learning on the piano for the upcoming junior band concert on her phone. She is fucking phenomenal at the piano. I missed half of what she told me since all I could think about was my feelings for her.

This admission could fuck up everything we have been planning for. It may change the entire dynamic of our friendship. Callie, Aubrey, and I are applying to the same colleges in hopes we can all stay together. We're all hoping to get accepted into a local college here in Connecticut. I don't know what distance would do to our friendships, but I don't exactly want to find out either.

"Have you talked to your prom date lately? What was his name? Chris, something?" I asked, trying to keep the tone of my voice even and calm. I didn't want her to think much of it.

She gave me a weird look, and I realized asking like that was pretty stupid. It was entirely out of the blue. She answered after hesitating for a moment.

"Alvarez, and no. He was nice, but we were too different. He isn't into music or anything that I enjoy, so we had nothing to connect on. I didn't see it going anywhere. He was fun to hang with while my two best friends ditched me for each other," she laughed.

"We didn't ditch you, but whatever," I said with an attitude.

She smacked my shoulder lightly. "Oh my God, Nick, you so did. You guys were all googly-eyed with each other and having fun. It surprised me I didn't get a text saying something *more* happened between you."

"Me and Aubs? Sweets, I could never date her. She's like my sister." I omitted the kiss information since Aubrey and I had agreed we wouldn't ever mention it.

I couldn't tell if Callie was just stating facts or if Aubrey and I had genuinely hurt her by going to prom and having fun together. My stomach lurched because I realized now was the best time to tell her how I felt since we were already talking about dating.

"Hey Sweets, speaking of dating, I wanted to talk to you abo—"

"Oh my God, I didn't tell you." She turned to look at me.

The moment I saw the joy and pure excitement in her eyes, I knew I wouldn't be happy about her news. Don't get me wrong, I will always be happy for her when good things happen, but I know that look. She likes someone. The chances of that someone being me are slim to none.

"I started dating this guy I met at the restaurant. We met when I was working last week. He is so perfect. He does construction around town and has been coming in daily to see me for lunch since we met."

My stomach churned like everything I had eaten during the day was about to end up on the floor right there in front of me. "You're already dating someone?"

Callie gave me a baffling, offended look. "What is that supposed to mean?"

"You were just with that Chris kid. Now you are already seeing someone new?"

Her gaze remained unchanged after my explanation. "Okay. I repeat, what exactly is that supposed to mean?"

I looked away, found the remote control, and turned on the T.V., all while trying to hide my pure disappointment. "Never mind, forget I said anything."

I expected her to ask again, but she stood up and started yelling at me.

"I don't need to explain my dating life to you, Nicholas. Chris and I went to prom together. There was no dating and no fucking. We barely even knew each other. I haven't even had a serious boyfriend. So I'm not sure if you were trying to imply that I am a slut or something, but—"

I stood up, cutting her off. "Woah. I didn't say anything like that. Don't be putting words in my mouth."

"Yes, you did. You may not have said those exact words, but you implied it by wording your question that way."

I was going to clarify what I meant and clear the air, but my grandma's yell from the other room interrupted my thoughts.

"Lunch is ready. Come and get it!"

Callie and I looked at each other for one more moment before I turned and walked toward the kitchen. I quickly realized Callie wasn't following.

"Are you not going to eat? Come on, don't be dramatic." *Fuck.* I cannot believe I just fucking said that. "Cal, I'm—"

She put her hand up. "Don't."

She gathered her bookbag and phone and started to walk away from me with a sad look. "Tell your grandma I had to run. I will see you later. If Aubs shows up, tell her I'll call her later."

She began swiftly walking toward the door, so I ran after her. "Callie, come on. You know I didn't mean it like that. The news just caught me off guard. I'm sorry."

She looked at me in a way I didn't think I had ever seen. It looked almost like a glimmer of hope in her eyes, but it quickly faded back into anger.

"Why do you care, anyway? You have never cared before about who I was dating, or wasn't for that matter?"

My stomach dropped. I couldn't tell Callie the real reason I was holding back and being so jealous, so I did the only thing I could think of at the moment.

I shrugged, looked down at my feet, and then muttered, "I don't care. It was just really sudden, that's all." I looked back up at her just in time to see the disappointment in her eyes. *Why was she disappointed?*

She looked away from me and then nodded. "Got it."

She turned and walked out the door.

"Fuck," I yelled.

My grandma came running out of the kitchen. "What? What's the matter?" she asked with concern.

"Nothing."

She looked out the front window and then back at me. "Nicky. What did you say to that poor girl?"

"Nothing Gram. Sorry for yelling. Let's go eat."

She put her arm around my waist since she was so short and walked me toward the table. "Give her time. That girl likes you." She nudged me. "I also think maybe you like her a little bit too?"

I tried to protest, but her grin made me stop talking. "You think so?"

"Yes. Now eat and put some meat on that scrawny body so I can be right."

I put my arm on top of her head and scoffed. "Hey, don't call me scrawny. I'm working on it, plus I am taller than you, so I can't be too scrawny."

We both laughed. "Nicky, you are only taller because I shrank," she joked. "And you know what I meant."

"Gram, I am over six feet tall. I have been taller than you for a long time."

She patted my arm. "Sure Nicky, whatever you want to tell yourself to feel better."

After dinner, I went to text Aubrey and Callie in our group chat but saw Callie had removed herself, so I texted her separately.

I am really sorry, Callie.

Sweets

> Don't worry about it. Let's just keep our distance for a bit.

> I really like this guy and don't want you to be negative and ruin things.

> I deserve to be happy.

Distance from Callie is the last fucking thing I want. She didn't answer the next text I sent, and I'm pretty sure all my messages were about to go unanswered for a while. I should have told her the truth.

What the fuck did I do?

CHAPTER ONE

Callie

7 YEARS LATER- AUGUST

I never in my life would have imagined this would happen two weeks before my wedding. Although I guess no one really thinks they would catch their fiancé cheating on them with someone they work with, but I digress. As I lay here on my best friend's couch thinking about last night, I can't help but wonder why I didn't see all the signs earlier. Everyone else did, especially Aubrey and Nick. They better not say I told you so.

My best friend, Aubrey, lived with my fiancé and me earlier this year. She started talking about moving out when she caught a random woman leaving our house. When she confronted him, Jake straight up lied to her about it. His explanation made sense, but it raised some red flags—*red flags that I just ignored, of course.* I should have taken the red flags and Aubrey's concerns more seriously. Looking back, I realize I was being a complete idiot.

She officially moved out of the house in June when her boyfriend, Lincoln, surprised her by moving to Connecticut from Tennessee. It was an adorable, completely swoon-worthy romantic comedy moment with a song on stage at a concert, a heart-wrenching speech, and everything else she could have wanted.

They found a place together rather quickly. Soon after moving here, Lincoln accepted a job offer a few towns over. They are living together, acting all lovey-dovey, and are completely in their honeymoon phase. They are perfect for each other, and I love it. Although, I don't want to hear about anyone being happy. To be honest, I am a complete mess and absolutely miserable. My eyes are stinging with tears again just thinking about how lonely I will be for the foreseeable future.

Last night, the plan was to stay at Aubrey's because she was helping me with the wedding bouquets, but when Jake said he wasn't coming home and was staying in Massachusetts to finish up a job, I went home for some quiet time. I wanted to set up a little surprise homecoming for him. He had been acting off lately. I was sure it was just a case of the wedding jitters. Boy, was I wrong.

When I pulled up to the house, all the lights were on. I knew immediately something was off. My body felt like it was going into fight mode. No one should be here. I thought I shut the lights off, and Jake said he was working late on a project and would stay at a hotel near the work site since it was over an hour away in Massachusetts.

After walking in, I stood silent momentarily to see if I could hear anything, but it was quiet. When I realized the only thing that seemed off was the lights being on, I chalked it up to being forgetful and leaving them on. I entered the kitchen to grab a water bottle before heading upstairs to the music room. I heard a loud thump from upstairs just before turning the lights off. I froze again, like not moving could make me hear better or something. It was silent for a few seconds, but then I heard it again, and again, and again. I heard what sounded like a low moan right after the thump. *No fucking way.* As I ran up the stairs, the moaning grew louder and more frequent.

"Yes. Jake, Yes...right there," the woman's voice desperately moaned.

I flung the door open, hitting the wall behind it.

There he was, underneath a skinny brunette, driving his dick into her. I couldn't see her face, but when she heard the door hit the wall, she jumped off him and flung herself to the side with her face in a pillow.

"Ca—Fuck—Callie. What are you doing at home?" My fiancé, I guess now EX-fiancé, said as he fumbled out of the bed, tripping over himself and trying to cover up with our sheets. Why do people do that when they get caught cheating? Like, I've seen you naked hundreds of times, you fucking asshole. What the fuck are you hiding?

I looked at him in disbelief. "Me? What am *I* doing here? You're seriously fucking asking me what I am doing in my home." I took a breath. "What the fuck are *YOU* doing here, Jake?"

He started toward me, so I stepped back, putting my arm out between us. "Don't you dare fucking touch me."

He stopped walking and looked down at the floor.

"I... I don't think I'm ready to get married."

My eyes burned with unshed tears. I looked over at the dumb bitch still on my side of the bed, hiding her face. Then I saw it. The uniform from my mom's restaurant was on the floor. Everything clicked.

"Sara?" She didn't move for a moment; then she nodded her head yes, removed the blanket, and sat up. "You're fucking Jake? How could you do this to me?"

She got up in a rush, trying to walk over to me just like Jake had. What in the hell is wrong with the two of them? Why would they think I would want to be anywhere near their nasty, cheating bodies? I held my hand up abruptly, and she halted.

"Sara, I would stop right there. If you come any fucking closer to me, I will break your damn nose. Don't fucking test me."

"Callie, I am so, so sorry. This was the first time. I know that doesn't make it better, but I—"

I stepped aside, making a clear path from her to the door. "Get the hell out. I don't want to see you ever again. I will send your last paycheck to the address we have on file for you. Don't bother going back to work."

"Well, you can't fire me for this," she stated bluntly.

"Get. The. Fuck. Out," I yelled. That time, it worked. She quickly grabbed all her clothes, and then she smiled. She fucking smiled back at Jake before she left.

Jake started speaking as soon as she left the room. "Baby, please. Let me explain."

He had gotten dressed while I was yelling at Sara, so now he at least had a pair of shorts on. I sat on the end of the bed with my head in my hands, tears flowing freely.

I should have known something like this was going on. Jake has been so distant since proposing at Christmas last year. He has been worried constantly about my location and who I am with. It was guilt.

Sara has been a coworker for about two years. Her mom and my mom became friends when they moved here. Sara has been exceptionally friendly to me lately. That should have been a red flag. I can't fucking believe I was so damn stupid. Not only one person in my life was fucking me over. It had to be two.

I started speaking without looking up at him. "Tell me something, Jake. When Aubrey caught that woman leaving the house a few months back, were you sleeping with her?"

"Callie," he exhaled softly.

I looked him directly in the eyes. "How many people have you cheated on me with? And don't fucking lie to me again."

"Ten. I'm so sorry, Callie." He tried to hug me, but I stood up and stepped back.

I wasn't sure if I was angrier at the number of people he had slept with or the fact that he didn't even have to think about it before he answered. He didn't even hesitate.

"Fucking ten? So, you have fucked ten people while we were dating and while being engaged to me? How...when did it start? How did you even pull that shit off?"

He stood up to face me.

"Cal, I'm sorry. It started after I proposed. I proposed because I thought it was the right thing to do after we had been together for so long. I wasn't ready, and I freaked out. It never should have happened. I'm sorry."

It baffled me because I never, and I mean never, brought up marriage to him. We all joked about it occasionally, but I saw what marriage did to my parents. They fought uncontrollably all the time. My dad was an addict in every sense of the word, and my mom just dealt with it and ran the restaurant by herself while he wasted away at home. It was easier than trying to get him to want to be a good husband or father. I think they stayed together for as long as they did because of me. One night at dinner, when I was ten years old, I was so fed up with them fighting I blew my lid. I told them to get a divorce. My dad left that night, and I never saw him again. I was utterly content with never getting married. Now, I sure as hell never want to.

I took a deep breath to calm my racing heart and the internal rage that was flowing inside me. "Okay, so let me get this straight. Even though we've been together for over six fucking years, you couldn't tell me you made a mistake by proposing? You couldn't just admit you weren't ready to get married? Instead, you went along with this happily engaged facade just to sleep around with ten fucking women since December? It's fucking August, Jake." I couldn't believe I was having this conversation right now. "Not even a year ago, you poured your heart out to me in front of our families, and you seriously thought cheating was the better choice? How does sleeping with other people help with you not wanting to get married, Jake? We were still getting married in two weeks, were we not?"

"Yes, we are," he said.

"Were," I firmly corrected.

"Callie, come on. It was just a little fun before we committed our lives to each other. It would have ended the minute we got married. I love you."

Was he trying to make me feel better? I can't believe I wasted over six years of my life on him.

Wiping my tears away the best I could, I stared him in the eye. "I'm leaving. I will be by tomorrow to pack my shit while you're at work. Don't even think about staying and waiting for me. You can keep the house and whatever is left. The lease is in your name anyway, so you decide what to do with it. There are only a few months left, anyway." My voice got louder for the last part. "Since it hasn't even been a fucking year!"

He grabbed my wrist hard. "Babe, please don't do this. We're meant to be together. I know that now."

I tried to rip my arm away but couldn't, so I looked at him sternly. "Apparently not," I said sarcastically. "Let me go, or I will call the cops."

He did, and after rubbing my wrist, I removed my ring, placed it in his hands, and dropped my voice before speaking again because I meant every word of what I was about to say, and I needed him to really listen, "I hope you found whatever you were looking for in those ten other women, Jake... because now that is all you have."

After packing a bag, I called Aubrey on the way out. She didn't answer, and I didn't want to just show up, even though I often do that. I sat on the front steps with my head in my hands and started contemplating what I would do next.

I teach private piano lessons from home. I'm unsure where I will teach from now on since my mom lives in a one-bedroom apartment, and both of my best friends have their own lives.

Logically, I knew I couldn't afford to live in my house alone, so I'd have to get some shitty-ass apartment, and I'd have to travel to my students again, I suppose. Unfortunately, that will limit the number of students I can see.

I was not okay, so I called the only other person who I knew would answer, and he did immediately. He always does.

"I can't stay here. Can I spend the night until I figure out what to do next?"

"Come on over, Sweets. Do you need me to pick you up?" Nick's voice gave me a comfort I hadn't felt from him in a long time.

"Yes," I whispered.

"I'm on my way."

CHAPTER TWO

Nick

Callista Adriana Diaz, or Callie, as everyone calls her, is the love of my life, and I will die on that hill. We have been friends since I moved here to live with my grandmother when I was fifteen. Callie is a year younger, but we were in the same grade since I repeated a year when I was eleven. I had gotten sick when I was ten and missed a ton of school, so my parents held me back. It must have been fate.

My parents passed away a few days before my fifteenth birthday. They were killed in a hit-and-run accident. I was the only other person in the car with my parents and could give a vague description of the guy I saw running away. My description led officials to find him a few days later. I still carry a lot of guilt for surviving when they didn't. Although that was the worst thing that could ever have happened to me, it also led to the best—my *people*.

Callie and Aubrey have been my best friends ever since. I have never crossed the line with either of them unless you count the mutually horrible kiss Aubrey and I had after our junior prom. It was like kissing my sister, and she agreed. Out of the two, I have always been closer to Aubrey since I met her first. Callie and I were friends with Aubrey separately, so naturally, we became friends too. Callie and I have had a complicated relationship for years. At least on my end, I have this attraction to her I've just never been able to act upon, so it presents itself as me being a little standoffish.

I got up the nerve to tell her once when I was eighteen; she was seventeen. I told her I needed to talk to her. Before I could speak, she cut me off, telling me about Jake. That was the end of that. Ever since then, things have been a little weird between us. I always felt uncomfortable when he was around. Watching someone touch what you know belongs to you fucking hurts. Some may call it jealousy, but she and I constantly bickered like we were a married couple. I think she may actually hate me deep down, but I would never ask because that would break my fucking heart, so I just take what I can get.

Over the years, I've watched both my best friends fall in love. I watched Aubrey get hurt and find a new love with Lincoln, and I thought I was about to watch Callie marry Jake. Her wedding is two weeks away, but at the moment, she is sitting on my couch with my laptop, looking at apartments. She probably shouldn't be doing anything like that right now, considering she is drinking straight from a bottle of wine she opened not even an hour ago. It's almost gone. She is three sheets to the wind.

When she showed up last night, I didn't know what to do except hug her tightly. My heart was flooded with emotions and a multitude of thoughts. I was hurting for her. I hated seeing her like this. She is such a strong, independent woman, and she was breaking apart before my eyes. Selfishly, a part of me felt relieved. Does that make me an asshole for thinking that? Probably, but I don't think anyone would fault me for being happy that she won't be marrying that piece of shit. I knew he was cheating. I fucking knew it. Aubrey and I both did. We just couldn't prove it.

Callie fell asleep in my bed last night while I was consoling her. I got up and slept in the guest room to give her space. I didn't want to crowd her.

When Callie called me, I couldn't have been more grateful my grandmother left me her house in the will. I miss her like crazy, but she ensured I was cared for if something ever happened to her. She left me her life insurance payout and the house, which is paid off, so even though I make a measly teacher's salary, I am still pretty well off.

Callie has barely spoken a word to me today other than thanking me for helping her last night. She asked to use my computer and to bring my car to her house to help her pack some stuff, but nothing more. It's taking everything in me not to kick Jake's ass for hurting my perfect girl; he is lucky he wasn't home when I was there. Although I look skinny and nerdy, I can hold my own, and since I would do anything for her, I would kill him if she asked me to.

"Cal, why don't we put the wine away and talk."

"Bout what? I have nothing to say." She didn't even look up from the computer.

"Cal put the computer down. I need to talk to you."

She rolled her eyes and closed it. She twisted her body toward me and wrapped the blanket tighter around herself.

"I know you don't enjoy talking about your feelings, and I understand that, but we have to talk about this."

She was quiet for a second, and her eyes started to tear up. "Nick, if I talk, I'll cry, and I don't want to cry in front of you anymore. I'm embarrassed enough. I don't need you thinking any less of me than you already do."

My eyebrow shot up in confusion. "What are you talking about? Are you being serious? Do you really think that, or are you just trying to be annoying and push me away?"

She shrugged, giving me nothing else.

"Number one, I would never think less of you for crying. You are my best friend. You could cry all day and I would never think less of you. God knows you've seen me cry a few times over the years. Did you think any less of me?" I didn't let her answer. I just kept talking to prove my point. "Number two, your life just fell apart." She sniffled and let out a small whimper, so I grabbed her hand. "You're allowed to be hurt, and you're allowed to cry without judgment. However, I might judge you a little if you keep drinking that bottle of wine. It's almost gone, ya lush." I smiled to let her know I was joking...kind of.

She handed me the bottle with a smirk on her face, and I placed it on the table. I wanted to grab her and tell her she would never have to cry again, that I could make this all better, but I couldn't. I could solve her biggest issue, though.

"I have a solution to some of your problems if you want to hear them."

She rolled her eyes. "What could you possibly give me to help me get over being cheated on?" I smiled at her because she was slurring her words a little, and it was fucking adorable. She tends to conceal her vulnerabilities—rarely allowing herself to be seen in a state of fragility. She leaned forward and took the last few gulps of wine, emptying the bottle.

"I can give you the house, well, a room to work and live in, not the actual house," I chuckled.

Her smile dropped as she sat up and stared at me blankly. "Wha—what? You want me to move in?"

I thought about my answer before responding. "Want is a strong word, Cal," I said with a joking grin. "I want nothing from you. I want my best friend to have a safe place to stay and work without going broke. There is a guest room for you to live in, and you can put the piano in the sunroom and do your lessons there."

Tears welled up in her eyes. "Are you being serious? Please tell me you are serious because–"

"Callie, of course I'm being serious. Why would I joke about that?"

She stared at me with a look I could only describe as a happy sadness. I nodded my head yes to drive home the fact that I was indeed serious once again. The next thing I knew, Callie was flinging herself at me to straddle my lap. Her hands went to my cheeks while she studied my face quietly. Before I could even think about the fact that all the blood in my body had now rushed straight to my dick, her mouth was on mine. She kissed me...hard.

When my thoughts caught up to our actions, I pulled my mouth away and put my forehead to hers. Both of us were short of breath.

"Callie," I whispered.

"Don't push me away, Nick. I need to feel something good right now."

What am I doing? Callie kissing me and being on top of me is something out of my dreams, but I can't do this to her. "Not like this, Cal. You're drunk, and you will definitely regret this in the morning. You don't want me like this."

"No, you don't want *me* like this," she repeated.

That caught me off guard because having Callie like this is the only thing I have fucking wanted for years now. I put my hands to her jaw and ran my fingers into the back of her hair. One of my thumbs grazed her bottom lip as I meticulously thought about my next words.

"Callie, I've wanted you like this forever. Forever and always." I shut my eyes, cursing myself for saying that out loud. I hoped she would forget I said that. "But I can't do this to you. You are too vulnerable and you are drunk. I would never hurt you like that. You don't really want me. You want comfort."

She pulled back, almost like she just realized what she was doing. She looked mortified. Her hand covered her mouth, and she began mumbling. "Nick. Shit, I am so sorry. I don't know what that was. I am so sorry. Can we just forget that happened? I was just overwhelmed with excitement that I could stay here."

Her tan skin was deepening with a pretty pink color. I don't think I have ever seen her look more beautiful.

I wanted to lighten the mood even though I was kicking myself for pushing her away and being the nice guy once again. That kiss was something I've always craved and yet also something I will never forget.

I leaned in and gently kissed her cheek as I grabbed her hand. "Already forgotten, but I was serious about you staying here. We can rent a truck tomorrow and grab your piano, and call Link and Aubrey's dad and see if they'll help us move it."

She looked at me with hope in those caramel-colored eyes that I loved so much. "Are you sure? You won't hate me and kick me out after a week?"

I was trying my hardest to keep my emotions in check and just be her best friend right now. "I've never been more sure of anything. Plus, getting sick of you will take at least a month." I laughed as she playfully slapped me on the shoulder.

"I hate you, Nicholas James," she smirked.

"I know. I hate you, too. Forever and always, Callista Adriana." I smiled back.

I knew I would need help moving some of Callie's things, so I texted the crew.

> Hey. Who's free tomorrow?

> I want to move the piano ASAP.

> I don't want her to have to think about it anymore.

Aubrey

> Hell yes. I am so freaking in.

> I have a lesson early in the morning, then I can help.

> Just let me know what time.

Link

> I'm in. I will wait for Aubs, then head over.

> Will Douchcanoe be there? Do you think I should do it alone?

Aubrey

> Real mature Link.

> But really...will he be there?

> What do you mean, do it alone?

Brielle

> I have plans with Amani, so I will have to pass unless you absolutely need me.

> No worries Pip. I am sure we can manage.

Brielle

> I still hate that nickname.

> Oh Link, If you hurt him, send me pics. lol

> Pleeeeeeese.

Link

> You and Aubs should probably stay away, don't you think?

> I can call someone else to help me. You guys will try to kill him and go to jail. lol

> Brie I got you on the pics. But I will deny it if you ever tell anyone it was me lol.

Aubrey

> I mean, we can come up with a plan of attack. Literally lol.

> I wouldn't mind getting in a few punches.

I should have known this was going to turn into a shit-on-him fest. Aubrey was just as pissed off as I was.

> I would love nothing more than to hurt that mother fucker.

> But tomorrow is about getting her shit and making sure she never has a reason to contact him again.

It was a few more minutes before I got a text back from either of them.

Aubrey

> Link and I agree you are no fun, and we are both going. I am bringing the bat, just in case.

When we got to the house the next day, Jake was there waiting for Callie. He'd been calling her nonstop since she left. We purposely told Callie not to come because we knew he wouldn't respect her wishes of not being there. Link had to go in and pressure him to leave because Aubrey tried to attack him the moment she saw him, and although I thought I could handle it, I flipped the moment he tried to speak to me. I can't believe he could cheat on such a fantastic woman.

Luckily, it didn't take long, and Callie didn't ask questions when we returned home. While the guys and I moved things around to fit the piano, the girls got started on making phone calls.

Aubrey and Callie have a lot of phone calls to cancel everything for the wedding. Unfortunately, a lot of it is nonrefundable. Her rehearsal dinner and honeymoon were the most significant things. Callie spent everything she had on that honeymoon, which will probably be the hardest thing to overcome.

Once the piano was settled in the sunroom, I called and ordered some pizza for everyone as a thank you. I heard Aubrey and Callie talking when I walked past Callie's room to grab my phone.

"Callie, you will be okay. I promise I will help you through this. We all will."

"Aubs, my money is gone... all of it. I put it all into the wedding and honeymoon. Jake never gave me the money for it. I didn't think anything of it at the time. I had been using Jake's credit card for all the everyday spending because all my money went into wedding planning, and it was going to be our money anyway."

"Callie."

"Aubs, I looked at my account this morning. I have one hundred and seven dollars left to my name. I'm fucking broke. What happens when I need to give Nick rent money?"

"Nick would never accept money from you for you staying here. You know that, right?"

Aubrey is right. She will not have to give me a damn dime. I wouldn't take it. I hate hearing her so scared and hurt.

Even if she never wants more with me, she will never have to want for anything, never be hurt or scared ever again. I would give her the world.

After we all ate, Callie pulled me into the sunroom and asked me about scheduling some classes, saying she would have to double and triple up some days in order to make some money. I gave her the go-ahead, of course. It wouldn't bother me to hear her play; I could listen to her play all day. School starts at the end of this month, so I will be gone most of the day on weekdays, teaching at the local high school. Plus, even if I was here, that's what noise-canceling headphones are for.

Once Callie scheduled a few lessons for the upcoming week, she called the students who already had lessons scheduled and gave them my address as her new residence, and then she took a nap.

I pulled Aubrey aside and gave her a check to cash for Callie.

She looked down at it and then back at me. "Nick, this is five thousand dollars." She held it back out to me, but I didn't grab it.

"Yes, Aubrey, I'm glad those reading classes worked out for you."

She slapped me on my chest. The sound made Link look away from the game he was watching to ensure she was okay. That man is so protective of her that it's sickening, but I understand. Aubrey is one of the good ones. I would protect her without a second thought, no matter the situation.

"Link, she's fine. Go back to jerkin' off to your baseball players over there." Link gave me the finger. I let out a laugh and turned back to Aubrey. "She will never accept this. Especially from you," she said.

"No shit, Aubs, that's why you are going to deposit it and write her a check from your account. She never has to know it's from me. I just want her to feel a little less stressed."

"Nick, she won't take it from me either...you know she doesn't accept help unless absolutely necessary."

Aubrey was right, but she had to find a way to get her to take it. I can't have her stressing about money when she's trying to put her life back together.

"Make her. End of conversation," I said sternly.

I went to sit next to a very surprised Link on the couch, and as soon as I did, he leaned over and whispered, "You got balls talking to her like that. You are lucky she didn't kick your balls in."

Aubrey called out from the kitchen. "He won't have any balls left if he ever does again."

Link and I chuckled and went back to watching the baseball game. "I am one lucky motherfucker," Link said before sipping his beer.

I laughed. "Never let that one go."

Link side-eyed me with a smile. "Didn't plan on it."

CHAPTER THREE

Callie

It's been a week since I moved in with Nick, and surprisingly, we're not sick of each other yet. He hasn't been home that much since he had some faculty meetings for back-to-school, but he has been making it a point to be home on time so we can have dinner together. I don't know if that's more for him or me. Surprisingly, it feels kind of normal. I like it.

We're going to the casino about an hour from home tonight. I can't wait to let loose a little. I won't be spending any money because I don't have any to spend, but Aubrey insisted we go out for my birthday before the boys get busy with work and Brielle gets busy with school. Brielle is Aubrey's sister, who is basically my little sister too. Brielle has been doing an internship at some art gallery all summer. It seems like she's been working every time I try to talk to her. I miss her like crazy.

We all dressed up for the occasion. Aubrey hates getting all fancy, but she's making me go, so I'm making her dress up. I'm wearing my best black dress. Aubrey bought it for me at one of the shops in Tennessee when she met her biological dad for the first time. It's a bitch to get on because it's so damn tight, but once it's on, I look fucking hot.

"Nick, come zip me up," I yelled.

I heard his footsteps coming down the hall from the direction of his room. He knocked first and asked if I was decent. It made me smile. This man is always so polite and proper. It's hard to believe we're even friends because it is just another thing that makes him different from me. Aubrey and I are so not proper. We are the exact opposite. Nick keeps Aubrey and me in line, so I guess that's a good thing.

I had my back to him when he entered. "What did you—Oh damn."

I started looking around me, then looked at him through the mirror. "What...what's wrong?"

"You...You look—" Nick cut himself off and visibly swallowed. He ran his hand over the back of his neck nervously, and I could swear he was blushing. "Wow," he added.

I smirked. "I look hot. You can say it." I looked back at my reflection, trying my best to smile like I was unbothered. So far, it's working, I think. I am usually okay until I get into bed and I'm alone. When I'm alone, I cry for hours.

"You look amazing, Cal."

"You've seen me in dresses before...plus I'm not even fully dressed yet, weirdo. Zip me up."

Nick rolled his eyes, walked up to me, and looked at me in the mirror as he pushed my hair to one side. His scent clouded my brain for a moment. It was a citrusy, warm smell, like a late spring night.

"You are welcome for the compliment, Miss Priss," he joked. His finger brushed my neck. Goosebumps immediately covered my skin.

"Are you trying to pick someone up tonight or something?" he asked.

I turned to him, acting offended. "Are you saying I look like a hooker, Nicholas?"

"Yes, I am. You are going to have everyone gawking at you."

Looking back at myself in the mirror, I appreciated my curves. I noticed Nick was too, which gave me a weird but warm feeling in my stomach. "Perfect," I whispered. "Just what I was hoping for. Maybe someone will want to make out with me."

Nick rolled his eyes again. I could swear I saw him slightly blush, but he turned around quickly and told me to be ready in twenty minutes, or he was leaving without me. He wouldn't, but I'm sure saying it made him feel better.

We got into the car thirty minutes later.

"Couldn't leave without me, huh?" I gave him a huge smile.

"Fuck you," he retorted with a laugh.

I shrugged. "I hope someone will."

Nick's face quickly turned a light shade of pink. He seemed to shake off a thought. Then he looked me over, focusing on my legs. "Cal, are you sure you don't want to wear pants or something? Maybe you will be more comfortable."

I patted his cheek because his concern was so cute. "Thanks for worrying, *Dad*, but my legs will be fine. I might even find someone to warm them up."

He pushed my hand away and made a weird grunting sound. He mumbled something under his breath, but I ignored him and blasted my music through his speakers. I texted Aubrey to let her know we were on our way.

When we picked them up, I got in the back with Aubrey so we could talk a little. She couldn't get my deposit back for the rehearsal dinner, so we are still going to it and making it a fun dinner party with some free food for all my friends. I invited Nick, Brielle, her parents, my mom, August, and Liza to come for dinner anyway. August is Aubrey's biological dad, whom I met in January. They were coming for the wedding, anyway, so why should they not enjoy their time here with some good food? I was trying my best to make the best out of the shitty situation.

"So, what are we getting into tonight?" Aubrey asked, pulling me from my thoughts.

I gave her a weird look. "You mean, what am *I* getting into? Lincoln wouldn't let *you* get into anything other than his pants even if you tried."

We both let out a loud laugh that had both the guys looking back at us. Aubrey waved at them to turn around and mind their business. Once they did, she linked her arm to mine and lowered her voice so only I could hear. "Very true, but I wouldn't have it any other way. How about let's just celebrate your birthday and have a fun night at the casino. We can worry about everything else later? You deserve fun. If that involves a sexy man, cool; if not, I'll kiss you and tell you that you're pretty, okay?"

I smiled, "You're right. I deserve some fun. Let's do it."

Aubrey whispered in my ear. "Did Nick dye his hair? Or is it just the lighting? It looks so dark."

"Yeah. I haven't mentioned it. I figured he was going through a quarter-life crisis or something."

Nick's voice chimed in, and he looked at me in the rearview mirror. "If you must know gossip girls, I just wanted a change."

Aubrey and I righted ourselves in our seats and let out a laugh.

The ride seemed quicker than usual, thanks to the lack of traffic. When we pulled up into the casino parking lot, I saw the beautiful

Brie talking to her best friend, Amani, and a guy with neatly cut copper-colored hair. He looked like he could have been a lawyer or someone important. He and Brie looked awfully cozy, but I'd never seen him before.

Aubrey and I both screamed as we rushed toward Brie and Amani. We all started obnoxiously running slowly toward each other like we were from Baywatch. I've always told my students if they don't have friends that match their energy, they need to find new friends. This type of moment is precisely what I meant.

The guys did not pass the vibe check. They passed us by, stood at the elevators, and then just watched as the four of us girls acted like idiots...and you can bet your ass we made them wait.

We hugged the girls tightly. It felt good to let all my worries dissipate for a little while.

"Hey guys, this is Shane. He works at the gallery with me." Brielle then introduced each of us to him by our names.

"Now, Shane, make sure you remember all that. There is going to be a pop quiz later," I teased.

His eyes widened a little. I was joking, of course, but I actually think I scared him.

"Nice to meet you all," he said hesitantly. "Especially you, Aubrey. Brielle doesn't shut up about you."

Link cleared his throat, and Brie smacked his shoulder. We all broke out in a burst of laughter.

Aubrey and I gave Brie the look as if to ask if she was seeing him or interested in seeing him. She mouthed the word "gay" as she pushed her bottom lip out into a pouty face that made me chuckle. *Damn.* The four of us girls let out a loud burst of laughter and linked arms as we walked into the elevator.

"Are they always like that? I've never seen Brielle smile like that before," Shane asked. It made me smile.

"Yes," Lincoln and Nick said in unison in an annoyed tone.

We let out an even bigger laugh as the elevator door closed.

"Better get used to it if you plan on sticking around, Shane," Aubrey called out.

"Ain't that the truth?" Nick added.

We went straight to Margaritaville because we were all starving. Aubrey and I had chicken salads and shared an order of sweet potato fries, as we always do everywhere we go. We saved getting drinks for the nightclub to help us get our dance on. Aubrey reserved one of the VIP couch areas for us, which was really cool because I'd never done that before. The server brought over some light snacks with some beers and margaritas and a Shirley Temple for Brie. Before I could even get a sip of my margarita, Aubrey pulled Brie and me onto the dance floor while also motioning to Amani to join us.

Nick kept giving us dirty looks, but I think that's just his face. Nick and I have been friends for so long, and we have always had this annoying banter between us that makes it seem like we hate each other, but I could never really hate him.

Now that I have spent more alone time with him, I realize he is more awesome than I thought. It's nice spending actual time together. We haven't done it in so long. We used to be much closer than we are now, especially in high school. There was a brief, fleeting moment when I thought I liked him more than a friend. I almost asked him to prom. He asked Aubrey instead. That was the end for me. I pushed those thoughts straight to the back of my brain and tried never to think of him like that again. I was selfishly relieved when it didn't work out for them. I didn't want our friendship dynamic to change.

When I met Jake, everything changed anyway. Nick and I got more distant and less friendly. That's when the "hating each other" era started. I don't know if he or I pulled away first, but Aubrey kept us together, and I'm so grateful for that. I don't know where I would be without either of them.

Brie is the little sister I never had, but in a good way. Brielle was never that annoying little girl that bothered Aubrey and me. She's just always fit right in with us.

This night was exactly what I needed. I didn't think I would be laughing like this again for a long time. It was one of those laughs that made you cry and lose your breath. We were having so much fun. Even Brie was dancing with us. She's opened up a lot lately, but she's usually very guarded when we are in public.

Brie was assaulted when she was sixteen. I never got the full extent of what actually happened. I know she was drunk, and I know it had to do with her ex, but that's about it. Understandably, none of us really ever talked about it. Even to this day, she still won't let us. Aubrey has tried to tell me what happened a few times over the years, but she always stops herself and says it isn't her story to tell.

Brielle hasn't had a drop of alcohol since that horrible day, and she rarely parties with us, but I think her walls are finally falling a little, and I couldn't be more proud of her.

After a few dances, we returned to the boys to grab our drinks and snacks. Link, of course, took Aubrey onto the dance floor so he could put his hands all over her like he didn't do that enough at home. Those two are so in love that it's almost sickening.

Amani was chatting up some girl at the bar, and Shane and I talked about art and piano. Brie and Nick were talking about her parents when a skinny woman with black hair came over to talk to Nick.

"Hey, Handsome, wanna buy me a drink?" I looked away from Shane as soon as I heard the unfamiliar voice. The stranger cozied up to him on the couch and put her finger on one of his shirt buttons.

He looked down at her finger and back at her face. "I would love to, but I'm celebrating with my best friend tonight, so she's the one getting all my attention." He smiled. He said it so calmly. Her bony ass finger did not faze him at all. Her scrawny body didn't seem to interest him either.

She didn't even move away an inch.

"Are you sure I couldn't change your mind? I bet I could be a lot more fun than her."

The bitch didn't even look over at any of us. She bit her lip and was trying to be sexy. Honestly, although she could use some meat on her bones, she was kind of hot, but seeing her touch him made my chest feel weird.

He chuckled, and I felt almost dumbfounded looking at their interaction. I don't know if I have ever seen someone hit on him before, or maybe I just haven't noticed. I usually only hear about girls he's seeing. I've only met one of his girlfriends the whole time I've known him. Now that I think about it, he really doesn't bring girls around at all.

"Yeah, I'm sure. She is more fun than anyone else I've ever met." He pulled her finger away from his torso and placed it on her leg. "I hope you enjoy your night."

She gave him an irritated look, stood up, and walked away.

I stared at him for a moment.

"What?" He started wiping his face. "Is there something on me?"

"What? No. I just...I hope you didn't turn her down on my account. Go have your fun."

He was quiet for a beat. "Nah, that girl wasn't my type. I didn't actually mean any of that. That would imply I enjoyed spending time with you." He smiled, so I knew he was joking. I playfully threw a chip at him, and instead of dodging it, he caught it in his mouth.

"Thanks, Sweets," he said as he leaned back and took a swig of his beer. Then he hopped right back into conversation with Brie.

That weird feeling was still lingering in my chest.

Is the salsa giving me heartburn?

Chapter Four

Nick

I lied...horribly, I'm sure. I didn't have a type unless you counted "women you can't have, aka Callie," as a type. Pining after my best friend didn't exactly let me have any fun in the dating department because I was constantly comparing every woman I met to her, and they never measured up.

I didn't keep many things from my best friends, but one thing I'd always kept secret was that I'd never had sex. I was probably the only virgin I knew over the age of twenty. Logically, I knew it wouldn't always stay that way, but I always held out hope that Callie and I would end up together.

When she got engaged, I vowed to start seriously dating. I saw one girl I worked with a few times back in January, but I broke it off when she asked to be exclusive. As bad as I felt about Jake cheating on Callie, it gave me this newfound hope that Callie might finally see me as more than her annoying best friend. However, I was unsure of what to do with that hope. She had only been single for about a week, so I couldn't exactly bring up the fact that I loved her now, could I?

Link and I started watching the girls dance again, and Shane joined them this time. Although Link and I are having a full-blown conversation over the music, we have not looked at each other once. We couldn't take our eyes off them. The only time we looked away was when the server brought over another round of drinks.

After giving her a tip and picking mine up, I looked back at the girls and noticed they had attracted the attention of a group of men and women. I motioned over to Link, and he didn't waste any time going and claiming his girl. I'm jealous that I can't do the same.

My fist tightened around my beer bottle when two guys approached Callie and put her between them while they danced. She put her arms around one guy's neck. The other guy put his grimy hands on her hips and was grinding into her. I couldn't see everything, but I saw her look back at him with a sexy smile. It made my blood boil even more. A moment later, her smile was gone, and she was pushing him away.

I saw Callie mouth, 'What are you doing?' and that was my cue.

When I got to her, she was trying to wrangle her wrist from the guy who was originally behind her.

"You have one fucking second to release her and walk away before you no longer have fingers," I yelled sternly. The guy didn't move. He scoffed at me with a dumb smile on his face.

"Move on, beanpole, get your own fun for tonight."

I instantly saw red. No one will ever get away with talking about her like that in front of me. I grabbed his wrist and bent it backward. His eyes went wide. By this point, Link had come up behind the other guy, holding him away from Callie. I don't know what he whispered, but the guy got the message and started walking away, unlike his friend, who was about to have a broken wrist.

"Nick, don't," Callie pleaded. "He is just drunk. He will go away."

I looked at her, and she had a genuine concern in her eyes. Then I looked back at the douchebag. "Are you ready to leave, or am I breaking this wrist?"

"Dude, I didn't realize she was taken; you need to keep a better leash on your slut next time."

That was it. I let his wrist go, and my fist caught the side of his face. He recovered quickly and hit me back. The ring on his finger caught my eye pretty hard, but my second hit knocked him down. His friends rushed over, picked him up, and dragged him away. Callie and Aubrey were fussing at me because I was bleeding.

I just wanted to leave. Unfortunately, I wasn't drunk, so I was feeling all the pain and pressure of my eye swelling up. This was definitely going to hurt even more tomorrow, but I'm not sure what will hurt more, my eye or my ego.

CALLIE

The car ride home was quiet. I was very drunk about an hour ago, but that fight with Nick and those guys sobered me up real fast. We dropped Aubrey and Link off, then drove to Nick's in absolute silence.

I opened my mouth a few times to speak, but ultimately, I didn't know what to say. Nick still hadn't said a word to me. Saying thank you to him seemed kind of stupid at this point, but I was truly grateful for him stepping in. That guy was pulling on my dress and trying to cop a feel on my ass.

I unlocked the door, and Nick rushed past me to the bathroom before I could step inside. I put all my things in my room, and after about five minutes, I knocked on the bathroom door.

"I'm fine," he grunted.

"Nick, let me in."

"Cal, just go to bed. I'm fine. I will see you tomorrow."

"Nick. I will sit outside this door and wait, so you might as well just let me in."

He let out a loud huff and opened the door. I gasped, my stomach turning at the sight of his eye. "Nick, I'm so sorry. Here, let me—"

He grabbed hold of my wrist and pulled me towards him before looking into my eyes.

"Number one, this is not your fault. You didn't ask him to grope you, nor did you ask me to step in. I know you can handle yourself." He looked down, letting my wrist go, and then turned toward the mirror and looked back at me through it. "Number two, I'll be fine. It's just a black eye and some blood. I think his ring caught me or something. I can see fine. Just go to bed and get some rest."

I put my forehead on his strong back. "I know I didn't ask you to, but I am thankful you did, and I am really sorry it happened. I am so sorry you got hurt."

He turned toward me and smirked a little. "I think my ego hurts more than my eye." He looked down at his feet. A moment later, he pulled me into his arms. "I would do anything for you, Cal, no matter the consequence...forever and always."

Who is this, and what has he done with my best frenemy Nick? His words made my stomach do a little flip. I like this protective side. It's...Sexy.

Did I just think that Nick was sexy?

I collected myself and pulled away from the hug. "I can't just go to bed with you looking like Popeye. Let me help you. Meet me on the couch. I'll get you some ice."

He kissed my forehead. "Go to bed, Sweets," he whispered as he walked out.

I walked to the kitchen, thinking he would meet me like I asked, but Nick wasn't there when I entered the living room. Why does he have to be such a stubborn asshole?

I walked into his bedroom without knocking. He was in nothing but a towel. The view stopped me in my tracks. Damn, he's been working out. I don't think I've ever noticed how fit he is. I must have been gawking a bit too long because I only heard the end of what he said.

"What?" I asked.

He smiled. "I asked if you were going to take a picture or just keep checking me out while I changed."

"I have no shame in my game. You look fucking good. When did you get so damn hot?" I felt myself blushing a little. I was hoping he didn't notice, though.

"I don't know if I should be insulted or not." He laughed and walked into his closet to put on a pair of pants and a shirt.

I turned to give him privacy. "It was a compliment, not a dig."

He tapped my shoulder and sat on the end of the bed, putting out his hand when he was done.

"What?" I asked.

He shook his head with a small eye-roll and a smile. "Sweets, give me the ice."

I love it when he calls me that, but I'll never admit it out loud. I usually act like I hate it. It's the nickname he gave me in high school. I was—and still am—addicted to Smarties. I could eat them all day if it wouldn't put me in a sugar shock.

I sat on his bed next to him. "Don't leave it on there longer than twenty minutes at a time, twenty on, twenty off. Give it time to get back to normal temps in between."

He bumped my shoulder with his. "Thanks, Mom." He smiled and placed the ice on his eye. I was about to get up and say goodnight when he lightly gripped my arm. "You okay?" he asked in a serious tone.

I looked at him. "Yeah, why wouldn't I be?"

"Because that guy put his hands on you without you wanting him to. I just wanted to make sure you were good. He had no—"

I placed my hand on his. "I promise I'm good. Plus, some strong guy saved me and kept me safe." We smiled at each other. "I'm really grateful you were there, Nick. Thanks for looking out for me."

He smiled. "Forever and always."

CHAPTER FIVE

Callie

SEPTEMBER

Jake has been blowing up my phone today. Tonight is the night that would have been our wedding rehearsal dinner. I've been successful at ignoring him, but staying strong is getting harder and harder. For some reason, I miss that dickhead. Sleeping alone after this long is hard, but I'm focused on making it through the next few days. They are definitely going to be the hardest.

My mom called last night and told me she would need me at the restaurant since she couldn't be there. She was getting some new table tops from a few towns over for the remodel she was planning. As her unofficial second in command, I have to be in charge. I haven't returned to the restaurant since I found Sara in bed with Jake. I'm not looking forward to seeing her. Luckily, I only had one piano lesson I needed to reschedule.

I pulled up to the restaurant at four in the morning. I was pissed as hell already because I left my energy drink on the counter at home. When I got out of the car, Sara was already waiting in the parking lot. She froze when she saw me. I wish I could tell her to leave, but my mom and I have already had a lengthy conversation about it. I can't do anything about her being here. My mom made me promise I wouldn't start anything with her while at work. I would never jeopardize my mom's business over some stupid bitch anyway. Mom knows that.

"Hey, Callie. Glad you're back," Sara mumbled. She probably knew I wouldn't answer her, but I'll give her points for trying.

I walked by her without saying a damn word. I went inside, started all the coffee pots, took all the chairs down, and did all the quick opening duties. We got busy as soon as I opened the doors. Being busy meant there would be less standing around for Sara to do. I said maybe five words to her throughout the entire day, which is how I liked it.

I was just about done with my shift when the afternoon shift lead arrived to take over for me. I had to finish a few managerial things before I could get out of here. Luckily, most people here were and have been my friends forever. They all know exactly what Sara did and have been treating her accordingly. I eventually told everyone to cool it because I didn't want to stoop to Sara's level. I didn't want any drama starting while I was in charge.

I got a little overwhelmed throughout the day, but did okay after keeping my distance from her. When I finished with all my tables, I walked back into my mom's office and sat down, letting out a sigh of relief at being alone. It was short-lived because I heard the door shut behind me. I knew without looking it was Sara.

"Callie, can you please let me explain?" Her voice was quiet, almost strained and desperate.

I turned the chair and gave her a smug smile.

"You want me to let you explain why I found you in bed with my fiancé? Okay, go for it. I can't wait to hear this."

"He came in looking for you one day. You were busy, so he was waiting at the counter. I asked him if he could come over to look at something at my house that I needed to get fixed. So he came over that day when I got off work." She paused like she expected me to say something, but I kept staring at her, waiting for her to continue. "He offered to fix it for me, so we exchanged numbers. I promise it was purely for that reason. I had no ill intentions. He fixed it for me over the next few days. He mistakenly texted me a picture that night and said he meant to text it to you. I thought the conversation was over at that point. Then he asked how I thought he looked. One thing led to another, and he invited me to hang out the night you and Aubrey went to the concert." She paused again, looking down at her hands, twisting them together in front of her. "That's when it started, I guess. It just happened, Callie. I'm so, so sorry."

I felt an evil smile overtake my face. I just caught her in her own lie, and I didn't even have to do anything.

I leaned forward toward her, "You told me when I caught you that night it was the first time you had been with him, Sara." Her face went ghostly white. I leaned back, trying to hold in my anger. "Don't sweat it. You can have him. I hope you guys are thrilled to be together. He slept with you and nine others in the past eight months while he was also with me. Now, if you will excuse me, I need to get home and get dressed for my *wedding* rehearsal dinner." I smiled and ushered her out.

The minute the door shut, my fake smile fell as my knees gave out. I let out the uncontrollable sob I'd been holding in all day. I tried to be as quiet as possible. My back slid down the door until I reached the floor. Then I cried until there were no tears left.

When I finally collected myself and left out the back door, a bouquet was on my windshield. My instincts were to trash them immediately because I thought they were from Jake. When I picked the bouquet up, I realized they were Bluebells.

Nick.

Nick is the only person who gives me Bluebells. It was always our inside joke in high school because a guy I dated gave them to me. Blue is my least favorite color. The kid joked they were purplish-blue like that would make it better, but it didn't matter. Blue used to remind me of my dad, so I have hated every shade of it since. Nick made a joke that he would always buy them for me to piss me off when necessary. I honestly can't remember the last time he had gotten them for me, but I suddenly seemed to love this shade of blue. Bluebells signify kindness. They also represent gratitude for someone's friendship, love, and support.

There was a note attached.

SWEETS, I KNOW TODAY WAS PROBABLY A HORRIBLE DAY FOR YOU, AND I KNOW YOU'RE DREADING THE NIGHT EVEN MORE. I WANTED YOU TO KNOW I PROMISE TO GET YOU HOME SAFELY AND LISTEN TO YOU ALL NIGHT WHEN YOU'RE SUPER DRUNK. I'LL EVEN SHIT TALK WITH YOU LIKE OLD TIMES IF YOU WANT ME TO. I WILL BE OUT ALL DAY FOR A WORKSHOP, BUT I'LL PICK YOU UP FROM THE HOUSE AT SIX FOR DINNER. HUG THE PURPLISH-BLUE FLOWERS IF YOU MISS ME TOO MUCH.

SINCERELY, YOUR SECOND BEST FRIEND, WHO IS SLOWLY BECOMING YOUR FIRST SINCE I GAVE YOU A PLACE TO LIVE. FOREVER AND ALWAYS.

The smile that spread across my face made my cheeks hurt. This man is saving me in so many ways, and he doesn't even know it. When I got home, Aubrey was already waiting for me on the couch.

"What's got you smiling? I've missed that smile lately."

I didn't say a word and just showed her the bouquet.

She knew.

I asked everyone attending tonight to wear black. Since we are celebrating the death of my relationship, funeral attire just felt right. Nick made a massive deal about picking me up. He made it all extravagant and bought some cheap champagne. He also insisted we make a toast to my singleness before we left the house. Then he told me to wait two minutes before going outside, then kissed my cheek as he smiled before he took off outside. It was a little weird, but that's Nick for you.

When I walked outside, I saw he had taken red chalk and colored a "red carpet" on the stairs and sidewalk. He stood at the bottom of the stairs with his hand out.

"Your chariot awaits, M'lady."

I threw my head back and let out an obnoxious, loud laugh that made me snort. I took his hand and kissed his cheek. "You're such a dork."

He linked his arm to mine and opened the car door. He leaned down and whispered in my ear before he let my hand go, "You love it."

Shivers ran down my body as the door shut. I felt a warm, fluttering feeling in my stomach that I couldn't quite place. Was it nervousness? Was it excitement?

He got in the car and kissed my hand before giving me a once-over. "You look beautiful, Callie."

"Thank you," I smiled shyly.

Once we arrived, everyone seemed on edge about giving me their condolences and trying not to harp on the subject. Aubrey's biological father, August, was the first one to make me laugh by telling me he would put some termites at Jake's next job site if I wanted him to. He and his wife, Liza, are really the sweetest humans on the planet.

When Aubrey learned about her dad last year, I thought it would be absolute chaos. When she finally met him earlier this year, he and his wife became such a constant in her life and mine, and I'm so grateful for that.

Aubrey sat between Nick and me as she always does at any function we attend, but Lincoln was also between us this time. Nick and I usually end up bickering, but I was honestly sad he wasn't next to me.

Small conversations broke out as everyone arrived. I was joking with Brielle across the table when Aubrey's mom, Michelle, caught my attention.

"So, Callie, what will you be doing about the honeymoon?"

A few people, including myself, froze. I looked around before answering.

"Um, I haven't really thought about it, actually." I gulped my wine. "I guess I will just go anyway and enjoy everything I had planned. Getting away from here for a few weeks will be fun and beneficial," I said with uncertainty clear in my voice.

Aubrey paused mid-sentence while in an entirely different conversation with her dad, turning to me.

"You're going alone?" The question sounded judgey. She was definitely judging me.

"Who else am I going to go with? None of you can just up and leave for three weeks on such short notice." Nick and Aubrey were giving each other a look...I know that look. What are they planning?

I was pulled from my thoughts when I heard the server telling someone to stay out. I stood up instantly because I knew Jake was about to walk through the glass doors. Then the door opened.

"What the fuck is this?" Jake said rather loudly.

Nick, Link, and Aubrey stood up. I sat back down as if his presence wasn't going to affect me in the slightest, even though a red-hot rage was burning inside me. I kept eating without acknowledging him.

Nick spoke first. "We are celebrating our friend, and I am one thousand percent sure you were not invited."

"Excuse me?" Jake sounded a little hurt. "This is the dinner for my wedding." He sounded almost desperate.

Aubrey looked at me for a clue on what to do. Honestly, I am winging it just like everyone else. I motioned for everyone to sit down, so they did. I started speaking to Jake without looking up at him. I knew If I did, I might cry.

"Jake, I'm not sure what you're doing here, but I am celebrating my newfound singleness with the people who *actually* love me. Your name is not on the guest list, so if you will see yourself out, I would appreciate it."

I went back to eating. Everyone else remained starkly quiet for a few seconds.

"Cal, I need to talk to you," he said in desperation.

"I think you should go, son." Both of Aubrey's dads stood, but only August spoke. "Maybe you should contact her later when she's alone." He tried to grab Jake's arm to lead him out, but Jake pulled away.

"She won't talk to me on the phone. I had no other option."

"Wonder why," Nick mumbled as he rolled his eyes.

It looked like Jake was about to lay into Nick, so I stood up to get his attention to avoid a blow-up. I motioned toward the door and signaled for Jake to follow me. I knew if I didn't listen to him and get him out of there, he wouldn't leave. I gave him five minutes. I looked back at Nick; he was burning a hole through me with his fierce glare. I gave him a reassuring look, but his face remained unchanged.

I led Jake out to the front of the restaurant. I sat on one of the copper benches that I loved so much. This restaurant has been my favorite since I was a little girl. It was built to look like it belonged in Little Italy. The rustic feel is why I loved it so much.

My dad used to take me here for day dates when he returned from long work trips. It's one of my only memories of him before he disappeared from my life. We haven't seen or heard from him since I was young. I am pretty sure my mom knows more about him and his whereabouts than she has ever told me, but I stopped wondering about what happened a long time ago. I know from social media that he lives in California now, but that is the extent of my caring about him and what he's doing.

Jake sat down beside me but left some room between us. He started speaking, but I had drowned him out with the thoughts of my dad. His apology was the typical "I'm so sorry, please forgive me, and let's still get married in two days" conversation he'd been trying to have with me over and over for two weeks now. I'm not sure what part of him could even possibly think I would still want to marry him, but here we are.

I shook my head to clear my thoughts and spoke sternly, "Jake. Why are you doing this? Why can't you just let me and our relationship go? Move on with one of the other women you have?"

"Because they aren't you, Cal. You are my forever." He inched closer to me to grab me and pull me in. "I love you, baby; please don't do this."

I waited to feel something, anything, but this didn't feel like it used to. His hugs used to send my heart into a frenzy, but now that feeling was gone. I pushed away from him.

"Jake, I am not doing anything you don't deserve. I can't be with someone who claims that sleeping with another woman is their way of showing me they love me. Let's just get over the fact that we wasted all this time with the wrong person and move on."

His face fell, and then I saw the anger and rage take over. "Callie, you can't do this. We are made for each other. You will regret it if you don't take me back. No one can love you like I do."

I didn't know if he was just making a vile comment or a genuine threat, so I stepped even further away from him.

"Jake, I hope you are right about no one loving me the way you do. I never want to feel this worthless ever again. This is over. We are over. We have nothing left to talk about. My things have been removed from *your* house. I removed myself from *your* life. I will eat the cost of all the wedding stuff, and I need nothing else from you. You can be happy with all your women and have the time of your life. You'll never have to see or talk to me again."

"Callie, I—"

"Goodbye, Jake. Please don't contact me again." I turned around to return to my friends and family and found my mom restlessly waiting for me with open arms right inside the door.

I started tearing up immediately when I saw her arms outstretched. "Are you okay, baby girl?"

I fell into her arms and let it all out. I don't know how long we stood there, but my mom didn't say a word or pull away, which I appreciated.

My mom has never been a very affectionate person toward me. It's been her and I for as long as I can remember. She has had to work her butt off to take care of us, which took her away from home for most of my childhood. That is how Aubrey and I got so close. I spent most days at her house. Mom and I have grown a little closer as I became an adult.

To this day, she is still not the affectionate type, so the fact that she is here for me in such a way made me grateful. When I was finally done crying, I looked up at her.

"I'm not okay, but I will be."

When I finally returned to my friends and family, no one bothered to ask about what happened; we all just went on as if it hadn't happened at all. I looked at Aubrey, and she held up her drink in a toast. Nick didn't look at me once until we left for the night.

"Bring on the wine," I announced.

Nick

I told Callie I would get her home safely tonight, and that's exactly what I'm attempting to do. Now, if only she would just let me hold her hand and walk her out, we would be golden. She keeps trying—and failing—to walk herself out. She is stumbling more than a drunken sailor.

I got sick of her tripping over her own feet, so I picked her up and carried her over my shoulder. Aubrey was drunk, too, but Link seemed to have a good hold on her. We all said our goodbyes as I plopped Callie down into the car.

When I tried to shut the door, she put her hand out to stop it and looked at me through hooded eyes. "Nick, you are the best guy in the world. I hope you know that."

She patted my cheek, so I grabbed her hands, and I couldn't help but smile and move her hands to her lap. This was the real Callie. This was the Callie I always wanted to see, the sweet, kind version of her she tries to hide from everyone else.

I should have probably gotten the compliment she gave on recording so I could hold it over her head later when she's in a hating-me mood, but she's having a rough night, so I won't. I shut the door without responding.

When I started driving, she leaned her head on the door and exhaled like she had been holding her breath or something.

"You okay, Sweets?"

"No."

I was hesitant to ask because she hates when people pry into her business. Honestly, the last thing I want to talk about or hear about is Jake and how much he hurt her, but I asked anyway. "Do you wanna talk about it?"

I shouldn't have asked.

She spent the entire ride telling me every nasty, foul word and every shitty thing that man had ever said and done to her. I didn't know most of this shit, but why would I. Her being with him changed everything for us. *Us? Where the fuck did that come from?*

At first, it was simple things like making her do what she had asked him to do, like the lawn work and taking out the trash cans. She started telling me more serious things, like the names he called her and canceling dinners at the last minute. She also mentioned there were several nights that he chose to not even come home without letting her know.

"But that's how men are, I guess."

I must have zoned out on some of what she was saying because I barely heard the last part. I turned my head and gave her a puzzled look even though she wasn't looking at me and still staring out the front window.

"Callie, not even one of those things is normal. It is not okay for a man to tell any woman, let alone the woman he loves, that she is a lazy pig or anything even close to that. Why did you let him treat you like that? Why didn't you say something? Why didn't you just leave?"

"Nick, stop. It's not that easy when you love someone."

"Yes, it is Callie. Come on. I know you are not that naïve. I would never let someone speak to me that way, and I sure as hell wouldn't have stood by and let him treat you that way if I had known."

She was quiet for a second before she finally looked at me.

"Why would you have cared how I was treated? You made it clear a long time ago that you didn't want to know anything about my relationship with Jake. I barely saw you unless you were with Aubs the moment I started dating him."

Luckily, I was pulling into the driveway. I turned the car off before turning toward her in anger.

"Are you fucking kidding me right now? You're the one who became a different person as soon as you two found each other, Callie. You stopped calling me to hang out, stopped seeing me anytime I wasn't with Aubrey, and you acted as if you fucking hated me anytime I said a damn word. Plus, you know the moment you told me he even breathed funny toward you, I would have–"

"Shut up. I did not. It was all you. You didn't give a shit anymore."

I felt myself getting angrier by the second with every word that came out of my mouth, so instead of continuing this and turning it into a bigger fight than it needed to be, I got out of the car, walked to her side, and helped her out. She was drunk and wouldn't remember most of what was said tonight anyway.

"This conversation is over, Callie. If you want to talk more when you are sober, we can do so. Tonight, I'm done. We both need to cool off."

"I don't want to talk to you, Nick. You just don't get it."

"Okay, Cal, you're right."

"Fuck you, Nick."

I didn't bother saying anything else. I helped Callie up the stairs and held her arm while I unlocked the door. She didn't make it easy, trying to pull away every two seconds. Once inside, I locked the door behind us so we could both go to bed. I turned around, and she was still standing there, staring at me—closer than when we walked in.

"What are you looking at?" I asked in an irritated tone.

"You, you're...infuriating."

My eyebrows went up in surprise. "You think I'm... you know what, Callie, you're right. It's all my—"

She moved toward me, pushing me against the door. Her lips were on mine, cutting off not only my words but any rational thoughts I had left. My fingers dug into her ass without hesitation. I've never felt something more perfect in my life. I'd always wondered what touching her ass would feel like. I lifted her off the floor, her legs wrapping around my waist. Her thick thighs gripping my body made me feel even more at home. She fit perfectly against me.

"I fucking hate you," she murmured on my lips as I smirked. She kissed me again, harder this time. Her warm tongue tangled with mine, and she let out the sexiest moan. We made our way toward her bedroom. I placed her on her bed and kissed her even deeper. I never wanted to stop, but I knew I had to. She tried to pull me closer when I pulled away. I kissed her cheek and whispered in her ear.

"I don't hate you, which is why we can't do this until you are ready and sober." I gripped her chin with my thumb and pointer finger and made her look me in the eye. "When we do this, and yes, I mean when. You will be mine. There will be no going back." I grinned and gave her a peck on the lips before turning around and walking to the door. "Good night, Sweets. I will see you in the morning."

I went to my room and took the coldest shower I think I'd ever taken. I couldn't get the visions of what had just happened out of my head. Once I realized the cold water wouldn't help, I turned on the hot water and stopped torturing myself. I closed my eyes and gripped my cock while picturing Callie's curvy body wrapping around mine. I placed one hand on the shower wall, letting the hot water hit my back. As my brain wandered to thoughts of Callie, I started with slow strokes—the thoughts of her plump ass in my hands, her smooth lips on mine. I almost wished I wasn't such a nice guy. I wish I didn't stop her. I should be deep inside her right now, making her mine, but I could never do that to her unless she explicitly tells me that's what she wants while she is completely sober.

I surprised myself tonight by telling her some of that stuff, not that she will remember it in the morning, but I'm hoping I didn't just fuck everything up by saying something so intense like that too soon.

I gripped my cock harder and moved my hand faster to chase my release. I was picturing Callie on her knees, ready and waiting for me. Her plump lips wrapped around me. Licking the thick vein on the underside of my–"Fuck, yes, Callie." I practically yelled her name when I came. God, this woman is going to be the death of me.

CALLIE

Holy. Fucking. Headache!

What did I do last night? I don't even remember coming home. I lifted the blanket and saw I was still in my dress from last night, but my heels were on the floor. The faint smell of coffee and bacon made my stomach turn before I could enjoy it. I ran to the bathroom, hurling up my entire body weight in liquid.

When I could finally get my shit together, I changed into sweats, brushed my teeth, and headed to the kitchen. Nick was sitting there reading the newspaper with his glasses on the tip of his nose. It was cute, kind of like a little old man.

"I think I just got a vision of the future when you're an old man on Sunday mornings sitting there with your paper and coffee."

Nick looked at me and placed his glasses down on top of the rest of the newspaper. "Morning, Sweets. Are you saying you plan on waking up to me when we are old and gray?"

"Shut up. You know what I meant."

He sipped his coffee again. "No, I don't, but a guy can hope, right?"

He gave me another smug smile and then motioned toward the microwave. "I made you some bacon and eggs. You just have to heat it up." He stood and placed his dishes in the sink. "Don't worry about the dishes. I'll get them done after my shower."

He tried to walk away, but I couldn't let him go without talking about last night. I felt horrible for making him take care of me.

"Nick, thanks for getting me home last night. I'm sorry about that fight in the car. You were just trying to help. I know you care about what happens to me."

"I know, Sweets. Think nothing of it."

He tried to walk away, but I stopped him once again. "About the kiss...I...I'm sorry about that, too. Thank you for being a gentleman."

He called out from down the hall. "Don't sweat it, Sweets. It wasn't the first time and won't be the last...I promise."

My cheeks blushed, and I bit my lip with the memory of that kiss running through my head. I couldn't remember details of everything that had transpired, but I did remember kissing him at the door and then leaving me wanting. I'm trying to figure out why I really want to do it again.

After two failed attempts at holding my food down, I gave up and got ready for my piano lesson and read a little of my book before Aubrey came over. I figured I could just sip on water until I was ready to try to eat again. I was a little on edge getting ready because this was the first lesson since the breakup. When I broke up with Jake, I called and told all my students I had an emergency and needed a few weeks off. I am happy to be getting back into a routine again.

I heard the front door open just as I finished brushing my hair. Aubrey told me last night that she would stop by at some point today because she had something to give me in private. She looked a little uncomfortable about whatever it was, but I knew I would be able to suss her out as soon as she came over.

I walked into the living room thinking I would find her sitting on the couch, but the living room was empty. I looked around and realized there was an envelope on the table next to the napkin holder. It had my name on it in Aubrey's writing.

Weird.

When I opened the envelope, I was holding a five-thousand-dollar check. I sat down because I was taken aback by the fact that I was holding that much money. I tried calling her, but she ignored it. A moment later, a text came through.

Aubrey

No, I am not taking it back.

> **Yes, you are cashing it, or I will do it for you. It is for you to get back on your feet.**

> **And before you ask, no…you won't be paying me back.**

I gripped my phone and held it to my chest. God, I love her. I don't want to cash it, but I'm so broke I don't have a choice.

Today I was teaching my favorite student, Cooper. I couldn't wait to see his cute little face.

"Why are you in a new house, Miss Callie?" Cooper asked.

I wasn't sure how to respond to an eleven-year-old because he may understand what breakups are, but I didn't exactly want to be the one to teach a child about relationships and cheating. It wasn't my place to teach him that. "It was just time to move on, so I moved in with my best friend."

"Okay," he said, giving me a shrug.

He went right into playing. I could tell he had been practicing without me. I was so proud.

On one of the breaks, I could tell he still had a few questions to ask. "What's up? You look like you have another question."

"Where is your ring?"

I looked down at my hand, my heart aching a little. I sat next to him on the bench. "I realized it wasn't meant for me, so I gave it back."

He seemed to be appeased by that answer. He just turned back to the keys and continued playing.

Since Aubrey and I were both music teachers, we came up with the idea of doing a mini-music show once a year with some of our students. Nick has offered the school auditorium for us to use. I'm super excited about the kids being able to show off all the work they've put into music. I had about eight months left to prepare the kids for the show, which would be held at the end of May. I can already tell Cooper's performance is going to be great.

I had one more student after Cooper. Luckily, I made it through both lessons without throwing up. Note to self: do not get drunk the night before little kids are going to be banging on piano keys; you will regret your life choices and want to stab your ears with a pen.

I took a nice hot shower and was planning to relax until I realized we had absolutely no food in the house. I really should cook Nick dinner as a thank-you for last night's escapades. I texted him and asked if there was anything specific that he wanted tonight.

Nick

Hemorrhoid cream, thanks, Sweets. You're the best.

I am not buying hemorrhoid cream, asshole.

Do you need any food? I'm being serious.

Nick

No, whatever you make is good. You're no fun, lol. I was trying to make you smile, dummy.

He did make me smile. A smile seemed to be permanently stuck on my face, especially when he was involved.

I grabbed what I needed from the grocery store and headed home to cook. I figured tacos were a good thank-you meal since they are his favorite. I opted not to drink tonight so my body could recover a little since I knew I'd be drowning myself in alcohol again tomorrow on my would-be wedding day.

I still didn't know what the hell I was going to do about the honeymoon. Part of me didn't want to go alone, but the other part thought it would be great to have some fun alone and relax without anyone I knew.

That's when the best idea I've ever had popped into my head...*Nick*. I could also use it as a way to say, "Thank you for letting me move in when I was a complete and broken mess" type of thing. A big plus is that he will make sure I don't get lost and die in a foreign place. We could both enjoy the time off work in the warm weather together. I will book another room for him because one bed would just be awkward.

I had set the table and prepared the tacos when he texted me to let me know he was on his way home.

"Honey, I'm home," Nick said as he chuckled and shut the door.

I called out from the kitchen, "Sit. Your food is ready."

"Yes, dear." he chuckled.

I was quieter than usual as we ate. I was afraid to bring it up because I already knew he was going to refuse. I think he could tell something was off because he kept smirking. Once he finished his drink, he placed his cup down and stared at me. "Okay, spill. Something is on your mind. Let it out."

I smiled. "I have an idea that I think you're gonna like," I said.

"Do tell," Nick said, intrigued.

"Now, don't laugh. I'm being one hundred percent serious. I will get you your own room." Nick sat up straighter, his smirk becoming a look of worry, almost like he was scared. "Come on the honeymoon with me.

We can make it a fun vacation. Everything is already paid for; we can have fun doing best-friend shit."

He put his taco down and just stared at me blankly. "You're serious? When is it?"

"It won't be until October because we planned to go when Jake's work slowed down in the colder months."

"Where is it? I don't think you ever told us."

"The Bahamas, for a few weeks," I explained.

His face turned stark white, giving me a look I didn't think I'd ever seen before. "Callie, I can't."

"Why not? Please. Please come with me."

"Callie, I can't get on a plane. You know that."

"Oh, come on, you chicken. Do it for me."

"The answer is no, Callie, I just can't. I can't get on a plane. I'm sorry."

I can't believe he is turning down a free trip to the Bahamas because he's too scared to fly. I mean, I always knew he was, which is why we drove to Tennessee for our college trip. He's never come with Aubrey and me anytime we have traveled and needed a flight, but I didn't think his fear was that serious. His skin is whiter than a sheet of paper just talking about it. He looks like he's going to be sick.

"I'm done eating." Nick stood up and left his plate on the table. "Thanks for the food." He walked into his bedroom without another word.

Weird.

After I cleaned up the dinner mess, I was about to knock on his door, but my phone rang. It was my mom. She needed me to help her with something at her house. I left a note for Nick just in case he came out and realized I was gone.

I hope he's okay.

Chapter Seven

Nick

I heard the front door shut, so I assumed Callie left because she was mad at me. My assumption made me feel like an ass as soon as I saw the note about her mom. After doing the dishes, I sat down to play some video games. My playing was trash because I couldn't stop thinking about the trip. I would love to be able to go on a trip with her, but I can't fly. I just can't.

The first and last flight I ever took was when I was moving here. I flew here after my parents died. It was probably the worst experience of my life.

It was like anything that could go wrong happened all at once. My flight got delayed three different times, causing me to miss my connecting flight. At fifteen, I had to try to find a new flight and coordinate with my grandma so she'd still be able to pick me up. The turbulence was so bad it made me cry like a baby. To top it off, all of my bags got lost. Granted, I got them back a week later, but still, I didn't have them for the first week here, which made things very hard. I had taken only the most important things with me, like my pictures and important documents.

I had just lost my parents, and then I lost everything I owned. It wasn't a very pleasant time for me to say the least. I haven't flown since, and I wasn't planning to ever again.

I gave up on playing my Xbox and called Aubrey and Link and told them what Callie had asked me. I needed to know if I was being a complete idiot, and the two of them were usually very honest. Link and I hadn't known each other that long, but we got close fast.

As I thought, they didn't hold back. Link told me to stop being a little bitch, and Aubrey said the same thing, but with a little more finesse.

"Nick, come on. When are you ever going to get another opportunity to go to the Bahamas for free? Aubrey's voice got more serious. "Plus, it will give you some alone time to spend with her, and maybe you can finally tell her how you—"

"I'm not doing that," I cut her off. "I can't tell her. We have already had some weird, awkward things happen, and thankfully, they haven't ruined anything. I'm not going to press my luck."

"Nicholas," Aubrey screeched. "What happened? Why haven't either of you told me? Why am I the odd woman out? We are supposed to tell each other everything."

"I haven't told you because it's none of your business." I smiled because Aubrey hates being told something wasn't her business, and I knew it would set her off. "And she probably hasn't told you because she was so drunk both times. I don't think she even knows what happened."

She huffed into the phone, and even though we weren't on Facetime, I know she rolled her eyes because Link was laughing hysterically.

I was quiet for a few moments because, as much as I didn't want to admit it, they were right. I really do want to go with her, but I just can't get past the thought of flying.

"I will give you some Xanax if you go so you can knock yourself out on the plane. You won't even know anything is happening. It is a short flight anyway," Aubrey said. "I promise it will be worth it."

"I don't know Aubs."

"Bro, come on. Spend time with her and make her happy. Show her what she is missing," Link added.

"I don't know...I guess I will think about it."

After hanging up with them, I got comfortable and put on a movie I had no intention of actually watching. I laid down while trying to talk myself into going. *I don't know if I can make myself do this.*

I must have fallen asleep, because the next thing I knew, Callie was covering me up with a blanket.

CALLIE

I pulled into the driveway, and the lights were still on. I sat there for a few minutes, contemplating how I was going to apologize for being such a bitch before I left. I started feeling horrible for trying to pressure him.

I unlocked the door and saw Nick asleep on the couch. The view made me stop short in the doorway.

He looked so peaceful. He stirred when I shut the door, and the blanket fell to his waist. For a thin, lengthy man, he really does have some definition on him. You wouldn't expect him to look like that when you see him with clothes on, but Nick is fucking hot.

Lately, I had noticed small, new things about him, making me wonder why I hadn't seen these things sooner. Was I that oblivious?

Sadly, Nick and I haven't been able to have a real, true friendship since becoming adults, and being here makes me wonder if maybe we are getting back to the way things were before Jake. I wonder if we can even get there because my dumbass can't stop getting all horny and making out with him every time I'm drunk. If I don't stop, I'll ruin everything. I know he's just trying to be nice by making silly jokes about wanting me and kissing me again. He can't be serious, but I'm finding it hard not to think about it.

I walked over to him, trying my best to stay quiet and not disturb him. I put one of his grandma's quilts over him. He opened his eyes slowly as soon as I pulled my hands away.

"Hey, you," he said with a sexy, gravelly voice as he stretched and sat up. "Everything okay with your mom?"

I sat beside him because he wasn't acting angry. I thought it was safe. "Yeah, everything is fine. She just needed some help with a few things, nothing major." I paused, then apologized. "I am sorry I was trying to guilt trip you into coming with me. You have already done more than enough for me. I shouldn't be trying to force you into going with me. It will be fine. I will be okay alone. I promise."

When he stared at me, it felt like he looked deep into my soul. He looked like he wanted to say something, but he didn't. My skin was heating under his gaze.

"What?" I asked.

"Nothing." He looked away as he got up and started to fold the blankets that got messed up when he was asleep.

I didn't want things to get more awkward, so I said goodnight. I grabbed my clothes and went to shower. When I returned to my bedroom, I let out a loud scream because Nick startled me when he was sitting on my bed reading the book I kept on my nightstand.

"This book is porn." He smiled at me and sat up.

Even though my heart was racing, I started to laugh uncontrollably. "Why do you think I read it? I needed something to get me off now that Jake is gone." I regretted saying it the moment it left my mouth, and I instantly felt the heat racing up my neck and cheeks. I covered my face, making it super obvious.

"Yeah...not touching that one," Nick said with a chuckle. He started to walk past me and leave, but I realized he hadn't told me why he was in my room.

"Did you need something?" I asked.

He turned to me and smirked. "I will go with you on one condition."

My face perked up with excitement. I waited for him to continue without saying a word.

"No making fun of me when I cry or pass out from fear on the plane."

I jumped into his arms and gave him a huge hug. "Thank you. Thank you. Thank you. You are the best friend ever."

I let go after about twenty seconds, and he let me down. I looked up at him, realizing his demeanor had changed. I went to pull away but stopped because I realized he was studying me. He reached out his hand and brushed his fingers across my cheek, stopping right before running it over my lips. Surprisingly, I didn't pull away. It felt...intimate.

Nick smiled. "You are so lucky I l—." Nick cleared his throat. "Lucky I would do anything for you, Sweets." He turned and nonchalantly walked out the door.

What the fuck was that?

Today was supposed to be my wedding day. I was up all night dreading waking up today, though I should be glad I woke up and not the alternative. I finally fell asleep around four in the morning. I assumed it was later than my usual wake-up time. When I opened my eyes and looked out the window, there was a brightness to the day even though it was raining outside. Of course, it was raining. I guess it's a good thing after all that I'm not having the garden wedding I planned.

I looked at my phone and saw it was just after nine in the morning, so I was right. I had three missed calls from Jake and just as many voicemails. *I am definitely not calling him back.*

I was about to lie back down, but I heard voices in the kitchen, which piqued my interest. I put on my slippers and headed out the door. I stopped short when my friends and mom stared back at me. Everyone was here, and I mean everyone—Mom, Nick, all four of Aubrey's parents, Bri, Amani, and, of course, Aubrey and Link. Aubrey said a few people from the restaurant were also on their way.

"We were all planning to spend the day with you anyway, so we came together and made it a party. I hope that's okay," my mom said with a spatula in her hand. "Plus, we knew Nick couldn't cook you anything except eggs, and you need some sustenance today."

Everyone laughed.

I'm not usually an emotional person, but then I saw the vase with the fresh Bluebells. I looked at Nick, but he just shrugged with a smile. My eyes started to tear up as I placed my face in my hands. "I don't deserve you guys. You guys are so—"

"Aww, Cal, don't cry, babe; we all love you so much," Aubrey said as she embraced me. She pulled me into the living room, and my favorite non-romantic movie, The Pacifier, was playing.

I looked over at Nick and mouthed, "Thank you." He held up his hands and smirked again. He acted like none of this was his idea, but I know it was. I told him I wanted to be alone on my would-be wedding day. He hardcore called me out on my bullshit and immediately told me I shouldn't be alone and that he would make sure of it.

We watched a bunch of movies and ate a ton of Spanish food, which is my mom's specialty. Aubrey's parents left just after lunch, and my mom left a few hours later. We played a few board games once it was just my friends and me. Brielle won almost every game; she always does.

Aubrey's phone rang a few minutes after we started our game of Clue. When I looked up at her, I saw the worry in her eyes, but she didn't say anything. She got up, eyeing Nick, then answered the call as she left the room. Nick got up and followed her immediately. I excused myself from the rest of the group. I said I had to pee, but I was just being nosey. They were in Nick's bedroom, so I leaned against the door to see if I could hear anything.

Nick was doing his best to whisper.

"Fuck you for even trying to call today. You don't deserve to even breathe the same air as her. Don't fucking call this number again, you piece of shit."

I knew it was Jake. I opened the door without considering how close they might be standing to it. Aubrey jumped back, the door nearly missing her. She gave me a heavy-hearted look before pulling me back into the hall before I could even fully step into his room.

"I'm sorry. I tried to keep it away from you today, but he kept calling."

"I get it. You don't have to hide it from me, though. He called multiple times and left me messages this morning, but I didn't listen," I admitted.

"How? Didn't you block him?" she asked.

I felt a little embarrassed admitting I hadn't, so I shook my head and looked down at my feet. "I haven't been able to block him. I tried the other day, but it felt too...I don't know, final. I guess I should make it final?" I looked back up at her.

She shrugged. "Well, I kind of think so, but do it when you're ready, I guess."

Nick's voice came from the doorway. "Ready for what?"

"She was going to—"

"Make dinner. I was going to make dinner." I cut Aubrey off, and she gave me a weird look. We don't lie to each other; Nick is included in that. *Why the hell did I do that?*

He saw the weird look and gave one right back to the both of us. "Well, that was the worst lie ever, but I'll let it go because I know Aubrey will tell me later."

He walked away, whistling.

Smug bastard.

I turned and pleaded with Aubrey. "Please don't say a word to him about Jake."

She looked at me with pity. "I won't bring it up, but Cal, if he asks me, I won't lie. You shouldn't be talking to Jake at all. Block him, okay?"

I nodded. "I will."

NICK

I spent most of today ensuring everything was perfect for Callie. I didn't want her to spend any time thinking about the fact that it was supposed to be her wedding day. After everyone left, Aubrey and Callie went to get pampered. I scheduled a massage and pedicure for them right around dinnertime. Callie thinks her mom paid for it. I asked her mom to keep it that way.

Link stayed to help me clean up while he waited for Aubrey. When we were done, we sat down to play some Xbox. It is unbelievable how close he and I have gotten. I first learned about Link when Aubrey went to find her biological dad. The first time Aubrey told me she was dating him, she made a joke about dating a more buff version of me. I didn't believe her, but then I met him. It's scary how alike we really are. We have the same job, likes, dislikes, and even the same sense of humor. He fit into Aubrey's life seamlessly. The biggest plus about him is that he loves my best friend just as much as I do. The only significant difference between us is our experience with women.

"Cal told me you decided to go to the Bahamas with her." He looked over at me.

"Was that a question, or are you just letting me know?" I chuckled.

"I don't know. I just think it's great you took our advice and are going. I think you guys will have a lot of fun. Callie deserves to have some fun." He said it with a smirk, but wasn't looking at me. His eyes stayed focused on the screen. I paused it with my gaming controller to get his attention.

"What does that mean?" I asked.

"Nothing."

He was still smirking.

"Dude, tell me what that meant?" It came out like an annoyed child, and I honestly felt stupid because I knew exactly what he meant.

"Nick, you're in love with her. This trip is the perfect opportunity to tell her how you feel."

"I can't. She is too vulnerable right now. She got cheated on two weeks ago. Today is her fucking wedding day, for god's sake. I can't do that to her and confuse her even more." I turned back to the game and resumed playing. "Plus, I've been throwing playful hints around, but she doesn't seem phased. I can't ruin our friendship. If I lose Callie, I'll lose you all. Aubrey and Callie are soulmates and you know it. You and I are the secondary characters in their story."

He laughed, "You know Aubs would never leave you in the lurch like that, Nick. I don't think it would go badly, but that's just my opinion. You guys already fight like you're married anyway. You guys need a good fuck."

"I can't just fuck her dude, she's too special to just get it over with, plus it would be—"

Shit. I don't know how to finish that sentence without giving away that I've never had sex before, but I know he's going to ask. It's too embarrassing to admit.

Link was staring me down, waiting. I looked away and sipped my beer to give myself time. "You can't tell the girls. Promise me you won't fucking tell them."

He slapped his hand on the back of my shoulder. "Guy code, my dude. I got you. What's up?"

"I...I've never actually...ya know." I paused when Link's eyes widened. He was waiting for me to finish. "I've never fucked a girl before."

"No. Fucking. Way," Link said with a smile.

I immediately got pissed off because I thought I knew what was coming. "Don't make jokes, dude. I don't need that kind of shit right now. This is why I don't—"

"Nick. Stop." He cut me off. "I won't make fun of you, at least not yet." He smiled. "I have questions, though." He looked me right in the eyes, and I could tell he was being completely genuine. "How? You've had girlfriends, right? Don't you go on dates? How do they not end with sex at least once in a while?"

They are valid questions.

"Honestly, being with someone else never felt right. I have always compared everyone I met to Callie."

He seemed to think for a second, unsure of what to say, so I continued.

"I know what you are thinking, and yes, I've done basically everything else. Just no sex. I always stopped it before it got to the point of actual sex. They are always well taken care of and satisfied."

Link raised his eyebrows and slapped me on the back of the shoulder. "My dude," he said appreciatively. "I can't wait to hear how it goes with Callie."

I still didn't believe he wasn't going to break my balls, but I added fuel to the fire. "I know you probably think it's lame as fuck, but none of them were her," I shrugged. "I have loved Callie since I was eighteen—probably even before that, if I'm honest. I don't know how to explain it. It just always felt right to wait." I took another swig of my beer before looking at him again.

He was quiet, like he was thinking hard about something. A different smirk appeared on his face. I was about to protest whatever came out of his mouth until he surprised me when he said, "I get it."

"You do?" I asked with wide eyes.

"Just because you haven't hit a home run yet doesn't mean you haven't ever played ball. If I'm being honest, if I had known Aubrey sooner, I would have waited for her forever, too. Yeah, I was a player and slept with god knows how many people, but she changed it all. When you know, you know. You knew, so you waited. I get it."

I was in shock. "Um...thanks, I think."

Just then, the girls walked in. Link looked at me and made the zipper motion across his lips. He got up and pulled Aubrey into a kiss. I felt a rush of jealousy surge through me. We all talked for a little while longer before Aubrey and Link headed home.

Callie and I chatted over some leftovers. She told me Aubrey was taking care of some arrangements for the honeymoon for us, like getting us separate rooms, making sure our massages were separate, etc. The thought of doing things separately upset me more than I was willing to admit, but I guess it was probably for the best. I don't know what this trip will bring, but I'm excited to find out. Let the anxiety-filled countdown begin.

Chapter Eight

Callie

October

It's been about a month since my almost wedding day. Jake has called a total of four hundred seventy-one times since the breakup. Most recently, he called when he found out that his plane ticket had been transferred out of his name. I'm not sure if he thought he would still be coming or what, but he was pissed. I told him I had canceled them so I wouldn't have to answer more questions. I still can't bring myself to tell Nick or Aubrey that I haven't blocked him yet. I have zero intentions of picking up the phone, so again, I'm not sure why I haven't. Luckily, he has left Aubs and Nick alone.

Nick and I leave for our trip tomorrow. He got the approval to take a few weeks off from work. I was glad he had saved up all his sick and vacation leave time over the last few years.

I had been looking forward to this trip for so long. The reason for going may look a bit different, but I was going to spend this trip of a lifetime with one of my best friends by my side. I just knew it was going to be a memorable two weeks.

I was washing some dishes when Nick came up beside me and started drying them. For a split second, I thought he was just being nice, but then he began to bug me again, just as he'd done numerous times as of late. He's been up my ass about every little thing. He's driving me insane. He has tried to pawn off his place on this trip to Aubrey multiple times over the last month.

"You sure we can't go somewhere more local that we don't have to fly to?" Nick asked for the millionth time.

"Nick, it's tomorrow. Even if we wanted to, we couldn't change it without losing everything, so no, we can't go somewhere else."

I get it. He's scared, but he's being a complete baby about it all. I started hearing mumbles about the first and last flights he took being so horrible that it scared him for life. I couldn't make out the rest of it. I have asked him why he's so scared a few times, but he always seems to ignore me or change the subject abruptly.

"You will be fine."

He rolled his eyes. "Whatever you say, I will just take some meds to knock myself out, I guess."

"The flight is short. You probably shouldn't do that."

"I am doing it. I am going to sprawl out in my comfy chair and knock out."

Jake and I had splurged when we bought our tickets, so Nick and I will fly first class, which I think will help calm him even more. It will only be the two of us in our row, so I'm hoping the extra space will make him a little more comfortable. I am also hoping I can just get him to drink a little alcohol instead of knocking himself out entirely with the medication.

A few hours later, Aubrey came over. She and I were in my room doing some reorganizing. I had to change a few of the outfits I had originally planned out, especially what I had planned to wear to bed, which was practically nothing.

I went into the bathroom to grab my toiletries, and when I returned to my room, Aubrey was messing with my bag. She looked awfully suspicious. I couldn't immediately figure out what she had done just by looking at the bag, and I honestly didn't want to unpack the entire thing.

I looked at her with annoyance. "You're not going to tell me what you did?"

"I didn't do anything," she grinned. "You're just being paranoid."

I gave her a knowing look. "Aubrey Lynn Miller, if you fucked with my clothes, I'm going to kill you. I just spent the last hour specifically picking out every outfit. Please tell me what you did."

She laughed when she got up and gave me a big hug. "I will be here at five tomorrow morning to take you to the airport. Don't make me wait."

"You got it, Miss Priss."

She started getting up to leave, then stopped short. "Oh, wait."

She reached into her purse, pulling out an envelope. "Here is your itinerary. No opening it until you land."

"You know I hate surprises, bitch."

She put it out toward me, but quickly pulled it back.

"Promise me you won't check it until you get there. I want everything to be a complete surprise."

I rolled my eyes at her, but she kept staring at me. She knows if I make a promise, I will stick to it. I was about to respond when Nick chimed in from the hallway.

"Since you are torturing me with the plane ride, you can deal with waiting to open it."

Aubrey gestured toward him emphatically.

"I didn't realize we were five years old and going tit for tat," I joked.

"Sucks to suck, doesn't it?" Nick said with a chuckle and shrugged as he kept walking into his room.

I looked back at Aubrey. "I promise."

She is so lucky I love her. If she hadn't been such a big help, I think I would have pressed her more, but I didn't want to piss her off.

Since Aubrey made all the calls and was such a big help, the least I could do was wait to open the envelope. I knew the sleeping arrangements had been changed so Nick and I didn't have to share a room, but I was super excited to see what fun surprises she had scheduled for us.

Jake and I hadn't planned much except for a cooking class, which should be interesting since Nick is so horrible at it. Jake and I planned to spend most of our time on the beach. I assume Nick and I will do a little of that, too.

A few hours later, as I was just settling and getting ready for bed, Nick barged into my room holding a snorkel. I jumped up without thinking, smacking my hand on something. He had never just barged in like that before, so it scared the crap out of me.

"Cal, do I need this?"

After clutching my chest to calm my racing heart, I grinned at him. "First of all, did you forget how to knock? What if I was naked?" His eyebrow raised. "Second, do you plan on snorkeling, Nicholas? I sure don't."

"Why not? It might be fun."

I gave him a dumbfounded look. "So, you are not afraid of being eaten by things in the ocean, but you are afraid of flying in a plane?"

He rolled his eyes and knocked me playfully off balance onto the bed before leaving.

"Sweets, that isn't even close to being the same thing."

I couldn't help but laugh. I really shouldn't be making fun of him, especially since I'm the one scared of the ocean. But he doesn't need to know that.

NON-HONEYMOON DAY 1

The next morning, I got up at three to shower and make sure Nick and I both had everything all set. Nick was sitting on the couch like a statue when I entered the living room. He was ghostly white.

"Good Morning. Are you all set?"

I stopped walking toward the kitchen when he didn't answer. I looked at him; he was still looking forward to the front door.

"Nick, are you okay?"

He gave me a dirty look. "Do I look okay, Callie?"

"You look like you're about to shit yourself, honestly." I smiled, trying to make a joke, but he didn't think it was funny.

He looked away from me and back at the door. "I don't think I can do this." He looked back at me with anxiety clear on his face. "Will you hate me if I bail?"

I realized he was serious, so I slightly changed my tone. "Honestly, a little." I sat next to him. He looked so defeated.

"Callie, I can't do this."

I grabbed his hand and made him look at me. "If you really don't want to go, I won't make you...but I would love to spend time with you."

He squeezed my hand and stared at our intertwined hands for a few minutes, as we sat in silence. Finally, he looked back up at me and nodded.

"Okay."

I leaned in and kissed his cheek. "Thank you." I knocked our shoulders together and hugged his arm. "You are my new favorite best friend."

He smiled a little.

"I fucking better be. If we don't die, you owe me for this. You are lucky I like you."

Something passed between us when he said that.

I broke the silence. "We will have fun, I promise."

"I'm holding you to that."

Nick fidgeted the entire car ride to the airport. It was cute, honestly. We got through all the security checks without any incidents and were about two hours early. Nick spent almost an hour in the bathroom while we waited. I don't know if he was puking his guts up or if it was coming out the other end. I was really starting to feel horrible.

I grabbed some Tums from one of the stores just in case he needed them. When he came out of the bathroom and sat next to me, he looked a little green.

"Nick, I can't do this to you. Let's call Aubrey to come pick you up. I will see you guys when I get back. I'm sorry I made you do this. I don't want you to be this terrified."

I tried touching him to help him out of the chair, but he stopped me. "Callie, I'm fucking here, aren't I?"

"Yes, but Nick, you have been puking for an hour. I didn't realize you were that scared of this. I never would have made it such a big deal. I'm—"

"I am going. I don't like it, but I'm going."

I didn't say another word until we were on the plane.

Once we were seated, the flight attendants got Nick and me some wine.

"Nick, if you plan to take the medicine, you can't drink that." He tossed it back like I was going to steal it from him.

"I am a grown man, Callie."

"Sure... let's go with that."

He looked at me like he wanted to strangle me. "Don't be a bitch right now, please."

I ignored his comment and reached into my bag to ensure my phone was off. I put on my headphones and started watching the ads on the little TV in front of me.

The flight attendants had just finished their safety mumbo jumbo. Nick made me stay completely still and quiet so he could pay attention to the entire thing. It was kind of charming.

As the plane started taxiing onto the runway, Nick gripped the armrest so tight his knuckles went white. I tried to lift it so it wasn't between us, and he tried to fight me. When he finally gave in, I leaned into him and held his hand.

"I got you," I whispered. "You are going to be just fine. I promise."

He looked at me out of the side of his eye and nodded.

Once the wheels left the ground, he gripped my hand harder than before and shut his eyes. He wouldn't let me go, even once the plane was coasting. I ordered another mini bottle of wine for us both. Before I could even open mine, his was gone.

We were quiet for about thirty minutes, but I wanted to break the silence.

"You didn't take the medicine," I stated.

When he responded, he didn't look at me, but I saw him smirk. "You told me not to."

I hugged his arm and leaned on his shoulder. "I'm glad you're here."

I felt his lips kiss the top of my head. "Me too, Sweets."

He passed out about ten minutes later and never let my hand go.

CHAPTER NINE

Nick

I was awoken by my head falling forward and Callie rubbing my arm. It felt so calming. For a second, I forgot where I was.

"We're here," she whispered.

My eyes shot open when I realized we were still on the plane. She winced when I squeezed her hand. I immediately let go, I hadn't realized how hard I was holding her.

"Hey, hey. It's okay. We're here; you're safe."

I looked at her and then out the window. I slept through the entire flight.

"How...how did I sleep through it?" I asked.

She smiled. "It was a really easy flight. It was probably the best one I've ever been on."

"We made it?" It came out like a question. I think I was in a bit of a shock.

"We made it," Callie repeated. Her smile was contagious. She was smiling like she was so proud. It was seriously the prettiest she's ever looked.

We got off the plane and quickly grabbed our bags. We only had to wait ten minutes for our car to arrive to bring us to the resort. Things were starting perfectly.

"What do you mean the reservation is only for one room? We called and verified that we were supposed to have two rooms."

"Ma'am, I'm very sorry. We didn't receive a call about separate rooms. The only call we received was about upgrading your room to a suite." The hotel clerk repeated to us.

I stepped behind Callie. "Can you check again, please?". I put my hands on Callie's shoulders as she got her phone out to call Aubrey. I took it from her and called her myself. Callie was about to blow up, and knowing Aubrey, she would just hang up on her the minute Callie raised her voice. I walked outside the door where it was a little more quiet.

It rang one time, and she picked up.

"Mad at me yet?" Aubrey's sneaky voice came through the phone.

"Aubs...what did you do?"

"Oh, Nick?" she sounded surprised. "I didn't really have a choice. It is a couples-only resort, and they didn't allow me to change it."

"Why didn't you tell us? Callie is pissed. She's about to fight the front desk guy."

"Let me talk to her," she demanded.

I walked in and handed Callie the phone, and she walked outside to speak to Aubrey. I couldn't hear her from inside, but I could see her arms flailing. Her face was becoming more red the longer they spoke. I saw her say something about one bed.

I went up to the desk and apologized for the mix-up. I reached for the information pamphlets and keycards. The clerk abruptly pulled them away.

"Sir, are you two a couple?" I looked at him like a deer in headlights for a moment, and he continued, "Because it doesn't seem like it, and we have a strict couples-only policy. If you would like to sleep separately, I can arrange for you to stay about thirty minutes away at our sister hotel, but not everything would be included. There will be many events that you can only attend with a significant other." The guy gave me a knowing look.

I tried to play it off the best I could. "We will be fine; we are just fighting about her mother. It's no problem. One room will work great."

He seemed to believe me because he smirked and handed me the keycards.

He nodded, "Good luck."

I mumbled under my breath, "Thanks, I think I'm going to need it."

He must have heard me because he chuckled before turning to the next customer.

When Callie returned, I could tell she was about to go off again. I put my arm around her shoulder, kissed her cheek, and guided her toward the elevators. "This way, baby. We're all set."

She recoiled a little and looked at me like I just called her a bad name or something.

"Baby? What the fuck are you doing?" She whispered through clenched teeth, her eyes darting around the room.

"Just follow my lead."

I turned and waved at the concierge. He nodded. I turned and urged Callie into the elevator.

She looked up at me, so I leaned in. Our faces were only inches apart. "You have some explaining to do, Nicholas."

I kissed her forehead and grinned against it as I whispered, "I know."

She turned and crossed her arms in front of her chest, huffing loudly. I couldn't help but smirk.

When I shut the door to our room behind me, she immediately laid into me.

"What the fuck was that? Why would you let them do this to us? Why would you want to share a room? We can't share a room, Nick. We are going to be here for two weeks."

"Sweets, sit down. Let me get you a drink." I explained everything to her, and she just stared at me. "If you really can't deal with sharing a room, let's just go to the other hotel and call it a day, but you must admit this room is gorgeous. Plus, it isn't much different from you living with me in the same house. It just has fewer walls."

It's an extensive suite. It is a studio-style room with the living room and bedroom combined. The kitchen and bathroom are separated. There is a beautiful balcony overlooking the beach. I am praying she doesn't want to leave.

"No, I chose this one for the activities. I want to do it." She said in a bratty tone like she was throwing a tantrum again.

"Then we are officially together for the next two weeks and we get to enjoy this beautiful room. We also get to make it look like we are really a couple when we're out of this room," I said proudly.

"Get to?" she questioned. "What about *inside* this room? What are we going to do?"

I stared at her for a second, trying to gauge what she was asking, but she was genuinely confused.

"I will take the couch. Problem solved." I smiled and dropped my bag onto it.

"You shouldn't have to sleep on a couch for two weeks, Nick."

I sat with my feet propped up on the coffee table. I put my hands behind my neck and my elbows fell out to the sides. "Well, unless you're offering me the bed or you are letting me sleep in it with you, then we are at an impasse here, Sweets."

"Fine," Callie huffed.

I was slightly surprised but didn't want to sound too eager. "You want me in the bed with you?" I inquired smugly.

"No, you get the couch. I'll take it every few days to give you a break."

"I'm fine on the couch, Sweets. I won't need a break."

She headed into the bathroom with her phone in her hand. She aggressively swiped on the screen, and I knew that, at any moment, I was about to hear her yelling at Aubrey.

Chapter Ten

Callie

I tried calling Aubrey, but she didn't answer, so I texted her immediately.

> I hate you!

The bitch did this shit on purpose. I wasn't sure if I was really that mad, though. That was until Aubrey texted me back.

Aubrey

> Oh, shush. You love me and please promise to still love me when you see I mainly left only sexy jammies in your bag for you. Only one set of modest ones because I know you will be a prude tonight...

> Thank me later.

God, she's infuriating. I knew she'd done something to my bag. Although I probably wasn't as mad as I should have been, part of me couldn't help but wonder about this whole situation. Would Nick be a gentleman and keep his hands and eyes to himself if I let him sleep in the bed with me? *Do I want him to be?*

I shook off the thought and looked at myself in the mirror. When I walked into the room to work on unpacking again, Nick was watching some infomercial about a brand of tape that doesn't get wet. He started talking without looking over at me.

"What are we doing today?"

When I didn't answer, he looked over at me, and I shrugged.

"No idea. What do you want to do? I had planned on keeping the first day free because I figured Jake and I would be—never mind." I felt my skin heating as I turned away from him.

He gave me a big smirk as he wagged his eyebrows up and down. "We can do that, I don't mind."

I reached into my bag and grabbed something to throw at him. I realized after it left my hand that it was a tampon.

"Nice try," I said as it hummed right by his head.

He put up his hands in mock defeat. "Just offering. Just know the offer is there." He turned and went back to watching the television, then spoke again. "Hey, why don't you let me take you shopping? We can have dinner after, and if you still wanna be out, we can go to the welcome bonfire they are having later tonight."

I was quiet and stared at him in disbelief. How does he know what's happening here? We just got here. He looked over at me and shrugged when he realized I was silently questioning him.

"What? I read the brochures while you were in the bathroom."

When he looked at me, it made my stomach flutter a little. "I would like that. Sounds fun." I said apprehensively.

"Perfect, get yourself all prettied up, and we'll go."

I scoffed, keeping the smile on my face. "Nick, I'm pretty all the time."

"Yes, you are pretty all the time, Sweets, but go put on something comfortable, and we can head out. Maybe put on your swimsuit so we can go to the beach if we want to."

I stood at attention and saluted him. "Yes, sir."

"God, you take things so literally. Just go get ready, pretty girl."

He chuckled while he started looking for his swimsuit and then went into the bathroom to change. I touched my cheek and my skin was even hotter than before. His compliments never made me feel things like this. I sort of liked it.

Nick knocked on the door from inside the bathroom to ask if I was decent. I honestly never noticed how considerate he really was. I mean, obviously, I know he's nice because he's one of my best friends, but he's been extra nice lately.

Once I told him I was decent, he came out and started unpacking his suitcase, hanging a few of his things in the closet.

"Why are you being so nice to me?" I finally asked.

He stopped rummaging through his bag and looked up at me, concerned. "Am I supposed to be an asshole? Do you want me to be mean? Do you have a degradation kink or something?" He chuckled.

I blushed. He's right; why am I even asking? "No, I guess not. It's just weird. You are never this nice to me."

"I don't know whether to be offended or not." He let out an incredulous laugh.

I waved off the conversation. "Never mind, forget I said anything. I'm just a little in my feelings, I guess. I'm just not used to people being this nice."

His face changed to concern. "What do you mean?"

"Nothing. It's nothing; just forget it."

"Okay, if you say so."

He went back to unpacking. I know I should tell him. I was referring to Jake and how he was quite different from what people knew. Jake and I fought all the time, and he was quite controlling toward the end. Now I know it was just guilt that intensified his actions, but I never told anyone because I loved him and didn't want anyone to judge him unfairly. God, I was so stupid.

I was hoping this trip would bring me some clarity. I planned on using the time to make plans for my new life with new dreams and goals. I was determined to have fun here. Nothing and no one would stop me. I needed to stay focused on the future and stop bringing up the past. Nick is great, and I won't ruin this trip by talking about Jake all the time.

NICK

We had been shopping for over an hour when I realized we still hadn't bought anything other than candy and a new swimsuit for Callie. I was too preoccupied looking for the music store I saw in a pamphlet at the hotel. I'm not one who usually asks for directions, but I was determined to find it, so I asked one of the shop owners and was told it was a few blocks from the resort. By that time, Callie was ready to lay in the sun, so she won. I figured I would check it out after we ate.

We took a beach bag with a couple of towels and sunscreen with us so we could sit on the beach when we were ready. The beaches here were absolutely beautiful. They had perfect, soft, white sand and clear blue water. Luckily, the beach wasn't too crowded since it was the off-season, so we got a perfect spot near a cabana.

Callie asked me to put sunscreen on her back, and my dick stood at half attention as soon as she took off her shirt. I don't think she saw it, but just in case, I turned and laid on my stomach as soon as I was done rubbing it on her. My dick needed a moment to calm down.

"I'm going to put my feet in the water for a minute," Callie announced.

I nodded, and she took off. I sat up and watched her walk away. I definitely should have waited because all that time spent waiting for my dick to chill went to waste. She was wearing a bathing suit that covered just enough of her plump ass not to be indecent. It made her caramel skin glow even more against the bright pink color. I could see lighter stretch marks dispersed along her thighs, and I started daydreaming about running my tongue up and down each and every one of them.

I love how confident she is. I have very rarely heard Callie talk badly about herself, but it happens once in a while. It makes me so angry that she can talk badly about her perfect body for even one second. I much prefer this Callie when she is embracing her curves, stretch marks, and all.

I laid back and started thinking about what we could get into on this trip. I quickly realized it was going to be a long vacation with the torture of seeing her in a bikini every day.

"You need to stay calm and stop giving me trouble," I mumbled to my dick.

"What was that?" Callie's voice startled me.

"Nothin', I was just talking to myself."

She smirked. "Weirdo."

"Oh, be quiet. You love my weirdness."

"Sure, let's go with that."

About an hour later, I realized I was being burned to a crisp. I looked over and appreciated the sun glistening off of Callie's tan skin. She must have felt my eyes on her, because her head turned a few seconds later, and she caught me staring.

"You gonna keep staring or take a picture?" she laughed.

"I will take both, please."

"Oh shush. You're being a weirdo again."

I leaned up onto my elbow, placing my head on my hand. "Are you ready to head out? I am being burnt to hell."

She looked over again, "Poor, poor, Nicky and his pale skin."

I rolled my eyes. "I am leaving. Are you coming, sassy pants?" I sat up to put my shirt on.

She waved me off. "I will meet you up there in a bit. I just want to enjoy the warmth for a few more minutes."

"You sure? Do you have your phone on you?"

She held it up. "Yes, Dad."

I leaned over and kissed her forehead. "I am running to one of the shops, so I will be up there soon if you get there first."

"Mmm, sure."

I didn't really want to leave her there alone, but I also didn't want her to think I was being possessive. I found a chair at the cafe overlooking the beach so I would be able to see when she left. I just wanted to be sure she made it inside okay. Once she did, I went to the little shop next to the hotel to grab something that I knew would make her smile.

She came out of the bathroom just as I was walking into the room. Callie had on a light purple sundress, and her hair was down and curly. She also had no makeup on. I rarely get to see her natural beauty like this. This was the real Callie once again, my favorite. She looked perfect.

"You look beautiful, Callie."

Her cheeks pinked up. "What's that?" She pointed to the flowers I had in my hand. I handed them to her. She smiled as she smelled them.

"They aren't your bluebells, but they are blue," I said.

She blushed a little. "What are they for?" I shrugged. I didn't want to sound like a complete pussy and say it was because I just wanted to see her smile. "I still hate blue," she added. She smiled and looked at me.

"I know, but it's our thing." I smiled back.

"Thank you." She went up on her tiptoes and kissed my cheek. "They are perfect."

I tried to play off the thrill that just went through me and linked my arm with hers. "Are you ready to go, Sweets?"

"Yes, sir."

She was trying to kill me with all the "Yes Sirs". I didn't even know I liked that type of thing until she said it.

"Complimentary bottle of our best champagne for the newlyweds."

Our server held out the bottle to us, and Callie smirked at me, wagging her eyebrows.

"Very fancy, thank you!" she joked.

He poured us each a glass, then left us to figure out what we were eating.

Callie looked at the menu thoroughly. I don't know why she wasted her time. I knew she was going to get some sort of seafood. She always does when Aubrey isn't around. Aubrey hates even the smell of it, but Callie is obsessed.

"I think I'm going to get the Bahama Mama and a salmon dish." She looked up at me. "Let me guess, you are getting chicken?" Her proud smile was so fucking adorable. "My boring bestie, always sticking to his comforts."

I looked at her over my menu, "Don't act like you know me."

She leaned in with a knowing smile. "Okay. So, what are you getting, then?"

I covered my face with the menu and looked again. "Well, if you must know, I am getting a Pain Killer to drink, and I don't know yet what I want to eat."

"Mmhmm, sure."

We sat there smirking at each other like idiots. The waiter came over a few minutes later. "What can I get you, miss?"

"I will have the Bahama Mama and the Honey Garlic Salmon, please. Can you please make sure there are no mushrooms on that dish?"

"Yes, of course." He turned to me, "And you, sir?"

"Yes, I will have the Pain Killer drink. What chicken dish would you recommend?"

Callie pointed right at me. "Ha, I knew it." She did a little jig in her seat, showing just how proud she was.

The waiter chuckled and recommended the Spicy Bahamian Chicken. "Yeah, I will try that. Thanks."

The waiter left, and before looking back at Callie, I caught the guy who checked us in, staring at us. He was having dinner with another person who worked here. I wanted to make us look more like a couple, so I grabbed her hand that was resting on the table and kissed her fingers. She was about to protest until she saw him, too. She blew me a kiss across the table. I made a show of acting like I was catching it and holding it to my heart. She laughed at me and slapped my hand away.

"I don't know why you try to act like I don't know everything about you, Nick. Face it. We have been friends for too long."

I grabbed her hand in mine again, running my thumb over the back of her fingers. "Not everything, Sweets, but that's a story for another day." She didn't question me, but I could tell she was a little curious.

It was really nice sitting and talking with Callie. Even though we've lived together for the past few months, this was different. I feel like I'm seeing a different side of her, a more relaxed side. She has been so stressed out leading up to this, and now that we are here, she's finally letting loose.

We tried each other's food, and surprisingly, I actually liked the salmon. We took the leftovers back to our room while making a pit stop to freshen up so we could head to the welcome bonfire. Callie grabbed my hand once the elevator door shut. She laced our fingers together and leaned her head onto my arm.

"Thank you for coming with me. I am so happy you said yes. We are going to have fun, I promise." She looked up at me, and those caramel eyes did it again. My heart was instantly racing. "I will make this trip worth it for you."

I squeezed her hand. "I'm glad I came, too. I love spending time with you, Cal." We were both quiet for a moment before I gripped her hand and looked at her. "Just being with you makes the trip worth it."

Her breath hitched as the elevator door opened. "Nick."

I squeezed her hand. "I know, I know...I'm sweet."

CHAPTER ELEVEN

Callie

The bonfire was filled with cute couples cuddled together. I realized I must have missed a few people saying hello when Nick squeezed my hand to get my attention. My brain was in a fog after replaying what Nick said to me before we left. It was the sweetest thing I had ever heard him say. I almost wish he hadn't said it because looking around at everyone made me kind of sad. Seeing everyone smiling and cuddling with their spouses put me even deeper in my feelings.

Nick had his arm around me so we didn't look too out of place, but I felt like everyone could tell I was uncomfortable. I am not the best liar. Usually people can automatically tell when I am lying about something.

One of the few times I tried to lie to my mom, I felt so bad that I told on myself. I was out with a group of people I shouldn't have been, and Aubrey and I tried smoking a cigarette for the first time. When my mom asked how my night went, she gave me that all-knowing look like she knew I had done something bad, so I just blurted out, "I smoked a cigarette." My mom wasn't even mad. She just laughed. Lying just isn't my thing.

We sat down in empty seats and everyone was chatting about how they met and the details of their weddings. Not even a minute into us being there, we were being grilled with questions.

"How did you two meet?" The brunette woman sitting next to Nick asked. I didn't realize she was talking to us until Nick started speaking.

"We met when I moved in next door to one of our mutual friends when we were in high school. We became fast friends, and I had a huge crush on her from the moment I met her." He looked at me with a genuine smile. "It took her a little longer to realize she was made for me, though. She dated some tools along the way." Nick squeezed my hand and looked deeper into my eyes. "But for me, it's always been her. We couldn't be happier." He looked away from me and toward the woman who asked.

The woman clasped her hands together in excitement.

"Oh, that's so sweet. It's like the perfect best friend love story."

My throat went dry, and my skin was getting clammy. I couldn't get any words out, but Nick kept speaking.

"I always knew she would be my forever."

I couldn't help the tears that welled in my eyes. I slowly blinked and just let them naturally fall. Nick wiped my cheek with his thumb and brought my hand to his mouth for a kiss.

"Nick," I choked out.

He squeezed my hand again. "I know."

Things were getting a little too emotional for me, so I excused myself to the restroom to take a break. I stood in the bathroom in silence, staring at my reflection in the mirror.

"Get it together, Callie. It's fake. He is your best friend. He is just here helping you have a fun time. It's nothing more." I repeated those words out loud to myself a few times before I actually calmed down.

Right before opening the restroom door to leave, I paused and gave myself one more look. *Am I crying because I wish he wasn't just being nice? Why do I want to kiss him again? Callie, you shouldn't have these feelings about your best friend.*

When I returned to the fire, Nick handed me a drink. I smiled up at him. He read my mind; It was time to drink the pain away.

NICK

I knew it was time to go back to the room when Callie began getting handsy with the people next to her. She was touching the woman's hair and slurring her words. Knowing her, she would probably embarrass herself soon, so I wanted to prevent that.

When the elevator door shut, it was like I was physically burning her. She winced, then moved all the way to the other side and looked straight forward.

"You okay, Sweets?" I asked. I was about to reach for her, but she stepped even further away.

"Yeah, just tired, I think," she slurred her words a little and covered herself with her arms.

"Cal, what's wrong? I know something is up. Talk to me."

She was quiet the entire walk to our room. When I turned toward her, she was staring at me. Studying me intently.

"What? Is something on my face?" I rubbed over my scruffy face, making a mental note that I needed to shave, and she softly chuckled.

"You were joking, right? You didn't mean all that...right?"

My stomach twisted right away. I didn't have to ask. I knew what she was talking about, but I asked anyway to give myself time to think.

"Mean what?"

Callie stepped toward me, pushing me up against the wall. Before I could speak another word, she kissed me. I instinctively picked her up.

I pulled back, breathless, after realizing what I had done.

"Callie, what are you doing?" I asked against her lips.

"We're just having a little fun, Nick. Just make me feel good. I miss feeling good."

She went in for another kiss, but I turned my cheek. "Callie...I can't." I swallowed the lump in my throat.

She put her hand on my chest and looked into my eyes. "Why not? We trust each other, right? There is only one person in this world I trust more than you, and if I kissed her, Link would probably kill me."

She lightly laughed. I put my hands on hers and really looked at her. I was trying to figure out why she was asking.

"I can't just do this to have fun, Callie. If we do this, I want you to want it for real. I want you to want me."

She walked closer to me as her eyes traveled up my body, her eyes landing on mine.

"What if I did want you?" she whispered.

My heart began racing, and I felt the desire rushing through me. "Callie," I pushed her hair behind her ear and away from her face. "Don't say that unless you mean it. We can come back from a few drunk kisses and stay friends, no big deal, but if we do something more," I paused. "Sweets, if you say you want me, you are mine forever." I grabbed her face so my hands were cupping her cheeks. "I've been waiting too long to make you mine, and I will not fuck this up by just fucking around with you... you mean too much to me."

She stepped back a little. "You meant it?" I gave her a curious look, and she continued. "You actually meant what you said outside?" Then she repeated what I said, "'But for me, it's always been her.'" She just kept staring at me. "You meant that?"

I couldn't tell if she was asking me or telling me, so I just nodded.

"Nick, we can't date," she said.

My heart instantly sank, but I didn't want her to notice and feel guilty, so I leaned forward, kissed her forehead, and then moved away. I spoke as I was facing away from her.

"That's why we can't do this, Sweets. I will wait until that changes."

"But—"

I changed the subject because I didn't want her to feel guilty or cry. Seeing her cry breaks me every time.

"I'm heading into the shower. Do you need to get in there before I do?" I stopped and turned slightly to get her response.

She sat on the bed and shook her head. I continued into the bathroom without another word. I closed the door and let out a loud, suppressed sigh. That rejection fucking hurt, but I knew I'd done the right thing.

CALLIE

When Nick was done with his shower, I walked by him and into the bathroom without even acknowledging him. I was mortified. When I shut the door, I leaned against it and heard him putting his forehead against the other side.

"I'm sorry, Callie,"

I swallowed my pride and tried to sound as normal as possible. "Nick, it's totally fine. I'm sorry I came onto you like that."

I heard him whisper, "I'm not." Followed by the shuffling of him backing away from the door a bit. "I'm going to sleep, but I'll leave the light on for you. Wake me up if you need anything, okay?"

"Yeah, for sure," I answered.

When I looked at myself in the mirror, I saw how much of a mess I was. My makeup was smeared, my skin beyond flushed, and I looked way too sweaty. The only nice thing left about me was the color of my eyes. I guess I'm lucky that is one thing that doesn't change. With how I look, it's no wonder he turned me down.

After getting in the shower, I just stood there, letting the warm water flow over me. It felt so good. I rubbed my hands down my body, and my mind started to wander.

I can't date Nick...right? What if I could? Is it too soon? I know I've only been single for about two months, but I've known Nick forever.

My mind went through about twenty other questions. I started replaying his sweet words in my head. My mind wandered to his touch on my skin, his mouth on mine. It was getting a little too hot, and I had to sit down. I ran myself a bath to relax away all this stress.

My hands traveled to where I needed them most. I looked up, realizing there was a detachable showerhead. I reached over and grabbed my phone to play some music to drown out some of the sounds I was about to make. I tried my best to hold the moans in, but I was definitely not being quiet by any means. "Fuck...Nick," I moaned. I tried to muffle my sounds with my other hand, but a few seconds later, Nick gently knocked on the door, jolting me from my thoughts.

"Cal, did you call for me?"

I sat up abruptly, making the water slosh everywhere. "NO! I'm fine, go away, I mean goodnight. Sorry, I will turn the music down. Must have been that." I heard him chuckle and mumble something, but I couldn't hear what he actually said.

He fucking heard me. Now I just wanted to die. My body dipped under the water up to my ears like I used to do as a child to drown out the noise of my parents fighting. Tears filled my eyes once again. I wasn't sure if I was crying because I was alone and embarrassed or because I was thinking about my mom and dad together. One thing I do know is that I'm stuck here until Nick falls asleep. I cannot face him right now. I need time to get this crying under control and get over this embarrassment.

After about twenty minutes, I heard the T.V. click off. I knew he would knock out soon after that, so I stood and took an actual shower to wash the day away. I never understood how people could sit in their own filth and then not wash off afterward.

I don't know what happened between Nick and me tonight, but I know that things are changing, and I think...I think I kind of want them to.

Chapter Twelve

Nick

Callie was moaning my name. The beautiful, perfect girl in the bathroom was thinking about me while she was… "Fuck," I said audibly with a chuckle as I backed away from the bathroom door. My cock stirred as I walked back to the couch to sit down. I wish I hadn't interrupted her. I should have just sat there and listened, but I didn't realize what was happening until I had already knocked. It would have been very wrong to listen, but God, do I want to hear her moan my name again, maybe even louder the next time and without a door between us.

I draped my arm across my eyes as I lay on my back on the couch. I can't believe I was so stupid. After a few minutes, I turned the T.V. off and turned to face the back of the couch, trying to get comfortable. I am not short, and this couch was not built to sleep on.

I heard the water in the shower shut off. I got as comfortable as I could, facing away from the bathroom. I pretended like I was sleeping when she came out because I didn't want to make her feel any more awkward than she probably already did. I never wanted her to feel bad or weird about us. Like I told her, a few drunk kisses here and there was something we would be able to come back from. I know we can't be more than friends right now, no matter how much I wished that wasn't the case, but I can't live without her, so being friends has to be enough.

She put on some light music, and I heard her getting into bed. She must have drifted off to sleep rather easily because I heard her lightly snoring. Her snores were soothing, enough so that I finally drifted off to sleep as well.

I woke up to being jostled around. I opened my eyes to Callie standing over me.

"Come over to the bed," she whispered.

Then I heard a loud boom of thunder and sat up. I was still pretty out of it and was rubbing my eyes.

"Wha—what? What's wrong, Cal? What time is it?"

"It's only four, but the thunder woke me up."

I was thoroughly confused. I clicked on the lamp next to me. My eyes took a moment to adjust, but there she was, standing in front of me, wearing almost nothing. I shook off the dirty thoughts that were forming and got back to figuring out why she had woken me up.

"What...what do you need? Are you okay?" I felt like I was asking the same thing over again. She pulled me up, grabbed my pillow and blanket, and moved it to the bed.

"Just come to bed, please," she huffed. "You are making this more difficult than it has to be."

"Fine, just let me use the bathroom first."

When I got up, she let out a profound gasp. I immediately started looking around, thinking, once again, something was wrong. Then I realized her eyes were locked in on my lower half, where my dick was standing at full attention. I looked down and laughed.

"See something interesting?" I asked with a tired smirk. She was staring directly at my erection that had fully tented my pants. Her eyes darted back toward mine, and I saw the moment her walls went back up.

"No, not really. I just expected it to be bigger," she smirked. "Now hurry up, put that little thing away, and get in bed so I can sleep."

Another crash of thunder hit and she scurried over and got under the covers.

There's my girl. I knew the awkwardness would pass quickly. I walked to the bathroom, almost in tears from laughing so hard at her attempt to insult me. I'm not exactly sure where she's expecting me to put it, but I have some ideas. It will go away on its own...I hope.

I turned off the bathroom light and walked over to the bed. She was sitting up with the covers pulled back for me. Then another crash of thunder hit and she sunk down into the blankets.

I slid into the bed beside her, laying on my back, not sure if she wanted me facing her or not. I still wasn't sure what was happening or why she'd asked me over here. She immediately pulled the blankets over us. Her arm went over my stomach and her nails dug into my side like she was holding on for dear life. She pulled her head back to look at me.

"Jesus, Nick, when did you get so solid?"

I chuckled. "You have seen me with my shirt off a lot lately, Sweets. Plus, I've always been ripped. I work out every day. Haven't you ever noticed?"

She rolled her eyes. "No, I haven't. I don't watch your every move."

"Maybe you just need to touch me more often." I gave her a sly smile and shimmied my shoulders.

She slapped my chest and scoffed before smiling and putting her head on me. Once she was settled, I moved one arm over my head and the other under Callie's head in order to get more comfortable. After a few minutes of silence, I thought maybe she had fallen asleep, but then she spoke.

"Thanks again for coming with me," she said hesitantly.

"Thanks for asking me." I pulled her in closer.

"Nick..."

"Yeah, Sweets?"

"We're okay, right?"

I couldn't say what I wanted to say out loud, so I just said what I always say when I need to stop myself from telling her that I love her. "Forever and always." I kissed her head. "Get some sleep. We have a busy day tomorrow."

"Good night, Nick."

"Night Sweets."

She was snoring again within minutes. The breath from her nose lightly brushed my chest. Now, if only I could get my brain to shut off and stop thinking about her touching me, we would be golden.

Chapter Thirteen

Callie

Non-Honeymoon Day 2

The sound of deep snores woke me up. I felt his every breath on my head. I must have held onto him and not moved. One of my legs was sprawled over both of his, and my hand was resting on something hard.

OH MY GOD! I snatched my hand away and sat up. He shifted, turning toward me, but his eyes remained closed. I was glad because if they had opened, he would have caught me staring at his dick. It looked like it was going to pop out of his pants. I started thinking about what could be going on in his head to make him that excited. His mouth fell open with his snores. I couldn't help the light giggle that erupted from me.

A flutter arose in my stomach at the realization I really enjoyed waking up next to him. It was a weird feeling, but good. A piece of his hair was falling over his forehead, and I couldn't help but reach out to gently move it. I found myself just staring at him with admiration.

I leaned over him to grab my phone, which was on his side table since mine didn't have an electrical plug. We had about an hour left if we wanted to grab the included breakfast. We are supposed to be at a cooking class at eleven and possibly a couple's hike or beach trip later this afternoon. We will see what we feel like after the class. If I let him sleep through breakfast, we could just pick something up when we headed out.

I was so lost in my own thoughts as I leaned over him that I didn't even notice his eyes were now open.

"Mornin' Sweets, you trying to cop a feel or something?"

I immediately abandoned grabbing my phone and sat back, pulling the covers over me. He chuckled and sat up against the headboard.

"What's got that beautiful brain going a thousand miles a minute?" He playfully tapped his index finger on my forehead.

I lightly pushed his hand away, and he chuckled again as he got up. I was staring again. He caught me, again.

"You gonna stop ogling me like a piece of meat?" he said with a smirk-filled grin. "I mean, I don't mind it, I guess."

"Fuck you," I smiled. "Do you want to get the included breakfast or stop somewhere later?"

I was trying to ignore his question. Luckily, he let me.

"It's your honeymoon, babe. You choose what we do."

He immediately looked regretful.

"Fuck, Callie, I'm sorry I shouldn't have—"

I held up a hand. "It's fine. Don't worry about it."

I said it more curtly than I intended to. He's right though, it is my honeymoon, but I'm doing my best to forget that. Although it's been nothing but weird since we got here, it's been nice spending time away from home. It's been even nicer that I'm here with Nick.

I was rummaging through my bag, and Nick came up behind me. He put his hands on my upper arms to settle me, then slid them around my midsection, hugging me tight. As he leaned down, he put his chin on my shoulder and propped his big ol' head onto mine. I could feel his breath on my neck, and I was trying my hardest not to shiver.

"I really am sorry, Sweets." He kissed my cheek. "Forgive me."

He sounded a little worried. I smiled and turned in his arms, and he stood up but didn't let go to give me room. I looked into his perfect blue eyes, then hugged him tight because his gaze was too intense.

"Of course, it's okay. Don't worry about it," I assured him.

He kissed my forehead and made his way into the bathroom to change.

When he came out, he was wearing blue swim shorts and a Hawaiian shirt with his sandals that he bought at a local shop when we first got here. He had a bit of sunburn on his nose, so he sort of looked like a tall, skinny Rudolph, but I gave him a break and didn't make fun of him.

Who am I?

I put on my favorite yellow bikini with a pair of white shorts and a yellow halter top. This bikini always made me feel rich. The pattern has always reminded me of the diamonds on a Louis Vuitton purse.

"You ready to act like my man?" I asked him jokingly as I hip-checked him.

He put his arm around my shoulders. "Forever and always, Sweets."

He opened the door for me and then moved his arm down to my lower back to usher me out the door.

Forever and always. I love when he says that to me. I always thought it was kind of weird that he only ever said it to me, but when I finally got the courage to ask him about it, he stopped. It was right around the time I met Jake. I think it was a respect thing, but I'm really glad he's saying it again and has kept it as our thing. It makes me feel special. My insides were twisting in all kinds of knots as soon as his hand grazed my back. As he let go, my body shuddered, already missing his warmth.

We thought we were going to have to buy breakfast, but luckily we caught the end of the resort's inclusive one. A few of the people from the bonfire were there and invited us to sit at the table with them.

"Hey newlyweds, how was your night?"

I looked at Nick, hoping he would answer, but he was already talking before my eyes met his. It was like talking about us as a couple came naturally to him. He didn't even bat an eye.

"It was perfect. The only issue was the thunder. It scared my beautiful girl here. I didn't mind, though. I got extra snuggles."

Nick pulled me in closer and kissed the top of my head. He and everyone else chuckled a little.

"You sit, Sweets. I'll grab your food."

I smiled and sat down without saying a word.

"He is so sweet; you found a good one, girl." I looked over at who was speaking, and it was the same brunette that spoke to us at the bonfire. I looked back over at Nick walking away.

"Yeah, I guess I did."

"So when did you know he was the one?" she asked.

"Huh?" I turned to look at her again. I heard her the first time, but I was trying to give my brain time to come up with something.

"When did you know he was it for you? Was it love at first sight or—"

I cut her off with my laugh. "Oh god, no. We used to be at each other's throats all day, every day. I think he may have even hated me at one point. I had a major crush, but never told him. He took our other best friend Aubrey to prom becau—"

Nick's voice cut me off. "Because you were already going with Chris Alvarez."

I turned to look at him holding both our plates. "What do you mean?"

Nick placed our food down. He was looking at me like he thought I was joking. "I only asked Aubrey to prom because you were already going with that Chris kid. Plus, everyone kept pestering Aubrey and me about dating, even though we knew we didn't want to date each other. We were both going stag, so we just went together."

He sat down, never taking his eyes off mine, and I nervously slapped his shoulder.

"That's a lie," I chuckled. "I was literally waiting for you to ask me, and you didn't, so I said yes to Chris."

He gave me a quizzical look. "Cal, I didn't ask Aubs till three days before prom. I was too scared to ask you, so I figured I'd ask you to dance when we were there, but you went with Chris so I didn't wanna steal you away."

I looked around and everyone at the table had a look of awe. "You are joking, right?"

Nick shook his head no.

"I was so mad at you for asking her and not me. I thought I wasn't good enough." Looking around I realized people were starting to look concerned, so I hugged him. "Guess it doesn't matter now. I have you all to myself."

Nick had a distressed look on his face but returned my embrace. "Forever and Always, Sweets."

We fell into conversation with everyone, and luckily, the woman who asked me that question moved on and didn't push for a direct answer. Her question had my mind racing. If I misunderstood that situation back then, what the hell else did I miss?

"You ready to get to cookin', good lookin'?" Nick asked.

I chuckled at his corniness. When I looked up at him, he gave me a chaste kiss on my lips. Before he could pull away fully, I pulled him in for a deeper kiss. One of his brows went up in surprise, but he recovered quickly, leaning into the kiss as his hand went to my jaw. I heard awes coming from the other couples around the table.

I pulled away, and his eyes had a hunger lingering in them. They were becoming a darker blue. I was absolutely speechless. That kiss was as close to perfect as it could get.

Nick tried to clear his throat quietly. "Callie."

I turned and pulled him away from the table. "Let's go."

Chapter Fourteen

Nick

The cooking class was four couples in total. One was a couple in their seventies that I overheard saying they were here celebrating their fiftieth wedding anniversary. They were telling one of the other couples that they came here on their honeymoon and this year finally made it back. *Goals.*

One couple was a funny-as-hell younger couple on their first vacation together. Miguel and Scott were their names. They were super friendly and introduced themselves right away. Miguel reminded me of Aubrey a little. He had this light about him just like she does. You could tell Miguel really loved cooking, and Scott was just there for the ride.

The last couple were newlyweds like us. *Like us? Why did I think that? News flash. Nick, she isn't actually your wife.* I shook those thoughts from my head. We found out in conversation that their names were Kelley and Matt. They were actually from New York, which isn't too far from where we live in Connecticut.

"You guys will totally have to come to our house and have dinner sometime. We can show you the real New York," Kelley suggested.

Callie looked up at me like a kid in a candy store. I nodded my head in agreement.

"Oh, we would love that. New York is beautiful. I've only been there a handful of times. One of my dreams is to go there for the New Year's Rockin' Eve party and see the ball drop," Callie said excitedly.

"OMG, you have to come."

This girl was as hyper as a kid on a sugar high. She just said OMG as a word. She seems nice, but she could tone it down a bit in my opinion.

"We definitely will," I added, pulling Callie into a side hug.

Matt leaned over to the other side of me. "Sorry, she gets a little excited about meeting new people."

We both laughed. "No worries, our friend Aubrey is the same way. I get it."

"OMG, bring her too. We will have so much fun," Kelley said.

The instructor walked in just as Matt and I began to laugh again.

The class flew by quickly. I missed most of it because I wasn't paying any attention. I was too busy watching Callie work. I got lost for a moment staring at her ass, when Callie's phone rang, jolting me from my thoughts.

Her eyes grew in what looked like concern, but she looked back at me with ease. "I need to get this; finish mixing this for me?"

She turned toward me, and she had flour on her nose. I tried to wipe it off, but she dodged me. She handed me a spoon thing that had a ton of slots in it. I think it's called a whisk or whip or something like that.

"You okay, baby?" I asked.

"Yeah, I just need to handle this," she kissed my cheek. "I'll only be a sec."

She walked out into the hallway as she took the call.

CALLIE

"Stop. Calling. Me," I yelled into the phone.

I didn't mean to yell it that loud, but he had called and texted me uncontrollably all morning.

"Callie, just listen. I need to talk to you."

"Jake, what could you possibly have to say?"

"Baby, I've been trying to find you for days. Where are you? I need you to come home."

"Jake—"

"Baby, please. I took this time away from you and found a therapist. I'm seeing him twice a week now. I want to be better for you...for us. I want to show you that I know I fucked up. It was a mistake, baby."

"Sweets, they're about to start making dessert," Nick called out.

I covered the microphone the best I could before responding. "Be right there. Give me one minute," I called back.

Nick promptly went back inside.

"Is that Nick?"

"I need to go. I am in the middle of something." Ignoring the question, I changed the subject. "This relationship is over, Jake. I'm glad you're getting the help you need, and I hope that goes well for you. I really do."

He was quiet for a moment. "Callie...are you fucking him? Have you been sleeping with him this whole time?"

"Excuse me! You did not just ask me that."

"Yes, I fucking did. You always told me I had nothing to worry about. Were you lying to me during this entire relationship?"

I scoffed at him. "Have a glorious life, Jake."

His voice got less tense, but he was still being a bit crass.

"Callie, hold the fuck on. Where are you? I need to fucking see you. I need to fix this. Let me come see you and apologize properly."

The conversation was going nowhere. "I'm out-of-town Jake. I will talk to you later."

"Where? I will come to you." He sounded like he was pleading now.

The fact that he doesn't even remember we are supposed to be on our honeymoon right now tells so much about the relationship he and I had in itself.

"I will see you in a few weeks. Goodbye, Jake." I said sadly. I had no intention of seeing him, but I really needed to go.

"Callie plea—" I hung up and shut off my phone.

I walked back in and tried my best not to show how upset I actually was. As far as Nick knows, Jake is blocked, and I haven't spoken to him in over a month.

"Hey, Sweets," He pulled me into a hug. "That seemed intense. Do you wanna talk about it?"

I looked up at him with misted eyes. At that moment, I didn't want to be anywhere else but in his arms. "No, it was just Aubs. She just wanted to tell me something stupid Link did. Then we had a disagreement about something that upset me. Nothing important."

I felt horrible lying to him, but I couldn't have this conversation right now. His face fell a bit, looking concerned. He leaned down and kissed my lips softly.

"Okay. Let's finish this, then we can head to the beach."

I looked up at him with admiration. "Sure, I'd like that."

He wiped something off my nose, then kissed the clean spot.

"What are you doing?" I whispered.

He placed his mouth near my ear. "Everyone is staring. I am making it look good."

"Oh, yeah. Of course."

After making the dessert, Nick started cleaning up the supplies. I watched him for a moment. He really is clueless when it comes to cooking and kitchen stuff. I don't know how he survived without me. *I wonder what life would be like if he didn't have to.*

Chapter Fifteen

Nick

Callie lied.

When she came back to the class, I knew something was wrong. When I asked her what happened on the phone, she lied about it. She told me it was Aubrey, which I know was a lie because Aubrey was texting me asking how our trip was going when Callie was outside.

I don't think she has ever lied to my face like that before, at least not that I know of, but I guess I wouldn't know if she had. I'm not sure when I want to bring it up to her, but I know I have to ask her about it.

We were quiet on the walk to the beach, and she immediately started reading her book porn while I was just relaxing with my eyes closed. It was only day two, but it felt like our time here was flying by, and I didn't want to waste my time wondering why she lied to me.

She, once again, looked perfect in her bikini. It covered her ass a little better than the one did yesterday, unfortunately. She also had some weird wrap-type of thing around her. She placed it over her legs, using it as a blanket while she was reading. She said her legs got a little burned yesterday. Not sure how a translucent wrap will help, but I just let her live.

We relaxed on the beach in silence for a while, taking in the surrounding sounds. I am not someone who's able to sit still for very long, so I eventually got anxious and broke the silence.

"So, what do you want to do tonight?" I asked without looking over.

"Hmm?" she said, also without looking away from her book.

I glanced over, and she was biting her lip. I sat up and snagged the book from her.

"Hey, give me that. I am just getting to the good part."

I held it away from her as I read the first few lines.

He trailed his hand down my body, and his fingers entered me. I was so wet; I was dripping...

"Fuck, that's hot," I commented.

She leaned into my chair to reach for the book. Her chest brushed my arm. I felt her pebbled nipple through her bikini top. My dick reacted before I could even try to hide it. I was hoping she hadn't caught it.

"I know. That's why I'm reading it. I'll take that back now."

She snatched it and moved back to her seat. Her cheeks were a little pink, but Callista Adriana is not usually shy about anything, so she just smirked and moved on. I gathered at that moment she saw my erection.

"You read that shit out in the open? If I was going to read shit like that, I would be so turned on I would need to have my dick out."

"You are disgusting. How are we even friends?" she chuckled.

"Oh come on, Cal. You can't tell me you have never gotten off to the shit you read. That shit is like fucking porn, no?" I was genuinely asking. I really wanted to know.

She put her nose back in the book and then spoke to me, "It doesn't matter what I've done or not done while reading. Leave me and my porn book alone."

I could tell she was smiling behind the book, so I put my sunglasses on my head to look at her.

"You have," I said slyly. "It's okay, you don't have to tell me. I can read you like a book, Sweets. No pun intended."

She just shrugged and pretended to ignore me, so I leaned forward and whispered in her ear.

"If you ever want to share any of that info with me, I'd be glad to hear about it." I lowered my voice even more into a growl, "or even help you with whatever you're 'not' doing." I put the not in finger quotes. Her body shivered, and goosebumps formed on her arm.

"Fuck you, Nick," she said with a smile.

"Exactly."

She slapped me on my bare chest. "Stop being a perv."

"Ouch, what the fuck? That stung," I laughed. "Ya know, hitting me won't get me to stop; I like the pain." I smiled and made a show of puffing out my chest to let her know I was joking, sort of.

"Shut the fuck up and let me read, or I'm making you sleep on the couch again."

That made me shut up because it caught me off guard. "Am I not staying on the couch anymore? I wasn't expecting that to change."

She looked at me over her sunglasses. "Be a good boy, and we will see." She smiled and went back to reading.

Fuck, I'm in trouble. This girl is going to be the death of me.

We ended up staying at the beach for two hours, then we went back to the resort and had a simple lunch. Once we got back to the room, we tried to watch a movie just to stay out of the sun for a bit since we were not exactly used to this kind of heat in Connecticut. Within minutes, we both passed out.

I woke up with her feet sprawled on top of my lap. I didn't want to move because she looked so comfortable. She had a piece of hair on her face that bobbed every time her mouth blew out a puff of air. She is the prettiest fucking woman I've ever seen, no matter what she looks like.

If I don't wake her up now, she will never sleep tonight. Callie is the second-worst napper I know, and she comes second only to Aubrey. When those girls take any length of nap, their moods are bad for days after. So waking her should be fun, for sure.

I leaned forward to tap her arm when her phone lit up on the table.

CHEATING ASSHOLE

Oh fuck no. She fucking lied about talking to Jake. It was him.

I pushed her legs off my lap, not even caring that she would wake up. She sat up groggily and started looking around. Before she could speak, I was in the bathroom changing into workout clothes. When I came back out she was standing there waiting for me.

"Where are you going?"

"The gym, the food here is making me bloat," I said curtly. "Be back in an hour or so."

"Nick wait, I will co—"

"I'm good." I cut her off and walked out the door.

CHAPTER SIXTEEN

Callie

What the fuck was that?

I tried calling Nick several times since he stormed out like a child, but he didn't answer. Hopefully, he won't be at the gym long because my mind is going crazy now. I'm trying to figure out what the hell that little tantrum was. I could go to the gym downstairs, but I don't feel like chasing him around in case he opted for a run outside instead.

I cleaned up a little while I waited. I threw our dirty clothes in the washer so that when he got back, I could throw in his gym stuff and do a load. Surprisingly, we had a lot of dirty clothes even though it was only day two. We have changed our clothes so many times already that I lost count. My thighs were not prepared for this heat, so I've been keeping an eye on the chub-rub, as I call it.

I got bored enough to do some dishes, which I hate. I heard the door open as I was washing the last water glass in the sink.

"Hey Nick, I'm in here," I called out to him. "Put your dirty—"

The bathroom door slammed. I went out there, and sure enough, he was in there with the door shut.

I knocked on the door, but he didn't answer. I tried the doorknob, and it was unlocked.

"Nick, are you okay?" I asked hesitantly. I didn't open the door all the way, but I saw his perfectly sculpted ass wrapped in a towel standing in front of the mirror.

"Callie, I'm good. I need to wash off the day, and unless you are joining me in the shower, I suggest you shut the door."

I'm not sure what came over me, but I stepped into the bathroom and shut the door. I never broke eye contact with him in the mirror.

He looked at me with a sense of outrage that I'd never seen in him before. "Callie, what are you doing?"

"You told me to shut the door," I whispered.

He was silent for a moment, then walked over to the shower and turned it on.

"Callie, just go. I need to get ready for dinner. Let me shower in peace, please."

He got into the shower and shut the curtain. He reached his hand out and dropped his towel onto the floor. It sent a small thrill through me knowing he was completely naked right in front of me.

"What is wrong with you?" It came out more judgmental than I intended.

He laughed. It almost sounded evil. "Nothing, just let me get ready, please."

"Nick—"

"Callie! Get. Out," he said sternly.

"Woah, asshole, first of all, calm the fuck down. I'm just concerned about you. I want to make sure you are okay."

He took a huge breath and opened the curtain to lean his head out. He still looked mad, but he lowered his voice exponentially.

"I'm sorry. Can you please leave so I can shower? We can talk when I get out."

"Fine." I turned and walked out without another word.

When he came out, my heart broke at how hurt he looked. When he was getting a shirt from his bag, I hugged him from behind, and I felt his body instantly relax.

"Are you going to talk to me?" I whispered against his back. He turned, so I started to let go, but he pulled me in and rested his lips on the top of my head. He held me close for a moment. I pulled away enough to look at him. "Are you okay? Did something happen?"

His blue eyes felt like they were staring into my soul. "You know you can tell me anything, right? You never need to hide anything from me."

I swallowed nervously. "Yes, of course I know that."

He backed up a little, putting about a foot of space between us. "Then why didn't you tell me you were still talking to Jake?"

"What?"

"You lied, Callie. Jake called you, not Aubrey."

"You went through my phone? How cou—"

He stepped back toward me and held up two fingers to my lips. "No, I didn't. I would never do that unless I thought you were in danger. I was texting her when you said you were on the phone with her, so I knew it was a lie."

Well, this is embarrassing.

"When I woke up earlier, I was trying not to wake you, and when I leaned over, your phone lit up. It was a message from Jake. I flipped. I was hurt that you lied."

He stepped toward me and took my face in his hands. "I'm sorry I spoke to you that way." He rubbed his thumb over my jaw like he was studying me.

I put my hand up to grab his. "Nick, I'm...I'm sorry." I stuttered a bit, but I wasn't sure what else to say.

"I know." He leaned in and kissed my forehead. "I shouldn't have blown up like that. No matter what I think, whoever you talk to is your business, not mine. I am here to support you forever and always, no matter what. Just no more lying, okay?"

I felt almost...relieved. I'm glad he knows now because I was dreading him finding out, and although he freaked the hell out, it was a lot less of a blowup than I expected. Now, I don't need to hide it, at least not from him.

"Can we keep this between us? Aubrey thinks I blocked him. I don't really want her mad at me, too."

He looked over and gave me a stern look. "I won't lie to her, Cal."

"I'm not asking you to lie. I'm just asking you not to bring it up."

He nodded in agreement, but his disappointed look still lingered.

We both finished getting ready. Before we headed out the door for dinner, Nick stopped me and turned me toward him.

"First of all, you look beautiful tonight." He lifted my hand and kissed the back of it. "Second, I won't tell you what to do or who to talk to because I have no right to do that, but I want to reiterate you can not lie to me again." He pulled me into his chest. "And I will kill anyone who tries to hurt you...Even Jake, got it?"

His curtness turned me on. I went from thinking aww, that's sweet to being turned on real quick. I swallowed the lump that had been forming in my throat.

"Thank you, I think," I said with a hesitant laugh.

He smiled and didn't say another word. He put his arm over my shoulder and guided me out the door.

CHAPTER SEVENTEEN

Nick

We finished dinner and made our way to the beach for a walk. I was pretty quiet the entire dinner. I know she noticed because she kept bringing up silly random things to get me to laugh or talk.

She grabbed my upper arm and leaned her head on me as we walked.

"It's beautiful here, huh?" she said with a relaxed sigh.

I looked down at her and then back at the ocean. "Yeah, it really is. It makes our beaches at home look like swamps."

She chuckled and shook her head, almost as if she was trying to clear a thought, then stared out in the same direction as I was.

Although we talked about it already, I still can't get this Jake thing off my mind. When I was in the gym, I started questioning everything Callie had ever told me. I started wondering if she had lied to my face like that before. It gave me a real sense of uneasiness.

I know I acted like a jealous boyfriend. Yes, she lied, but I didn't even give her a chance to talk to me about it. I just assumed the worst. I don't know if she read my mind or it was just impeccable timing, but she stopped us and looked up at me.

"Do you want to talk about it?"

I knew she was talking about Jake, and I knew this was her reaching out in a way, but all I could say was, "Do you?"

"Well, no…not really, but you deserve an answer as to why I lied to you. If you want, we can talk about it."

"Sweets, you don—"

She covered my mouth, and I smiled against her hand.

"I do. Sit with me?" It was a question, not a command. She gestured to the sand, and we sat. She took off her sweater so she could sit on it instead of directly on the sand.

We sat down, and she leaned her head onto my shoulder again. I couldn't help myself; I kissed her head before looking out in front of us. No matter how mad I was at her, it changed nothing about my true feelings for her.

"He's been calling me a few times every day," she mumbled.

"What's a few?" I asked.

She looked up at me and smiled. "Ten or Twenty."

I looked at her in disbelief. "How long has he been calling that much?"

"Daily since I left." She looked down and kicked some sand with her shoe.

Of course, I was angry that he was bothering her so much, but damn, she was distracting. "Cal—"

"I know, I know," she said in an ashamed tone.

"Why haven't you blocked him? What could he possibly want?"

She chuckled and rolled her eyes. "Gee, way to make a girl feel special. Thanks, best friend," giving me a look like she was offended and nudged her shoulder into mine, making me laugh loudly.

I looked her directly in the eyes, letting my smile fall a little bit. "Callie, you are everything any guy could want. What I meant was, why is he calling? What does he say when you answer?"

She blushed. I'm not sure if it was my comment or something she was about to tell me.

"Well, the last time I talked to him before today was the wedding rehearsal."

I gave her a disbelieving look. "He's been calling you every day since, that much, with no answer?"

She nodded without saying a word.

"Callie, you need to block him. Why haven't you? That is not okay. What did he want when you answered today?"

"He said he's changed and is doing well in therapy. I was happy for him, but I still couldn't forgive him. I told him I want nothing to do with him."

I was hesitant to ask again because she ignored part of the question a few moments ago, but I asked anyway. "Then why haven't you blocked him, Cal?"

She was quiet and let go of my arm. She started running her finger through the sand like she was mulling something over in her head. I don't think she was drawing anything in particular; just thinking. I let her sit in the quiet for a moment before speaking again. "You don't have to tell me, Cal. Forget I asked."

"No...I want to. I'm just trying to figure out how to say it without sounding pathetic."

I grabbed her hand and made her look at me. "Sweets, you could never be pathetic to me."

Her eyes glazed over a little, and she looked down, causing a tear to fall. I lifted her chin and wiped it away with my thumb.

"If I block him, it's final," she whispered. "It means the last six years of my life were a waste. For the last six years, I loved someone who didn't love me back, someone who lied to me daily. I could have had a completely different life. I could have found someone who loved me for real." She looked up at me. "I think...maybe I was blind to a lot of things. Now I'm so afraid to find out that I—"

She paused to catch her breath. Then she looked at me with more tears forming in her eyes. She looked different. Like a weight had just been lifted or something.

"Kiss me."

My stomach jolted. I don't know if it was excitement or fear.

"What?" I asked. I heard what she said, but I was trying to buy time to cure the lump that had just clogged up my throat.

"Kiss me, Nick."

I know she saw the surprise on my face, but I was hoping it didn't look like disgust. "Callie, we can't—" She placed her hands on both sides of my face, cutting off my words.

"Please," she murmured even quieter as she leaned closer. She waited for me to acknowledge her, and when I gave a slight nod, her lips were on mine. It was hesitant, but perfect. I pulled her into me, kissing her with all I had. Soft and slow. I don't know how long the kiss lasted, but it would never be long enough for me.

When she finally pulled away, her lips lingered near mine, our breath commingling. She raised her eyes to mine.

"I'm sorry," she said breathlessly.

I moved a hair off her forehead and looked into her eyes. "I'm not."

Chapter Eighteen

Callie

"I kissed him for real," I whispered into the phone.

Nick and I walked back to the room in silence after our earth-shattering kiss. I ran to the bathroom to gather myself. He knocked and told me he was running to get some ice, so I called Aubrey.

"What do you mean 'for real'? You guys have kissed before, dummy. A few times, actually, from what you both have told me," Aubrey said smugly.

I scoffed. "What do you mean 'what we both tell you'? What does he say about me?"

"Callie, can we focus, please? What are you calling me for? And why the fuck are you whispering?"

"What I mean is, I let my emotions get to me, and I basically told him I regret wasting time on Jake because I wished I was with him that whole time. I literally almost said it to his face. I was crying about how blocking Jake makes this all so final and all this other stupid crap I was feeling, and then I asked him to fucking kiss me. He was hesitant, but then I kissed him." I said it all in one breath, trying to get it out as fast as possible.

The phone was silent for about thirty seconds. I was just about to ask if she hung up when she spoke. "You are still talking to him? You told me you blocked him. Bitch...did you lie to me?"

"Calm your tits. I know I fucked up, okay? I just...I can't."

"Do...do you want to get back with him?" she asked quietly.

"No. Absolutely not."

"Okay," she whispered. Her tone took me aback because Aubrey was not usually someone to give one-word answers or whispers, for that matter.

"Tell me what you want to say. Be honest."

"Callie, he hurt you, and a lot of us knew it had been going on for a while. You just wouldn't admit it. I think I'm just worried you are going to fall into old habits, and I can't watch—"

"I won't...I promise. Aubs, I want to talk about what I said to Nick."

"What is there to say, Callie? You finally admitted you are in love with the man. He has to be so fucking excited...No?"

"I never said I loved him," I said curtly.

"Well, you do, don't you?

I was silent. I couldn't say no because I do love him. He is one of my favorite people in this world. I also couldn't say yes because...Well, I don't know if that would be a lie, too. She wasn't asking if I love him as a friend, and I'm just not ready to admit something like that.

I heard the hotel room door open, so I whispered into the phone, "Gotta go. Love you."

Before I could hang up, Aubrey whispered back, "Tell *him* that, not me." It made me smile as I hit the *end call* button.

I exited the bathroom and found Nick making our drinks.

"Hey, how's Aubrey?" he asked. He wasn't looking at me, but I could tell he was smirking.

"Why would you think—" He turned and looked at me with that knowing smirk. I smiled. "She's fine."

He handed me a drink, and I took a sip. I made a funny face when I tasted it.

"What is this?"

Nick laughed. "It's this amazing thing called lemon water; they just invented it."

"Asshole," I muttered. I took another sip. "I just wasn't expecting it."

Nick kept laughing and started getting his bed ready on the couch.

"What are you doing? I asked.

Nick looked around the room and then at me. He pointed to the couch. "Getting ready for bed. Why?"

"No reason," I said quickly.

I returned to the bathroom so I could change into my pajamas. I walked out to grab a hair tie out of my bag and he was sitting on the couch, smiling. When I walked back into the bathroom to brush my teeth, I watched him in the mirror as he passed by the open door. He was bringing some cups and things we had left around the room into the kitchen.

He was wearing gray sweatpants that fell just below his hip bones, his bare chest was on full display. Staring at him had my mind buzzing with the memory of our kiss. I bit my lip, thinking about how his hands fit in my hair. How his lips overtook mine and put the perfect amount of pressure on mine. The way his tongue entered my mouth with such care. The way his dic—

"Sweets. Did you hear me?"

I was pulled from my thoughts and turned to look at him. "Wh-what? Sorry, I was lost in thought." Shit. Did he see me staring? *Of course he did, dumbass.*

He chuckled, "I see that. I said I was going to leave the radio on so you had some noise. I know you didn't like the silence last night."

The smile forming on my face couldn't be hidden. "Um, yeah. That's great. Thank you."

We were both staring at each other, smiling like idiots, not saying a word until he finally looked away. "Okay, well, I'm going to try to get some sleep. Wake me if you need me."

He didn't wait for a response and walked into the living area. I looked back at my reflection and started giving myself a silent pep talk.

You can do this. It's Nick, He is your best friend. If things don't work out, you can just go back to being friends. Grow some balls, Callista. You are sexy as fuck, and he wants you. He has made that clear. Just do it.

I walked into the room and he was already facing the couch. I walked over to his phone and looked down at the playlist he chose. It was named "Forever & Always".

My body thrummed with excitement. Or was this desire? Did he make that for me? Have I really been so fucking blind I couldn't see this amazing man in front of me?

I stood there for a moment, just watching him. He stirred, so I ran over to the bed like a coward. When I finally looked back over, he was still facing the back of the couch. I let out a small breath.

Fucking do it.

Before I could think anymore or talk myself out of it, I walked over and shook his shoulder. He turned toward me.

"Hey, what's up?"

I swallowed the lump in my throat as I looked into his perfect blue eyes. I felt my body trembling a little. Nick must have seen it too, because he stood up and grasped both of my hands.

His voice was quiet and deep. "Hey, what's wrong? Are you okay? Did somethi—"

"Sleep with me."

Chapter Nineteen

Nick

"What?"

Callie did not just come out and ask me to sleep with her. There is no fucking way this is real life. If this is a dream, I hope I never fucking wake up.

"Wait, no," she bit her lip, and I could see—even in the dimly lit room—that her cheeks were pinking up. "I meant to sleep in the bed with me. There is no reason you should suffer on the couch."

I grazed my fingers over her knuckles, but I was not going to let her change her mind on me. "Okay. Let's go to bed."

She let my hands go and walked over to the bed. We both got in silently. For a moment, I thought she was going to just lay with her back to me, but as soon as I was settled, she turned toward me with the blanket bunched under her chin, staring up at me.

"We should talk about it, right?" Callie whispered.

I snuggled in closer and put the blanket under my chin also to mock her. I knew it would make her laugh.

"Do you want to?"

She smiled and then covered her mouth with the blanket, probably hiding her smile. She looked at me silently for another moment.

"I like kissing you," she whispered behind the blanket.

It felt like my heart was pounding out of my chest, but I didn't want to scare her by getting overly excited, so I did my best to keep my voice calm. I moved the blanket away from my face so she could see I was serious. I loved this understated side of Callie. She was usually so bold and unafraid. Seeing her timidness made me feel a new kind of desire toward her. I don't think I have ever wanted her more than I do right now.

I gripped her chin lightly with my thumb and pointer finger. "I like kissing you too, Sweets."

She shifted a little, a piece of her hair falling over her forehead. "But I'm scared," Callie admitted.

"Can I ask why?" I reached out and tucked the hair behind her ear. As I pulled my fingers away, I instantly missed the feel of her on my skin.

She cleared her throat and moved the blanket. "I'm scared to want you. You're my best friend. I'm scared that I will lose you."

She bit her lip, and my eyes went wide. That was not what I was expecting her to say. I was about to speak, but she continued. She looked at me like she could see right through me.

"I want you so bad, Nick. I think I always have."

"Baby, I want you, too." I caressed her cheek, then rubbed my thumb across her bottom lip. She closed her eyes at my touch. My fingers traveled down the column of her throat, slowly making their way to her sternum, right between her perfect breasts. She was melting under my touch. I mindlessly rubbed the back of my nail up and down until she opened her eyes to look at me again.

"I'm so scared I'm going to fuck this up," she whispered. She grabbed my hand, holding it to her chest.

Leaning forward, I kissed the tip of her nose. I pulled her into my chest, and she relaxed in my arms, which made me relax as well. I could smell her shampoo and body wash—she smelled like jasmine. I kissed her head and spoke against it.

"Then we wait. I've waited a long time for you to be mine, Callie. I will wait forever if I have to. There is no one else for me, never has been."

She leaned away and looked at me. "What? What do you mean? You have been with other people. I know some of them." She leaned back down but kept her gaze on me. She had a puzzled look on her face.

"Callie…I…It's always been you, baby. I've waited for you." I ran the back of my finger over the swell of her breast, my eyes never leaving hers. When I reached her collarbone, she gasped. "Callie, no matter who I was with, I was always thinking of you. I never gave away what is yours."

She almost looked scared when she said, "Nick, I…I don't understand what you are saying."

"I'm saying we can wait as long as it takes for you to decide to be mine forever. I only want you. I've tried to see other people, and it's never been right…they weren't you."

I could see her eyes glossing over. A single tear ran down her cheek. "Nick."

I leaned forward and put my lips to her cheek to kiss her tears away. "Shh, baby. It's okay. No crying. I'm a patient man."

I laid down on my back as Callie rested her head on my chest.

We lay silent, and I tried not to react to her rubbing circles on my stomach and tracing my abs while I ran my fingers over her hair.

"Nick?"

"Yeah, Sweets?"

"What if I am ready now?"

My entire body stiffened. I looked down at her, and before my brain could catch up to what she said, Callie's hand traveled down my body to the top of my sweatpants. She was lightly dragging her finger across my skin.

I grabbed her hand. "Even if you were ready, that's not how this is going to go, baby. I want to be really sure you are ready."

She sat up and looked at me. Before I could say another word, she was swinging her leg over my body to straddle me. She caught my lips in a passionate kiss.

My hands went to her hips to hold her steady. My fingers dug into her curvy ass. She pulled away but kept her face close.

"Sorry, I forgot I was heavier than you."

She tried to pull her body off mine. I grabbed the back of her neck and kissed her again. When I pulled away, I made her look into my eyes. "You will never apologize for your perfect body ever again, do you hear me?"

She nodded her head.

I squeezed her ass lightly. "Use your words, baby."

"Okay," she whispered as she swallowed hard.

My fingers were framing her face, and I ran my thumb over her bottom lip again.

"Now, use your words and tell me what you want."

Her eyes were searching mine. She tried to nod again, but I stopped her.

"Words, baby. I need to hear the words." I smiled up at her. "If you say the words, Callie, you are mine. There is no going back from this. You agree to let me worship you forever. I need you to be sure because I've been sure since the moment I met you."

"That is a lot of pressure, Nick."

"I know. That's why I am okay with waiting as long as you need," I assured her.

She stared at me for a moment, then placed her hands on my chest. "I want this. I want to be with you, Nick."

I pushed a piece of hair behind her ear. "Callie, please be sure."

"Kiss me, Nick."

That was all I needed to hear. I sat up with her still straddling me. I took her lips against mine once again. It felt like everything was falling into place for me. My hands went into her hair and pulled her body even closer to mine. I felt like I couldn't get her close enough. I wanted to be consumed by her.

Suddenly, nothing else mattered. It was like my world was finally right. All the wasted time with other women meant nothing. The agonizing days of watching Callie and Jake together were erased from my mind. The moments I laid awake telling myself to give up and move on, that she would never care for me the way I did her, were gone. It was all for this moment right here. Callie was mine now and always would be, forever and always.

CALLIE

The feel of Nick's warm hands exploring me was like nothing I had ever experienced. It was the sexiest feeling in the world. It felt like he was lighting my body on fire. His hands were rough and warm. He slid them up my back and into my hair. I'd never felt this much built-up desire in my entire life. Our lips fit perfectly together. As his tongue entered my mouth, I felt a rush of courage and rotated my hips on the bulge forming underneath me.

"Fuck," Nick moaned. "Sweets, if you keep doing that, this will be over way too fast."

We both smirked at each other. As he went back in for a kiss, I ground my hips down onto him again and bit his bottom lip. He smirked again, and it surprised me when he flipped us over so that he was now on top of me.

He leaned down to my ear and whispered, "You like being a bad girl, huh?"

The gruffness of his voice sent shivers through me. My body was humming underneath him. I couldn't speak, so I nodded with a grin. Nick gripped my chin.

"Words, baby. I want to hear you when I make you scream."

"Yes, I like—" My words were cut off by his mouth once again. He traveled down my neck to my breasts. He kissed over my shirt, taking my pert nipple in his mouth through my clothes. I moved my hand to try to lift my shirt for him, but he stopped me.

He looked me in the eye as he lifted it himself. "You don't do any of the work tonight. You let me take care of you. Do you understand?" I let out a small moan when he latched onto my other nipple.

"Fuck, that's my favorite fucking sound," he growled between kisses. He kissed further down my body. "Do you understand, Callista? This body is mine to worship tonight. You do not lift a finger."

"Ye—Yes," I moaned. His use of my full name melted any resolve I had left in me.

He looked up at me from my stomach. "Good girl."

I moaned as his mouth reached my hip bone over my bottoms. My hands were gripping the sheets tighter and tighter as his mouth traveled further down. He slowly pulled my shorts down my legs.

"You are so perfect, Callie," he groaned against my skin.

"Nick, I need you."

I moved one of my hands into his hair and pulled. He smirked against my hip and bit down, immediately running his tongue over the bite.

"You have me, baby." Nick traveled back up my body. I leaned up and let him remove my shirt.

He looked at my chest and back at my face. Instinctively, I tried to cover myself since he could now see almost all of me. I was suddenly very self-conscious. He grabbed my hand, which was covering my left breast.

"You never have to feel self-conscious around me. Never Callie." He pulled my hand away, leaned down, and took my nipple into his mouth again. I pulled his head into me.

When he looked back into my eyes, it looked like he was going to say something. I felt his hand rubbing right below my belly button.

"Tell me you're mine." He leaned down, kissing my jaw, then down my neck. "Tell me you will be mine forever." His hand slid further down, just above my underwear. When I didn't speak, he moved his hand lower. I gasped.

"Fuck, you are so wet for me, baby. I haven't even touched you yet."

"Nick," I gasped. "What the hell are you doing to me?" He rubbed his fingers up and down my slit over my underwear. My breathing got more labored. It felt like my heart was going to beat out of my chest.

His gaze was intense. "I have been waiting forever to make you mine," he groaned.

I leaned up and into him, kissing him harder than ever. Pulling away, I looked into his eyes again as he dragged my underwear down my legs.

"Make me yours," I whispered. I leaned back onto my pillow as he pushed his finger into me. I gasped, a moan escaping my mouth just as my eyes rolled back.

He leaned down and spoke into my ear before biting down on it. "No one other than me will ever touch you here again." He added another finger, which made me moan even louder. "This is mine," he growled.

I was nodding my head in agreement. He stopped and removed his fingers. I whimpered at the loss.

"Words, baby. I want to hear that beautiful mouth tell me this is mine."

"It's yours, I'm yours," I said breathlessly. Before I could even finish my sentence, he was curving his fingers perfectly into my G-spot, taking my breath away.

This man knew what he was doing. I was mentally kicking myself for not giving in to him sooner.

I watched as his eyes grew darker and darker with desire.

"Cum for me, Callie."

My legs shook, toes curling as my release hit me fast and strong. It was so intense; I started crying. My walls contracted around his fingers. I let out a noise I had never made before, almost as if I was gasping for air.

Nick leaned down and kissed my temple as he helped me come down from my orgasm, fingers still inside me. When he removed his fingers, he did the hottest thing I had ever seen in my life. He licked his fingers clean while staring right at me.

His eyes rolled back in his head. He let out a sexy, low groan as his tongue licked up every drop of me. His enjoyment turned me on all over again. He walked to the bathroom and grabbed a damp towel to clean up my inner thighs. I was watching him in absolute awe. He just kept that same sexy smirk on his face.

He got back into bed and laid on his back, pulling me closer to him and kissing my forehead. We fell into a comfortable silence immediately. He closed his eyes as I was still staring at his erect dick, wondering if he was just going to go to sleep or if he was waiting for me to do something. My question was answered when he spoke.

"Good night, beautiful girl."

I was immediately confused. "What? What about you? Don't you want anything?"

He looked at me from the corner of his eye. "What do you mean?"

"Like, don't you want me to...you know, take care of that? I owe you now, no?" I gestured toward his cock and the fact that it was making itself very well-known.

He sat up a little to look at me more head-on.

"Callie—" He rubbed his thumb over my cheek. "What did that man do to you?"

I blushed. "But I can—"

"Callie, you will never owe me a God damn thing for making you happy. Especially in the bedroom. I will worship you every fucking night if you will let me. I did that because I wanted to, not because I was expecting anything back. Just being here with you is everything I will ever need."

"Nick—" I stopped talking because I didn't trust what I was about to say. I leaned in and kissed him.

"Good night, beautiful girl."

As I put my head down on his chest, he whispered, "Forever and always."

Chapter Twenty

Callie

I woke up in Nick's arms the next morning. As soon as he realized I was awake, he kissed my head and told me to stay in bed and relax. He got up and made us breakfast. He acted like nothing had changed and it was completely normal we woke up in that state. He went to shower while I ate.

He opened the bathroom door but didn't exit. "What do you want to do today?" He was turned away from me, drying his hair with the towel. When I didn't answer, he turned to face me.

"Callie, didn't we have an entire conversation last night about using your words?" He plastered a sexy smile on his face.

I stood up. "Is that what we're calling last night, a conversation?"

He frowned a little. "What do you mean?" he walked up to me pushing his hands into my hair at the nape of my neck. He stared into my eyes for a few seconds and then rubbed his thumb over my bottom lip. I shivered. "Was last night not fun for you?"

"Oh no, it was definitely fun for me. It was perfect actually, but..." I tried to look down, but he held my face up toward him. "Nick."

"Yes, baby?"

I put my hands on his. "Are we really doing this? Like, are you going to tell people we are dating? What are we supposed to do when we get back? Am I supposed to move out? Do we—"

He cut me off with a kiss. "Callie, we don't have to do anything just yet. Let's spend this time together and worry about home when we get there. Okay?"

"But—" Another kiss cut me off.

"But I will answer a few of those questions. Yes, we are dating. I told you, no one else gets to be near you. As far as moving out, the only place you will move is into my bed. You're welcome to keep your room, so you have a private place to go when you need it, but you sleep with me in *our* room. Does that help clear things up a little?"

"Don't you think that's a little quick?"

He gave me an evil grin and made it clear he knew I was breaking his balls. I smiled and leaned into him. His arms wrapped around my waist, and I leaned up for a kiss. "So, is that how this relationship is going to be? You tell me what to do, and I just agree? You know I'm not a very agreeable person, Nick." I was half joking.

"I don't know. Do you want to boss me around instead, Sweets? I can get used to having a sexy, bossy girlfriend. I've known you for over ten years. You bossing me around and getting me to do things for you is nothing new to me." He chuckled and kissed my nose. "Here's the deal. I'll do anything you say, anytime. But in that bedroom, you listen to me and get worshiped. Understand?"

A rush of desire ran through me, heating my skin. I leaned in to give him a passionate kiss. He picked me up, and my legs instinctively wrapped around him. He walked me over to the bed and laid us down. When he broke the kiss, I was beaming with mischief.

"Anything I say, huh?"

He kissed me. "Anything, baby."

"Hmm." I stared off to the side, tapping my chin like I was thinking. "Wear my underwear today for the massage." I began laughing uncontrollably but was cut off when he replied without missing a beat.

"What color?"

I looked at him in surprise. "Nick, you are not wearing my underwear." I was smiling so hard my cheeks hurt.

"If you want me to, I will," he said with a grin.

I smacked his shoulder. "Shut up, weirdo."

His face got a little more serious, and he lifted my chin. "Callie, I will do anything for you...anything."

The look he was giving me was too intense. I didn't think I was ready for the feelings he was bringing up, so I leaned in and kissed him.

He wrapped me in a hug before I could pull away. "We will be fine, Sweets. I promise this will work."

"I know it will."

After lunch, we made our way to our massages that were scheduled by Aubrey and Link. That was one of their gifts for Jake and me. She told me she called to change it to single massages when we planned for Nick to come with me. I was quite excited to get some time to process last night alone.

"Are you beautiful people ready to massage each other?" The brunette woman holding our robes was only looking at Nick when she spoke. Nick's gaze turned to me.

"You didn't tell me we were massaging each other, darlin'." He dragged out the darlin', making me laugh.

I looked back at the woman I assumed was our masseuse. "I'm sorry, but we should just be getting separate ones. We called to switch it."

"Oh, of course, let me look again," she said way too eagerly.

"Thanks." Nick placed his arm over my shoulder and leaned down to my ear.

"What, are you afraid of me getting my hands on you again?" His smirk was devious.

I looked at him with a questioning stare. "Did you change this?" I asked.

"Not me, Sweets. I'm just here for the ride. I didn't do any of the planning, remember?"

The brunette woman spoke again. "Sorry, ma'am. It says someone called and changed it. They asked for it to be our honeymoon package. For that package, we show you a few different types of massages, and then we leave you and your partner to do the rest." She winked, and my stomach fluttered. I didn't exactly hate the idea of Nick's hands on me again, but I didn't want to seem too eager.

I looked at Nick to ask if he was okay with this, but I knew he would be.

"I am here for the ride, Sweets; I will do whatever you say." He leaned down and kissed the top of my head.

When I looked back at the woman helping us, she was looking at Nick like he was a snack. A rush of jealousy ran through me.

I looked back at her with determination and pulled him into me. "It will be perfect. I can't wait to get my hands all over him."

"Oh, really?" I heard Nick whisper.

I pinched his side without looking at him, and he winced.

Before leaving us alone in our private room, she explained to get undressed and lay down. She acted like we were idiots who didn't know how a massage worked. I didn't even acknowledge her snark before she left, because I was too busy thinking about Nick touching me again.

The memories of his hands all over me last night were turning me on all over again. My heart raced as arousal formed in my lower belly. I clenched my legs together to get some small amount of relief. I was pulled from my thoughts when I saw Nick staring at me.

Nick stood in the corner, just watching me. He removed all his clothes except his boxers, then covered himself with one of the robes. Just knowing he was practically naked made the blush continue to cover my body.

The masseuse knocked and came back into the room. I heard her voice mumbling words. My mind was so filled with anticipation that nothing else was processing. She showed Nick all the oils and lotions he could use, then moved to teaching him a few different massage techniques on my back, thighs, and calves. When her hands left me, I didn't hear them talking for a moment. I looked over and she was whispering in his ear. I felt my cheeks get hot as a furious rage coursed through me. He laughed, breaking my thoughts.

"Oh, I definitely won't have that problem with her, and that was wildly inappropriate, but thank you," Nick retorted.

She leaned away, blushing, then nodded before saying, "I'm sorry." She cleared her throat. "So, that's everything. Do you have any questions, sir? This controls the lights and music." She pointed to a switch on the wall by the door.

Nick was smiling from ear to ear, giving me a hungry look. "Nope, I have everything I need right here." He looked back at her. "Thank you."

I turned my face back into the little hole in the chair I was lying on. I heard the door shut. I was anticipating Nick's voice, but he didn't speak just yet. The lights dimmed and some relaxing music started. I was just about to move when I felt his breath on my ear.

"Let me know if I hurt you, okay? Don't forget to use your words."

An instant flood of arousal hit me. I had no idea how I was going to get through this massage session without fucking him right here on this table.

He started at my ankles, lightly rubbing his fingers in soft circles. My body trembled at his touch. As he traveled up my leg, I felt myself getting more relaxed. He was kneading my calves with the perfect amount of pressure. Muscles I didn't even know I had were relaxing under his touch.

"Is this okay?" Nick asked.

"Mmm, perfect." It came out more like a moan than I intended.

His hands abruptly let go of my calf, and he leaned his body over mine. He groaned into my ear, "If you keep moaning like that, this is going to change directions very quickly."

I felt my body flush and stayed quiet. His hands began traveling up my legs, and then he was kneading the back of my thighs right under my ass.

My ass was covered with a towel, and he kept slipping just under it.

"Can I remove this?" He flipped the corner of the towel, and I nodded.

He slapped my ass playfully over the towel. "Words, Sweets? Let me hear you say it's okay."

I swallowed down the lump in my throat and pulled my head up to gaze at him. "Yes, remove the towel."

He smiled and lifted the towel as I put my face back into the chair hole.

A moment later, he groaned. "Fuck baby, you are so fucking perfect. Look at this." He gripped my ass cheeks, kneading them with just the right amount of pressure. Then he moved both hands to one ass cheek, then the other, giving them each their own attention. My whole body was like putty under his touch, that was until he leaned down and bit my right ass cheek.

"Ouch," I giggled as I jumped. My body tensed in the best way at the feel of his mouth on me. He immediately ran his tongue over the bite.

"Your skin tastes amazing," he murmured.

I leaned up, holding the towel over my breasts to my chest, turning my head so I could look at him.

"I thought I wasn't allowed to moan because we didn't want this turning into something else?"

He walked over to the top of the massage chair and lifted my chin to kiss me. "I never said I didn't want you to moan. I said it would become something more if you keep making all those amazing noises."

I rolled my eyes at him and tried to lie back down, but before I knew it, he lifted me up and flipped me over onto my back.

"This view is much better."

I struggled to hold on to the towel covering me, but it didn't fall fully. I grabbed the towel that had been covering my ass that was sitting off to the side and rushed to get it over my lower half.

Nick laughed at my nervous movements. Once I was settled on my back, he moved behind my head so I was looking up at him. He kissed the tip of my nose. "You are so beautiful."

"Thank you," I whispered.

He began at my shoulders, taking each arm and massaging them thoroughly. I felt myself becoming more and more tranquil every time he massaged somewhere new. My body felt amazing.

I don't know if I fell asleep, or was just that relaxed, but after what seemed like an hour, Nick finally pulled his hands away.

When my eyes opened, he was grabbing my robe and placing it on the head of the massage table.

"You ready to go, Sweets?"

I sat up and put the robe on and tied it tight.

"Thank you, that was perfect."

I was still sitting on the table, so he placed a hand on each side of my legs and leaned closer to me. "It was my pleasure. Literally."

My eyes traveled down his body, but the robe was too fluffy to make anything out. I teased him the way he was teasing me. I pulled one of the ties holding the robe together, and I saw the mask of confidence on his face slipping a little.

"So, what did that bimbo whisper to you before she left?" I pulled the second string, but didn't open the robe.

"Um," he swallowed, "she told me they had a no-sex and no locked doors policy." I was rubbing my finger down the opening of the robe down his torso. "She said if I needed any help to let her know."

"Then what was so inappropriate?"

He visibly swallowed again. "She told me if I get bored with this, she could come help me out."

Jealousy rose inside of me as I hopped off the table and went to lock the door. I turned back to him with a devilish grin.

"Your turn."

Chapter Twenty-One

Nick

Callie's hands on my body were the second-best feeling in the world. I reserved the first for when I truly made her mine. Making love to Callie, and really making her mine, will be the best thing that I ever get to experience in my life. I have waited too long, and imagined too many perfect scenarios, for it to happen any other way. Since it will also be my first time in general, I have a feeling that will make it even better.

"Do you like this?" she asked.

Playing the piano has made her hands fast and light. Her fingers digging into my leg muscles gave the perfect amount of tender, firm pressure. I was so deep in thought, I just grunted. She stopped, then leaned toward my ear and mimicked my words, "Use your words, darling"

Her laugh was contagious. She was trying to be sassy, and it was working. It was also hot as fuck. She had been acting so timid since last night, and I was starting to worry for a second. Callie is not a timid woman by any means, and I don't want us getting together changing that fact. I don't want us getting together to change much of anything. Except, of course, the added benefit of making love to my dream woman.

"Ya know, you have a very flat ass, Nicholas," she laughed.

I turned my head and peered at her over my arm.

"Are you making fun of me, Sweets?"

She moved her hands onto said flat ass and tried to squeeze it. "Maybe a little," she winked.

There's my girl. I put my head back down. *My girl*. Callie is finally mine, and I can't fucking wait to tell the whole damn world. She put her hands on my lower back and kneaded her fingers into my tight muscles. She gave my back attention for a few more minutes before asking me to flip over.

"I don't know if that's the best idea at this moment." I gave her a side-eye.

"Why? Is little Nicky coming out to play?" she mocked. She was laughing at her own joke until I grabbed her arm and pulled her toward me. I sat up and put her hand just hovering over my lap, but not quite touching me. I heard her breath catch.

"Do you want to see just how not little 'Little Nicky' is?"

She stared into my eyes and gave me silent permission. I used my other hand to push her hair away from her face and placed it behind her ear.

"Words, baby."

She never took her eyes off me. She bit her lip. "Yes, I want to feel you."

I lowered her hand onto me. She instinctively gripped me through the towel. I let out a low growl, bit down on my bottom lip, and let my eyes roll back. She let out a whispered gasp.

I looked back at her and my voice came out strained. "Not little, baby. Especially not when you have had your perfect hands all over me."

"Not little," she repeated. She was staring into my eyes, and she moved her hand up and down, increasing and decreasing the pressure she was using. The towel was still between us. It was causing a bit of friction. She must have noticed my wince because she dragged the towel away, and my dick jutted toward her.

Before putting her hands back on me, she asked, "Ready to continue?" Her voice sounded uneasy.

"Yes, ma'am."

Without taking her eyes off me, she gripped my length and ran her thumb over the tip, capturing the small bead of pre-cum that had developed. She put her thumb into her mouth and sucked.

"You are so fucking sexy." I pulled her toward me, claiming her mouth. She put both her hands on my bare chest and pushed back, breaking the kiss. She moved her mouth toward my ear.

"It's my turn to make you feel good."

God, I love this woman.

She grabbed the body oil and looked at the label. I was about to question her, but then she put a drop in her hand. She wrapped her hand around my cock and began stroking up and down. My eyes rolled to the back of my head again. The warming oil felt so fucking good.

"Lay down," she whispered against my ear.

"I can't—fuck, I don't want you to stop," I said between heated breaths.

"I won't."

She kept one hand on my cock as she guided me onto my back. I closed my eyes so I could fully enjoy her hands on me. One hand continued to stroke me while the other was massaging my shoulder, then down to my peck.

"Does that feel good? Are you relaxed enough yet?"

"Fuck yes." I opened my eyes and peered at her. Her bottom lip was pulled into her teeth with a playful smile. I closed my eyes, and she removed her hand from my cock. I started to protest until she leaned down and her hot mouth wrapped around me.

"Holy fuck." My hand instinctively went into her hair. "Baby the... the oil is..."

My body felt like it was on fire. I couldn't believe what was happening. I was trying to keep my noise to a minimum, but she was so fucking good at it. She pulled her mouth off me with a pop noise and laughed.

"The oil is safe for me to swallow. Now, push my head down."

I let her head go, and my eyes went wide. "What?" I chuckled. I thought I was dreaming for a second.

She looked me in the eye. "I said, Push. My. Head. Down. I want to choke on your cock." She lowered her mouth, put my hand back into her hair, and pushed down. I took over. When I hit the back of her throat, it was like a lightbulb went off for her. She became a different person. She started taking me deeper and deeper each time. Within minutes, I knew I was about to cum.

"Baby, if you don't...fuck, if you don't stop, I'm going to cum in your mouth."

She hollowed out her cheeks and took me deeper. I took that as the go-ahead. My balls tightened, and I was cuming down her throat. She was working her mouth up and down, working me through it.

Once she was done, she looked down at me, panting. Then she wiped the side of her lip with her thumb, licking anything she wiped away, making sure she didn't miss a drop. The sight made me thrum with more desire.

I stood up shakily and lifted her onto the table. I pushed the robe open around her legs and stood between them. I took her into a deep, passionate kiss. Her hands went into my hair, and we kissed like we were going to die without each other.

"I want you so bad, Nick," Callie whispered.

"Callie, you have always had me. Forever and always, baby." I took her back into a kiss and ran one of my hands up her thigh. In between kisses, I took her face into my hands and looked into her caramel eyes. I ran my thumb over her bottom lip. "Tell me this isn't a dream. Tell me you are finally mine for good."

She leaned into my touch. "I'm yours, Nick." She looked at me with so much care. "Forever and always."

Hearing her use my 'forever and always', even though she couldn't know the real meaning, set something off inside of me. I knew I would never be the same now that she was mine.

"Forever and always," I whispered.

✿

CALLIE

Nick and I returned to the hotel room soon after our massage. We stopped at one of the local food stands and grabbed some jerk chicken kabobs, which were phenomenal.

The tension between us was loud. I was trying everything I could to calm myself down on the walk back to the room, hence the stop for chicken. I knew that as soon as we got back to the room; it was do or die. We were going to have sex.

The moment the door shut, I jumped into his arms. His hands went up my back and into my hair.

"Callie," he moaned.

I would never get sick of hearing my name come out of his mouth in that raspy tone. We were becoming ravenous. He placed me on the bed and kept kissing me until I pulled away. I was nervous, but I looked into his eyes and whispered in my best sexy voice, "Fuck me, Nick."

He stilled. His body got tense above me, and I thought something was wrong.

"Now?" he asked.

I was a little thrown off by the squeaky decibel in which the word came out of his mouth.

"Um, yeah, I was thinking now." I was very confused. "Did you want to wait till tomorrow or—"

"No," he said curtly. "I'm just," he moved from above me and sat next to me, grabbing my hand. "I told you I waited, so I don't...I don't want it to suck for you."

"Wait," I sat up, gazing at him. "That's what you meant by there has never been anyone else? You can't be serious." It came out in an almost mocking tone.

"Damn, Cal," he moved away a little. "You don't have to say it like that. I kind of thought it was romantic."

He pushed my hand away and got up to walk over to the ice bucket. He spun around to face me and simultaneously rubbed the back of his neck. "I'm going to grab some ice. Need anything?"

"Nick. You know I didn't mean that the way it came out."

He turned toward the door. "Yeah, I just need a second. I'll be back."

"Nick, come on, the bucket is full." I got up to follow him and grabbed his arm. "Talk to me. We don't need fucking ice right now."

"Apparently, we don't need fucking at all because you find it funny."

With that, he walked out the door.

What in the world just happened? Nick couldn't be a virgin. I mean, I knew some of the girls he'd dated. Not once did they say anything bad about him or mention that they didn't have sex. I've only heard good things, actually. It always made me feel weird hearing about him being with other people. Although, now that I think about it, they never said anything about actually sleeping with him.

I sat back on the bed, my mind swirling with confusion. Once the confusion cleared a little, the realization hit me once again.

He waited. Even though I was marrying Jake, he waited. I don't know whether to absolutely melt at how fucking charming that is or cry my eyes out because I feel horrible that I didn't give in sooner and share my genuine feelings with him. Our lives could have been so different.

I heard the lock on the door click. I sat up, and he put the bucket down on the side table next to the door. He leaned on the door with his arms crossed and his head looking down. "Sorry. I shouldn't have run out like that. I was embar-"

I got up while he was talking and took his mouth in a sweet kiss. When we broke the kiss, his eyes went down again, so I lifted his chin.

"You waited," I whispered.

A small smile grew on his face before he nodded. "I would have waited forever for you."

I gripped his hands in mine and started leading him toward the bed.

"What...what are you doing, Cal?"

I looked up at him with admiration. "We're going to bed. Today was a lot. You are going to hold me, and we are going to sleep. Everything else can wait until tomorrow."

We stopped next to the bed, both still fully dressed in our day clothes. I laid him down, covered him up, and snuggled into him.

"Callie, It's six o'clock, we haven't even eaten dinner. If we go to bed now, we will wake up at two in the morning."

I smirked at him. "Two in the morning is tomorrow."

I kissed his lips softly.

He remained quiet for a few minutes until I felt his body moving. I realized he was laughing, so I sat up to look at him.

"Are you laughing?"

He pushed the hair out of my face and behind my ear. "Yes."

"Okay, I'll bite. Why?"

He pulled me in closer and kissed me deeply. "I just wanted to ask if I could set an alarm for midnight since you didn't specify when tomorrow and didn't seem to care how early it was."

I started laughing so hard I couldn't even answer him. As funny as it was, I don't think he was joking.

Chapter Twenty-Two

Nick

Since I didn't set the alarm, I woke up at three-thirty the next morning, and Callie was snoring away. It sounded like a small freight train was in the distance. It took everything in me not to laugh, even though my stomach was growling almost as loud as Callie was snoring. I grabbed an orange we had sitting on the kitchen table and scarfed it down before heading to the bathroom. I needed to wash my face, brush my teeth, and maybe even get into something a little more comfortable since I hadn't changed before we fell asleep.

Showering was next on my list so I could wash all this oil and lotion off from the massages, but I didn't want to wake her with the sound of the shower water running. I made a mental note to make sure we asked for a set of new sheets later today.

Just as I finished washing my face, the door opened and Callie stepped in. She winced at the bright light, and her appearance made me chuckle. Her hair was disheveled and falling all over the place, which was surprising because I hadn't felt her move much, and when I woke up, she was still on my chest.

I stared, appreciating the view. I was waiting for her to say something, but she just smiled and walked farther into the bathroom. She started undressing slowly like she was putting on a show for me. My heart rate quickened, followed by my cock hardening more and more with every item she took off.

She walked toward the shower, putting her perfectly curvy body on display for me. Her body was fucking perfection, but her ass was like a fucking wet dream all on its own. She opened the shower curtain. Before she fully got in, she turned with the sexiest grin I'd ever seen and said, "You coming?"

Fuck yes, I'm coming. Hopefully, in more ways than one. I started undressing immediately without saying another word. Once we got into the shower, she ran her hands up my torso and around my neck, digging her nails into the hair at the nape of my neck as the water cascaded over us. I let out a low groan as I pulled her into my embrace and kissed her softly.

"How did you sleep?" she asked.

"Perfect, with you next to me. How about you?" I kissed her again before she could answer. Kissing Callie was my new favorite thing to do. I pinned her up against the wall. Just as I was about to pull away from the kiss, she did and whispered, "I want to make you feel good, Nick. Will you let me?"

I searched her eyes for any ounce of the hesitation I had seen over the last few days, and there was none. It was gone. She was just as sure as I was. I ran my fingers over her features. I was studying every inch of the beautiful face I had come to love so much. I was delicately tracing every freckle I had imagined kissing. Every laugh line that made her face just that much more beautiful. Then I looked into those hypnotizing caramel eyes again.

"You will have to show me everything. I mean, I get how it wo—"

She cut me off with a finger over my lips. "I'll show you anything and everything, baby. We will go as fast or slow as we need to."

She ran her finger down my body until she reached my cock and ran her finger over my tip, causing me to release a breathless groan.

"Fast, we go fast," I blurted.

She kissed my chest and licked my nipple playfully. "Let's get washed up, and then we can go as fast as you want...on the bed."

We spent the next few minutes hurrying to wash each other. It was taking everything in me not to make love to her in the shower. We toweled each other off in a hurry.

"Callie?" She looked up at me with sultry eyes. I ran my fingers through her hair. "You are sure about this, right? Because I'm nervous as fuck, and I want this to be perfect for–"

"Shh," she put her finger over my lips, then leaned up to kiss me. "I am more than sure."

As she led me to the bed, my skin heated to an uncomfortable temperature. I was desperately trying to swallow the lump of nervousness in my throat. Once we reached the edge of the mattress, she stood on her tiptoes to kiss my nose.

"Thank you," she whispered.

I was breathing heavily, praying she couldn't hear my heart pounding out of my chest. I was hearing it in my ears. The adrenaline was radiating throughout my entire body. "For what?" I breathed out.

"Waiting."

She smiled up at me, kissed my lips softly, and lowered back onto her feet. She held her hands flat on my chest, almost as if she was waiting for me to move. The air between us was full of so many unspoken words.

I took a seat on the edge of the bed and started nervously playing with my sweaty hands. Sweat dripped down my forehead as my heart pounded rapidly. I could lie to myself and say I was just hot from the shower, but I could hear my heartbeat in my head. This moment is something I've thought about a lot, and I thought I would be able to handle it with a little more finesse than this.

Callie positioned herself in front of me, discarding her towel and straddling me, all while maintaining eye contact. I slowly and carefully looked over her body. Before my eyes could even take her all in, she was touching me. She ran her hands down from my face to my neck and continued slowly down my chest. When she reached my torso, my heart felt like it might actually explode out of my chest at any second. Callista Adriana Diaz was naked and on top of me.

I ran my hands through her hair on the sides of her head. She leaned her face into one of my hands. "I feel like a fifteen-year-old about to cum from my crush's touch," I admitted.

She smirked and giggled a little. "The first time probably won't last long just because of the built-up excitement, but don't be embarrassed because we will be enjoying each other all day in this bed so that you can make it up to me." She pushed my torso back onto the bed and leaned down on me. "You have no say in the matter," she added.

The thrill I felt with her leaning on me was unexplainable. I wouldn't fight her about being in this bed, even if she wanted me to. I would spend the rest of my life buried deep inside her and doing nothing else if she would let me.

"I have condoms," I blurted in my nervousness. *What the fuck is wrong with me? Why do I need to be so weird right now?*

She looked sort of surprised, but not upset. "You do?"

I cleared my throat. "I didn't want to assume. I was just really fucking hoping. I always hope."

She shook her head from side to side with a seductive grin on her face. "We won't be needing those."

I sat up abruptly with wide eyes, catching her before she fell backward. "What? We have...Callie, we have to. I don't want to get you pregnant...not yet, at least."

That made her eyes go wide for a moment, but she recovered quickly. I would have missed it if I hadn't been looking at her already.

She pushed my back down. "Nick, I've been on birth control since I was fifteen. I've been tested multiple times since the breakup, and you are a virgin. We have nothing to worry about."

I winced at the word virgin. I mean, it was true, but it just felt weird to hear her say it. I believed I was the only man my age who was still holding out.

She continued, "If you want to use one, I'll go grab them, but I think they are unnecessary."

I pulled her down and kissed her deeply with all the passion I had pent up for this moment. My mind was racing with all the moments I'd dreamt of being in this position with her. Right as I was becoming overwhelmed with emotion, she started kissing me across my face and down my neck until she stopped with a nibble on my ear.

"Get me nice and wet for your cock," she whispered. "Or should I do it?" She put her hand between us and dipped her fingers into herself. I flipped us over with a newfound confidence. My cock was throbbing against her thigh as I pushed her hands above her head. I held both of her hands in one of mine.

I looked her in the eyes. "You're going to cum for me first. Then we'll worry about me."

"Fuck yes," she moaned.

I kissed her as my hand traveled down her body, dipping into her with two fingers. She let out another soft moan.

"Fuck baby, you are so wet already."

She wiggled, trying to get her hands free. I finally let her hands go and started peppering her body with kisses. I ran my mouth over one of her supple breasts, using my tongue to circle her dark pink nipple before taking it into my mouth. I removed my fingers from her pussy and rubbed her wetness over her other nipple, then sucked the excess off my fingers.

"Mhm," I groaned. "You taste amazing, baby. You are my new favorite thing to eat." I cleaned off her nipple with long strokes and sucked hard. She let out the sexiest moan, so I knew I was doing something she liked. I started to move my mouth further down her body. I nipped at her hip lightly, causing her to gasp. Her hands went into my hair, pulling with the perfect amount of pressure, making my cock even harder.

I finally reached her pussy. I kissed her inner thigh before running my tongue over the swollen bud that was begging for my attention and sucked it lightly into my mouth.

"That feels...Mmm fuck, keep going," she moaned as her hips arched off the bed.

I thrust my tongue into her, making her grip onto my hair tighter. I used two fingers to help me bring her to her release. I was getting into the perfect rhythm. The feeling of her holding onto me made me hum with my own groans. It must have caused the perfect amount of vibration on her clit because she came a second later, screaming my name. Her legs were trembling as I coaxed her through it. I kissed her inner thighs, then worked my way back up her body.

Callie wasted no time flipping us over to straddle me again.

"Fuck Sweets...what...Oh my god." She was using her own release to lubricate my cock, rubbing herself up and down my shaft.

"Are you ready for me, baby?" she said with a grin.

No words came out, and all I could do was nod. She leaned down and used some of my favorite words against me.

"Use your words, baby."

"Yes, I'm re—"

She cut off my words by lifting herself up and dropping down onto my cock. I was only about an inch in, but the feel of her pussy gripping me made me go numb. I couldn't get any words out other than a long drawn-out "Fuuuck."

"You are so damn big," she moaned.

I smiled. I was trying so hard not to thrust my entire cock up into her. Instead, I let her take the lead and acclimate to my size. This was the best day of my fucking life, and I refused to rush it.

My hands were gripping Callie's hips so hard I knew I was leaving a mark, but she didn't seem phased. I think she enjoyed it. Knowing her, she was getting off on the pain.

That's my girl.

Her moans were getting louder with every new inch she took in. I cupped Callie's breast in my hand and then pulled her forward to take her nipple into my mouth.

This new angle sent sparks of fire down my spine. Callie was very right; this wasn't going to last long. Once my cock was fully seated inside her, she began to twist her hips, stretching herself out using my cock. It felt incredible to be moving inside of her. This had to be the best fucking feeling in the world. Her pussy was my new favorite place to be.

"Fuck Callie, you feel so good. You are so tight, baby." I was trying to talk through each of my grunts. I could feel my balls tightening with every move she made.

She leaned down and moaned as she said, "I can't wait to do this every day."

With those words, I thrust up into her as deeply as I could from this angle. I got a rush of confidence and flipped us over. Being on top of her was the answer to all my fucking dreams. I pulled my cock almost all the way out of her, my eyes never leaving hers. I spread her legs even further and thrust into her, hard.

She screamed my name the moment I thrust into her completely. There were no words for what I was feeling at that moment. I only got a few more thrusts in before my balls tightened, and I came harder than I had ever experienced before. I pumped into her a few more times to get myself through my orgasm. We both moaned, followed by Callie letting out the sexiest whimper.

"Fuck, baby. I—"

I almost told her I loved her. That would have scared the shit out of her, I'm sure.

I pulled out of her and watched as my release covered her pussy and thighs. I laid down beside her, panting, with my arm covering my face. I heard her breathlessly panting as well. A huge grin was forming on my face because I could feel her staring at me. I moved my arm, and sure enough, she was up on her elbow, staring at me with a smile, biting her lip.

I pulled her in close and kissed her like there was no tomorrow. "You are amazing, Callie."

She was quiet, just looking at me for a moment. My inner thoughts started creeping in. *Oh my god, she hated it. It sucked. She doesn't really want this. Fuck, why did you do this? You just fucked it all up.*

"It was amazing, huh?" she whispered.

Her response surprised me.

"Well, not for you, but for me, yes. I promise next time you will—"

She sat up a little more. "Nick," I looked at her and waited for her to continue. "It was amazing. I've never felt like that during sex before." She looked up at the ceiling and fell onto her back. Her pert nipples pointed straight up. "It was..." she looked back at me, and I moved onto my elbow to get a better look at her. "I felt so in sync with you. It was..." I swept a piece of hair off her forehead, and she leaned into my touch and smiled up at me. "Perfect, you were so perfect." She ran her fingers through my hair.

I gave her a smile. "I appreciate the vote of confidence, baby, but that was nowhere near perfect for you, and I know it. I didn't even get the job done for you."

She placed her hand on my chest. "Nick. It was perfect, and nothing you did or didn't do will change that. It was the best sex I've ever had. And it was with my favorite person in this entire world."

I licked her bottom lip, making her moan greedily. I spoke against her mouth before kissing her.

"I am about to make it even better, baby." I trailed my fingers down her torso and found her clit. She was right again... we would be enjoying each other all day in this bed so I could make it up to her. I was going to enjoy every fucking minute of it.

Chapter Twenty-Three

Callie

I thought this would be different. I thought I would feel awkward. I honestly didn't think I was ready to take this step, but I knew he was, so I did it for him. I said all the right things and made him think I was confident. I was still afraid this would change everything, and I guess, in a way, it has.

Sex with Nick was more than I ever could have imagined. Yeah, I didn't climax during sex, but I never have. I always had to finish myself off after Jake finished. Jake never cared to take care of me the way Nick does. That sex wasn't earth-shattering by any means, but it was still amazing. I'd never felt how much someone cared about me like that during sex, and I was with Jake forever. Besides Nick, Jake was the only man I had been with.

My thoughts were cut off by the amazing tingling Nick was giving me between my legs.

"Nick, yes. Right...right there," I moaned. "Nick, you don't have to...I can finish myself."

His entire body froze. He removed his mouth from my breast where he had been enjoying lapping at my nipples and looked into my eyes.

"What did you just say?" His voice sounded a little stern. I leaned up on my elbows to look at him.

"I can finish myself off. I'm used to doing that after sex. It's no big deal. Plus, I really have to pee." I laughed and rolled over to hop up and run to the bathroom. When I came back out, he was staring wide-eyed at me.

I stopped and looked around at myself, thinking something was wrong. I started feeling all over my body.

"What? What's wrong? Is there something on me?"

"Say it again." Nick retorted.

"Say what?" I walked over, straddled him, and kissed his neck just under his jaw. I didn't know what it was, but the urge to touch him was so intense.

"You are used to finishing yourself off after sex?" It wasn't a statement. It was definitely a question.

"I'm just used to it. I never actually get off during sex. I didn't want you to be upset by it. I can do it. Actually, I can do it right here if you want me to." I reached my hand between us, finding the pulsing bundle of nerves. It felt so good to touch myself. Nick's eyes were locked on mine, and then he swatted my hand away and flipped me over to get on top of me.

"Oof, ouch, Nick. What was that for?"

"Baby, I know I am kinda new at this sex thing, but there will never be a moment that you'll *need* to get yourself off. If you *want* to, then go for it. I will gladly watch that shit all day long and then clean you up with my mouth, but you will *always* be satisfied with me.

"What—" He moved his body, and I could feel his heavy erection on my leg, hard and ready once again. "How are you ready to go again already?"

He kissed my temple and down my body to my breasts. He took my nipple back into his mouth and then spoke around it.

"Baby, there will never be a moment when I am not ready and willing to make love to you. You turn me on just by fucking breathing."

When I didn't respond, he looked at me with concern. "Sweets, did you hear what I said?"

I nodded my head, and he smiled as he leaned down to kiss my lips.

"Use your words, Callie," he whispered. I felt his erection nearing my entrance. "Can I make love to you again?"

"Ye...yes. Please."

"That's my perfect girl."

His girl.

"How are you...how are you so good, and how do you know so much if you were a virgin?"

"Sweets, I'm not a fifteen-year-old virgin. I am a twenty-six-year-old man who has had experiences and fun with women. I'm not new at everything." He smiled and kissed me again.

A pang of jealousy ran through me hearing about him being with other women, but of course he was. I was wasting my time with the dick of the century. I was about to say something, but he continued.

"I just saved the most enjoyable and rewarding thing for my forever girl." He kissed me again. This time, it was rough and passionate. His erection was hovering over my entrance. "I still know how to take care of my partner and make sure they are happy."

My mind was whirling with thoughts and trying to catch up with itself. He looked me in the eye once more.

"Nick, I don't want you to get upset if it doesn't happen during sex. It is hard for women to orgasm during sex sometimes. Like I said, it's never happened to me before. I've always just taken care of it after the fact."

He kissed my nose. "Maybe you're right... maybe it won't happen this time, but..." He smiled really big as he lifted one of my legs over his shoulder and slowly pushed his erection inside me, then whispered, "I will have so much fun trying."

My eyes instantly rolled to the back of my head because the pressure and fullness he gave me were literally mind-blowing.

"Fuck," I moaned out.

I felt every inch of him as he slid inside me, making sure I could take him in again. Once he was fully inside me, he gave me a moment to adjust, pulled out, and thrust inside me, causing my body to jolt with pleasure and my back to arch off the bed. I could feel my release building already. His thrusts were perfectly timed with each beat of my racing heart. Some were gentle, while others were rough. Every single one made me grip him harder. I knew my nails were leaving marks, and I honestly couldn't wait to see my nail marks on him.

I was moaning so loud it was nearly a scream.

"Use your words, baby; let me hear you."

"Oh fuck," I love this dirty side of him.

I didn't think it could get any better, but then he said the magic words, "You take me so good, baby."

My walls began to pulse around him. He leaned down and whispered, "I wanna feel you cuming on my cock."

He moved one hand down to my clit. His thumb circled it while he thrust in and out once more. With the feel of him inside me and his perfectly skilled fingers on my clit, my release came with a loud scream.

Heat spread throughout my entire body, and I was seeing stars. Moments later, I felt Nick's release fill me once again.

He pumped in and out of me a few more times, working us both through our orgasms. He pulled out of me and lay beside me, his chest rapidly rising and falling. My legs were shaking with aftershocks, and I began laughing loudly.

Nick looked at me with concern. "Are you seriously laughing right now?" he asked with a smirk. I nodded my head. "I don't know whether to be offended or happy that you are happy," he chuckled.

I leaned over and kissed his chest. "Happy, I'm very happy."

I felt myself becoming overcome with emotion, and tears were pricking my eyes. I got up to pee and hide my tears, but Nick grabbed my hand before I could get far.

"What's wrong?" His smile dropped.

"I'm fine," I said, wiping away a tear. "Happy tears, I promise."

He got up and pulled me into a hug. "Talk to me, baby." He pulled away and took my face in his hands.

I swallowed the lump in my throat and grasped my hands around his wrists. "That was just...unbelievably amazing. I've never...it's never felt like that before. I don't know how anything will ever top how perfect that was."

I looked up at him as he leaned in to kiss me. He gave me a peck and then whispered against my lips, "I can't wait to have many more perfect moments like that with you." He pulled back and stared into my eyes again, rubbing my bottom lip with his thumb. "Forever and always, baby."

Chapter Twenty-Four

Nick

I tried to coax Callie into laying down with me right away after we made love because we were having such an emotional moment, but she insisted she pee first. Apparently, that's a thing girls need to do right after sex. I guess I still have a lot to learn, even though I did tons of research. I'm really glad that she is going to be the one teaching me from now on.

Instead of continuing our moment when she returned to bed, she snuggled into me and kissed my chest. I kissed her head and started to ask her more about why she was so emotional. It honestly made me nervous that something was wrong, even though she assured me that wasn't the case. Before I could even finish my sentence, Callie's beautiful snores were filling the room.

We woke up a few hours later, both still completely naked. I was grateful because it gave me a moment to admire her without her knowing and getting all self-conscious.

Callie's body was fucking perfect. She had flawless, light caramel skin and eyes that she got from her mom. Her ass was phenomenal. It's just the right amount to get a good grip on. Her breasts were full, with dark pink nipples. They were just bigger than my hands, which was the perfect amount for me.

She had light pinkish stretch marks on her breasts and over her hips and lower stomach, some of which she covered with floral tattoos. Although I'd known her forever, I'd never actually seen that much of her body. She always hid her stomach under clothes, even in a bathing suit. She wore what she called a high-waist bathing suit, whatever that meant. I could see the petals of the flowers peeking over her bathing suit bottoms, but that was it. It's a very beautiful tattooed piece. Although, now that I was thinking about how someone else was so close to her pussy, I was starting to get heated.

She had very little pubic hair, and what she did have was very well maintained, so I could see every perfect inch of her. It's so mesmerizing. Thoughts of tasting that perfect pussy again were rushing through my mind. My mouth was practically watering from remembering the way she tasted.

"Creeper."

Callie's voice brought me out of my thoughts. My eyes trailed back up her body, and I saw that she was smiling. I leaned down to kiss her, and she quickly turned her head so my lips caught her cheek.

I looked at her, pretending to be offended.

She covered her mouth. "I have morning breath."

"So?"

"Wait five minutes, crazy, then you can kiss me all you want."

I got on top of her and moved her hands over her head. I leaned down till my lips were barely touching hers.

"Or I could do what I want, and you could be a good girl and just take it."

Her eyes went wide. I lost a tiny bit of confidence in that moment, but I wasn't going to let her know that. Instead of kissing her mouth, because I would never forcibly make her do anything she didn't want to, I began by kissing her neck and moved down to her chest. I took her nipple in my mouth, and she hummed with excitement.

I continued down her body and spoke against her stomach. "Callie you have exactly three minutes to do whatever you need to do, then I'm going to make love to you in the shower. If you are late, you get nothing." I kissed the top of her pubic bone right above where I knew she was begging for attention the most. I got up and grabbed a few towels.

"Wait," she protested. She sat up a little. "That was such a damn tease." She had the sexiest fucking pout on her face.

I smiled and walked into the bathroom. I turned to her and leaned against the door-jam. "You didn't let me kiss you when I wanted to, so you have to wait to cum till after we shower if you're late."

She huffed as she got up out of bed. She stopped right in front of me and looked up. "You're an evil, evil man, Nicholas James Clark."

I looked at my wrist with my non-existent watch and tapped it. "Two minutes, Sweets."

She pushed me out of the way with a laugh.

She wasn't late.

CALLIE

After an hour of steamy shower sex and multiple orgasms, the water went cold, forcing us to get out and talk about what we were going to do today.

I went with a pretty yellow sunflower dress with my favorite Greek-god-looking sandals. When I finished getting ready, I plopped down next to Nick, who had been ready and waiting for me for about forty-five minutes.

"Okay, where to, sir?"

He looked over at me with a sly smile, and his eyebrows went up in question. "Sir?" He put the newspaper he was reading down and pulled me onto his lap. "Sweets, if you want to go anywhere today, you can't call me sir while looking that delicious."

I slapped his arm playfully. "Stop it. We need to do something else. My vagina needs a break."

He leaned in and bit my earlobe. "I'll give it a break anytime you want, baby."

"Nicholas," I screeched. I slapped his arm again, harder this time. I got up off his lap. "You knew what I meant," I laughed. "New rule for today: no touching until we get back to the hotel; kisses are an exception." I smiled, thinking he was going to give me shit for it.

His sexy smirk was back on his face. "Hmm, is that what you really want, Sweets?"

I nodded in agreement, even though that smirk quickly depleted my confidence.

He stood up and kissed my cheek. "Game on then, Sweets."

We found something to eat and then headed to do some shopping, but the weather took a turn, and it began to thunder and lightning. I absolutely hated thunderstorms. I hated that Nick had held up his end of the no-touching rule up to that point, especially when the thunder boomed and the lightning was striking. I just wanted to snuggle into him.

"How about we go see a movie?" Nick suggested.

"Can we omit the touching rule?"

He smiled big. "No can do, Sweets. You made the rule: no touching other than kisses until we get back to the room." He kissed the top of my head.

I looked up and gave him a peck on the lips. "I changed the rules. Touching is fine." I tried to give my most innocent smile.

"Sorry, Sweets. You will just have to survive without my hands all over you." He smiled and began walking toward the front door of the resort.

The resort shuttle took us to the theater. Luckily, the movie we wanted to see had a few more tickets available. We got hotdogs, popcorn, and blue slushies. Nick brought me some sweet tarts from the room to have as my sweet treat. How did I not see how perfect this man was?

My senses heightened when he asked to sit at the back of the theater. I was really hoping that meant he would break the no-touching rule and caress me in all the right spots. Just the thought made a rush of heated desire travel through me.

Turns out, I was wrong.

We sat there chatting about the trip home. Nick seemed less nervous this time, but still a little apprehensive. I tried to touch his hand to comfort him, but he pulled it away.

"No touching." He grabbed the popcorn from me.

He took a bite from his hotdog and had ketchup on his lip. I realized very quickly that it was on purpose because his tongue darted out and licked his lip in the sexiest, most seductive way he could have possibly thought of. Then he let out an exaggerated moan. More tingles ran through my body, and I felt like I was on fire with lust.

A switch flipped inside me. I was ready to play this game, too. I will get him to touch me. It's my new goal today.

I looked around to be sure no one was looking and took the hotdog into my mouth. I pushed it back as far as I could and moaned as I bit it. Nick's eyes went wide. I don't think he was expecting me to do that. I saw his Adam's-apple bob as he swallowed. His eyes continued watching me as I deep-throated my hotdog. I licked the entirety of the hotdog before each and every bite. He watched me as I ate the entire thing. Once I was done, I sucked on each finger, followed by a low, sultry moan.

I saw the growing bulge in his pants, so I sat back and sipped my slushie. "Checkmate," I mouthed. I looked back at the screen, thinking he was for sure going to reach over and touch me now.

Damn it, I was wrong... again.

He smirked and bit his lip. Leaning into me, he whispered, "Not even close, baby. I'm going to make you beg me to take you back to the room and fuck the shit out of you."

I gulped down the slushie that was in my mouth. Nick and I have always had this crazy banter as friends. Now that I thought about it, it was more like sexual tension and hate banter mixed into one. This banter now is different, very different. This type of sexual tension is something I've never experienced before. Now I know what it feels like to be with him, and I know that he's not lying when he says he's going to fuck the shit out of me.

We both sat in silence, waiting for the other to move. Then he picked his hotdog back up and started to lick the ketchup from it slowly and seductively. I watched his tongue work its way up, lapping up the ketchup drop by drop. Then he bit the hotdog with an intensified moan.

"This bun is so good. Super soft and plump, just like your ass in my mouth," he whispered. I turned back to the movie and squeezed my legs together to try to give myself some relief.

A few moments later, I felt his hot, wet tongue lick up the side of my neck and take my earlobe into his mouth.

"So fucking good," he said in the sexiest groan.

"No touching," I said weakly.

Somehow, his voice got even deeper and sexier when he said, "You said kisses were okay. By extension, anything with my mouth is okay as long as I don't use my hands to touch you."

I looked at him and realized he was not kidding. *Fuck*, this is going to be the longest day in history.

Chapter Twenty-Five

Nick

Callie eating that hotdog was the most irresistible thing I'd seen in a long time. My cock was weeping for her. I had to resort to tongue fucking some ketchup just to hold it together because in reality I wanted to take her right there in the movie theater seat. I wanted her to be just as turned on as I was.

We both sat there in silence for the rest of the movie. I saw her squeezing her thighs together a few times, and I couldn't help but chuckle. When the movie ended, I was thinking of anything and everything to keep us from going back to the room. I was going to win this fight.

"Where to, Sweets? Want to see if there is another class we can do?"

She looked at me deadpan. "We're going back to the room, aren't we?"

I laughed and kissed her cheek. "Oh no, Sweets, you are going to be waiting all day for me to allow that pussy some relief, and then when you can't take one more second, I will make you scream my name."

She gave me a look like a petulant child who was about to throw a temper tantrum. I shrugged.

"Your rules, I'm just abiding by them, baby. You did tell me you wanted to be in charge, remember? The bedroom is the only place I get to dominate you."

She was speechless.

We walked to the shuttle to head back to the resort. Once we were seated, she finally spoke.

"I'm tired, and I have a headache."

I turned to her and smiled. I knew she was just trying to get me back to the room. "If you need to go back to the room, you can go take a nap. Wouldn't want you to be in any pain." I grinned.

"Will you come with me?"

I shook my head. "Oh, Sweets, I wouldn't want to interrupt your sleep now. Since the sun has started to shine again, I think I'll go do some shopping, and that'll give you plenty of time to rest up and feel better."

"What? No, that's not...damn it."

She was so cute when she stammered. Her face was flushing a light pink, and she gave me her best pouty smile.

"I will meet you back in the room later, don't worry," I assured her.

"Nevermind, it's fine, let's just go shopping. Then we can go back to the room. I can wait a little while."

"You sure, Sweets? I want you to get your rest. Your vagina *is* broken. Don't forget." I said it rather loudly by accident.

She slapped my bicep. "Nicholas, cut it out; we are in public."

She opened her water to take a sip. I looked over at her with the most serious face I could muster. "I thought you like being watched."

Water shot straight out of her mouth. I was trying hard to keep my composure, so I began whistling as I walked ahead of her with a huge ass smile on my face.

After striking out at a few different stores, Callie dragged me into what looked like a department store with only women's clothing. She called it a boutique. It had a name I couldn't pronounce because it had accents over some of the letters. I gathered she was going to make me suffer just to get back at me.

Callie walked around, putting clothes over her arm. Once she had a few things, she looked over at me.

"Arm, please."

"What? I'm not touching you, Cal. Your rules, remember?"

"Nick, put your damn arm up like this." She showed me her arm holding all the clothes so I copied her, still confused.

She transferred all the clothes she had onto my arm. "Hey, what the fuck?" I chuckled. "I am not your butler."

She looked at me seductively. "No, you're not." she got closer. "You're my big, strong boyfriend, and those were heavy, so be a good boy and hold them for me."

All the blood in my body went rushing straight to my fucking cock. "You little fucking she-devil," I muttered.

She smiled and shrugged. "It's okay. You love me."

Both of us gasped when she said it. I was about to say, 'Yeah, I do', but stopped myself. That was not how I was going to tell her I loved her. She began to stutter and backtracked her statement.

"I didn't mean...I meant like...shit."

"Callie," Her face began to flush again, and she looked down. Keeping with the no-touching, I bent down to get her to look at me since I couldn't lift her face with my hand. "I knew what you meant. It's okay. Let's just keep shopping."

"Sure," she answered.

She grabbed a few more things and then went to the dressing room. The guy bringing us back was clearly staring at her ass and didn't care that I was right there.

"Here you go," he gestured to the room marked with a number two. Then looked at me. "You have to stay out here. Only people trying on clothes and employees are allowed in the rooms." He looked back at Callie. "If you need any assistance, just call out. I'd be glad to help you."

"Wow, you are fucking bold, dude," I said, a little too loud. I took one step closer to him, and he didn't back up, but his stupid fucking smile fell a little. "In what universe would I ever let *you* in a dressing room with my girl?"

He didn't say a damn word. He just turned around and walked away.

I looked back at Callie. "The fucking nerve of that guy." I was red hot with rage.

Callie placed her hand on my arm and then removed it quickly. "I will ask you if I need help, okay?"

"He better not even fucki—"

"He won't. Why don't you get some fresh air and call home to see how everyone is doing? Remember, not a word about us until we get home next week."

"Good idea." I kissed her forehead and made sure she got into the dressing room and locked the door.

When I got outside, I called Aubrey, but she didn't answer, so I tried Link.

"Hey man, how's the sex? I mean the trip." Link's loud laugh bellowed out of the phone.

"Dude, really?" I asked.

"What? You can't tell me you guys aren't doing it. How was it? I can't remember what my first time was like. That was so fucking long ago."

"Dude, I am not talking about this with you."

"So you did fuck?" He laughed.

"Fuck you, Link. Where is Aubrey? That's who I really wanted to talk to anyway."

"Her mouth is full," he joked.

"Lincoln Matthew, what has gotten into you?" I heard Aubrey yell with a mouth full of something. "I'm eating apples, not his small dick." I heard her laugh.

"Songbird, do I need to remind you what happened last time you called my cock small?" he threatened. I heard a slap, then Aubrey yelped. I could only assume he slapped her ass or something.

"Aaaanyway," I said. "Me and Cal are out shopping. She wanted me to check in on you guys. Ask Aubrey how Callie's mom is doing for me."

"Tell her she is fine. I have actually been helping her out with a few of Callie's shifts." I heard her voice get a little louder. "When do you guys come home?" Aubrey yelled.

"Friday of next week. We will need a ride when we get in around ten o'clock that night. Don't forget."

"We won't." Link answered.

"Okay, I gotta go. Callie is trying on clothes, and I am going to go take a nap while she does that."

"Sure, dude. Whatever you say."

"Bye, Link, give Aubs a hug for us."

"I'm going to give her way more than that for how sh—"

I hung up because I didn't need to hear the rest of that to know what he was going to say.

I walked back into the store and immediately knew something was wrong.

I heard a gravelly voice coming from the back. "Let me help you, beautiful. I can do so much more for you than that skinny asshole."

My vision clouded with rage. Without giving it a second thought, I told someone in the store to call the police and went running toward the dressing rooms.

Chapter Twenty-Six

Callie

"Stop! Please! What are you doing?"

The man had me pushed against the mirror, and he was trying to run his hand down to my backside. I was only wearing my thong and a thin tank top because I was mid-outfit change when he unlocked the door from the outside.

"Come on, baby, that loser left you here, and now we can have some fun."

"Get off me before I make you regret your life," I yelled.

He remained unmoved and gripped my ass cheek with one hand while the other traveled around to my front. He was holding me against the mirror, so he backed off a little to give his hand room to travel. He was definitely stronger than me, but I had the gift of long legs. Just as he was about to rub my front side, I kicked my foot up backward between his legs. I must have caught his balls just right because that man yelped like a little girl and keeled over, letting out a string of coughs.

"Ah fuck! You bitch."

He started to stand, but I was already moving around him to run and get Nick. Before I could turn the corner, I ran right into someone's chest. I started flailing, thinking it was another man trying to push me down.

"Baby... baby, it's me." I looked up and saw Nick. His eyes were dark like I'd never seen. "Are you okay?"

I didn't speak. I just wrapped my arms around him tightly. He pushed me back a little. "Callie, I need to go handle that. Are you okay?"

"Please don't," I whimpered. "I just... I need to go."

"Let me grab your clothes."

I heard the worker moan from inside the dressing room, and it made me wince.

Nick didn't say another word. He stalked toward the door and swung it wide open. I saw him cock back his balled-up fist, and then heard the guy make several "oof" sounds.

"You will never touch another woman again, especially mine." Another punch, and this time, I heard the mirror crack. Nick bent down and picked up my items along with my bag, then shut the door.

He rushed up to me.

"Baby, I am so fucking sorry. I can't believe I left you here alone. This is all my fucking fault. I made you come shopping instead of going back to the room. I am so fucking sorry, Callie."

His eyes went glassy, and I could only hug him tighter. This was not even remotely close to his fault. I couldn't get any words out, so I just cried.

A few moments later, the jingle bells jangled against the shop's glass door, and I jumped into Nick's chest.

"It's okay, it's just the police."

When did he have time to call them? It was like he read my mind because he answered the question I had asked in my head.

"I asked someone in the store to call when I ran back here."

"Ma'am, are you okay? Do you need medical attention?" I shook my head. "My name is Officer Malcolm Pinder. I am part of the Royal Bahamas Police Force. Can you tell me what happened?"

Nick spoke up before I could say anything. "I need to take her to the bathroom so she can get dressed. She has been humiliated enough, and she doesn't need the entire police force staring at her while she's exposed." He was almost yelling.

"Sir, I need you to calm down." He looked at me. "Ma'am, is it safe to leave you with him for a moment, or would you like to be alone?"

I didn't say a word. I just pulled Nick closer to me. The officer got the hint.

"I'll be right outside. Come out whenever you are ready to give your statement."

I nodded my head, and Nick said thank you and apologized to them for yelling.

As we were walking over to the bathroom, we saw two other officers dragging the sleazy worker out by his arms. His face was so cut up, I assumed from the mirror, you could barely see his skin tone through all the blood.

Nick opened the door for me and ushered me in.

"I will wait right outside the door. I promise I won't—"

Before he could finish his sentence, I pulled him into the bathroom and kissed him.

"Callie," he murmured.

I begged against his lips, "Don't leave me, please?"

"Never, baby. I will never leave you again."

He kissed me on my forehead as we stood there in silence. The only sound was the bathroom fan kicking on. After a few moments, I finally got dressed and walked out to the front of the store. The officer saw me and walked up to us. Nick instinctively grabbed my hand and moved me almost behind him.

"Sir, we need to speak with her alone."

"She will not be going anywhere without me. It's non-negotiable," Nick said sternly.

I'm not sure what changed the officer's mind, but it must have been a look Nick gave him because he agreed without argument. After giving my statement, they made me go to the hospital so they could check me out, but mainly to gather any evidence that might have existed. They needed to swab under my fingernails and take pictures of the bruises that had formed on my leg and neck.

Luckily, it didn't take too long. Nick got us a ride back to the resort. Before we could fully walk into the room, my legs collapsed, and I fell into Nick's arms and cried well into the night.

I woke up a few times throughout the night, but I was never fully able to get comfortable. One time, when I woke, I heard Nick sniffle. I was too afraid to find out if it was just a coincidence or if he was crying. Every time I moved, I felt him hold me closer and whisper in my ear.

"Forever and always, baby."

NICK

Callie cried for three hours before falling into a restless sleep. She had fallen into my arms right before I shut the door. I carried her to the bed, settled against the headboard, and held her. Silent tears ran down my face as I recalled every detail she had shared with those officers. I can't imagine how scared she was. I was thanking God he didn't get further than holding her down and grabbing her ass. I wish I could have broken his fucking hands, but his face was good enough.

I didn't know much about assaults, but I googled them on my phone while she slept. Now I felt even more scared than I had been before. The internet said this kind of incident could affect her in many different ways, ranging from nothing to giving her major PTSD. This kind of trauma could cause her to have all kinds of issues to deal with, and the effects could last years. I was scared for her.

I was so damn mad at myself for letting someone hurt my perfect girl. His nasty fucking hands were all over her body. She had bruises that formed around the back of her neck where he held her against the wall. I pushed her beautiful brunette hair off her neck and traced the finger marks with mine.

My thoughts began to wander. I started wondering how this was going to change things for us. Would this make her timid? Would she wake up and be worried that a man was touching her? Then the worst thought of all...would she realize this was my fault because I left her alone, and would she hate me so much that she would leave me because of it?

"Fuck." I realized I'd said it out loud when she moved a little.

She groaned a little, then opened her eyes. "What time is it?" She asked groggily.

"Seven-thirty."

I kept my hands at my sides, letting her determine how much she wanted to be touched. She grabbed my hand and kissed it.

"Thank you for being there for me today. I don't know what I would have done without you."

I was quiet and felt my eyes pricking with tears again. She sat up to look at me straight on.

"Hey, what's wrong?"

"Nothing, Sweets. I'm fine. I'm just so happy you're safe."

I tried to look away, but she grabbed my face in both of her hands. She wiped her thumb over my cheek, catching a tear that made its way out. "Nicholas James, talk to me right now."

I did my best to swallow the lump that was preventing me from speaking. "I just...fuck, Callie. I fucking left you alone with that guy. He...he fucking touched you. He fucking violated *my* fucking girl. You should not be the one comforting me right now." I loosely gripped her hands and pulled them down between us. "Callie, you are my life. You are my fucking everything."

Callie straddled me before I could get the rest of the words out. Before she settled fully onto my lap, she softly gasped.

"Sorry." I tried to adjust myself a little. Of course, I had to have a raging fucking hard-on right now. I get one anytime she touches me, no matter the situation.

She looked into my eyes, rubbing my cheeks with her thumbs. "I love you, too."

My whole body went rigid. I sat up against the headboard a little more.

"What did you just say?" I asked cautiously.

"Forever and always," she replied.

Words...what the fuck are words right now? Callie just told me she loved me, then used my version of I love you to reiterate it.

"Callie," I said hesitantly. "You just told me you loved me. You are not thinking clearly, you—"

She kissed me deeply. "Nicholas James. Listen to me, and you better listen good. I love you more than I have ever loved anyone or anything in this world. You are my safe haven. You are the person that lights up my world without even trying. I am sorry it took me over ten years to realize

I was made for loving you, but we have the rest of forever to make up for it. I have known from the moment I met you that you were something special, and I knew from the first moment you said 'Forever and Always' that you were trying to tell my stupid ass that you loved me. I'm sorry you had to wait, baby, but I am yours...Forever and always."

I took her face in my hands and kissed her furiously. "I fucking love you so much, Callie. Baby, there hasn't been a day since I met you that I haven't thought about you. I don't know what will happen in this life, but I know that I will be doing it with you by my side. Forever and always, baby."

My hands crept up her back and into her hair, pulling her into me. Between kisses, I told her again. "Callie. I am going to love you until the day I die."

"You can't die without me. If you're a corpse, I'm a corpse."

I leaned back. "Did you just turn a beautiful Notebook reference morbid?"

She kissed my nose. "I don't know whether to love you more because you knew it was from The Notebook or to make fun of you for it."

"I only watched it because it's your favorite." She looked surprised. "Callie, I told you I love everything about you. Even your shitty taste in movies."

She laughed and pushed me onto the bed, kissing me until we both snuggled in and fell back to sleep, wrapped in each other's arms.

CHAPTER TWENTY-SEVEN

Callie

The next few days went by in a blur. The morning after Nick and I declared our love for each other, my adrenaline from the assault had worn off. When Nick tried to get into the shower with me, I freaked out. I yelled at him, making a scene about how I didn't want to be touched. He barely spoke to me that entire day, giving me the space I needed. He even offered to sleep on the couch, but that made me feel even worse.

I knew Nick would never hurt me, but all I could muster up was hugging him or holding his hand. I was grateful he was being so understanding, but I felt like me being assaulted would eventually be too much for him, and change how he felt about me. I was afraid he wouldn't find me as desirable as before.

In the days that followed, we fell into a sort of routine. We'd wake up, he would give me the privacy to shower, and then take his own. We got breakfast at the hotel, then hung out until lunch. The days always ending with dinner and a beach trip or a show mixed in.

"What are you thinking about, beautiful girl?" Nick asked from across the dinner table.

"Nothing really, I've just been thinking a lot about Aubrey." He gave me a questioning look. "I should probably call her and tell her what happened. I feel weird about her not knowing."

That wasn't a total lie. I had been thinking about that since the morning after. We only had a few days left here, and I needed to tell her to help calm my own uneasiness. On the other hand, I knew she was going to have a fucking heart attack and would worry about me until she could hug me again.

Aubrey has experience dealing with someone she loves being assaulted. Her sister, Brielle, was sexually assaulted when she was younger. Neither of them has ever shared the exact details. I just happen to know that is why Brie doesn't drink anymore and it's why she rarely goes out with us now. I also know she doesn't date.

Brielle.

It was like a lightbulb went off. I needed to talk to Brielle. I stood quickly and looked at Nick.

"I want to go make a phone call. Are you okay if I head back to the room to have some privacy?

Nick gave me a worried look but didn't protest. "Sure, I can walk you there to make sure you get inside okay, and then I'll head to grab us some dessert. Is cheesecake okay?"

I grinned up at him and hesitantly laced my fingers with his. I am trying to touch him without issue, but I'm just not there yet. "Perfect."

I gave Brie a call, and she answered in a panic.

"What? What's wrong?"

"Hi to you, too," I chuckled.

"Tell me, Callie. Something happened to you, didn't it?"

I was quiet, trying to figure out how in the actual hell she possibly knew that. Did I let something slip yesterday when I texted Aubrey? How would she know that something was wrong with me?

"Callie," she called out again. Then she lowered her voice and softened her tone. "Tell me, please."

"Brie, how did you know?"

"First of all, you never call me unless you are looking for Aubrey, and you know she is visiting her dad and isn't with me right now. Second, I had a weird dream a few nights ago about Nick and you. You were crying, and he was holding you. Please tell me that wasn't real."

"Bean, how could you possibly...hold on. How is it possible for you to have a dream like that?"

She gasped a little when I used Aubrey's nickname. I rarely use it and always call her Brie unless we are having a more serious conversation.

"I don't know, Cal. I have this weird thing where sometimes my dreams come true. It's the scariest fucking thing in the world. I never know which ones will actually happen." She was quiet for a moment. "Callie," she whispered. "Did someone hurt you?"

"Yes," I whispered.

"Were you...r—"

"No," I paused for a moment. "I was sexually assaulted while trying on clothes at a boutique here a few days ago." I went on to tell her the whole story, and she kept quiet. When I finished, I heard her sniffle.

"Does Aubs know yet?" she asked.

"No, and I would like to be the one to tell her. Please don't tell her I called you first."

"Why did you?"

"What?" I was confused by her question.

"Why did you call me and not her?"

"I figured you might be able to tell me how to let Nick touch me again."

Her voice got louder. "Nick freaking touched you. He hur—"

"Hell no. Nick isn't the one who assaulted me. We sort of...shit. I'm fucking telling you everything before Aubrey. I will kill you if you speak a single word of this to her, Brielle."

"Lips zipped. I even made the motion with my hands, zipping it shut for an added level of realness."

That made me chuckle. She was so fucking sweet for someone who had dealt with so much shit in her life.

"Nick and I are together. It's been incredible. He is so amazing. We were having a fun day suggestively teasing each other. Then, this stupid guy at the boutique did what he did. That same night, I was fine with Nick touching me. I found it kind of weird, but I just figured maybe this just wouldn't affect me in a negative way. I even straddled him, and we had a beautiful moment of letting our feelings be known, but the next day I woke up and couldn't let him near me. Even his hugs completely overwhelmed me. We haven't talked about it since. I don't want him to think I didn't mean what I said or that I regret it. I know you went through something similar, so I felt like I needed to talk to you."

She sighed. "Callie, have you told him how you are feeling?"

"No, I'm scared. He has been looking at me with pity, and he is the last person I want to look at me that way. I know he probably doesn't mean to, but it makes me feel worse than I already do."

"He will. Everyone who finds out will. Honestly, it surprised me that you know about what happened to me. You've never treated me like you did."

"What is that supposed to mean?"

"It means that every time someone finds out you have been sexually assaulted, they will look at you like you are broken, which—in my case—I am, I guess, but this isn't about me. Make sure you are ready to tell people because once you do, everything changes."

"Bean, you are not broken. You are one of the strongest people in the world."

"Thanks, Cal, but that's the furthest thing from the truth. I am just really good at smiling to your face even if I am having the worst day of my life. Again, though, this isn't about me. What can I do to help you?"

"How do I let him touch me again? How do I work through these feelings without making him feel bad or unwanted?"

"Callie, I say this with love and a lot of it. But fuck Nick's feelings. None of this has to do with him. You need to share with him how you are feeling when you are ready. I know it's only been a few days, and I don't know where your mind has been, but I also think you may benefit from seeing a therapist regularly when you get home."

"I've never done therapy before. I was supposed to go as a kid when my dad left, but I never did. Mom didn't have the money."

"You can definitely get through it without therapy if you want to, but I think it would be beneficial for you to try. It has helped me so much. I've been going ever since it happened to me six years ago."

"Brie, I know you and I haven't spoken much about what happened to you before today, but I am so sorry you had to go through it. I know you had your parents and Aubs, but know you have always had me too. You are just as much my sister as Aubrey is. I love you, Bean."

She chuckled a little. "Why are you comforting me? This is supposed to be about me comforting and helping *you*." I heard her sniffle again. "Callie, I am so sorry this happened to you. I love you, too, girl. I am so thankful that you weren't r—" She cut herself off. "Fuck. I am just so glad you're okay."

"You will be, too. I am glad I have you to help me through all of this."

"I will always be here for you, Callie. No matter what."

"I know."

We were both quiet, just listening to each other cry. Once we calmed down a little, she spoke again.

"You should explain to him how you are feeling. He loves you, Callie. That man would give his life to make sure you were okay. I guarantee he isn't showing you pity. He is worried about you. There is a difference."

"I know...and I will. Thank you, Bean. You and I need to have a Brielle and Callie date when Nick and I get back."

"Deal. But you are paying 'cause I'm a broke college student," she laughed.

"Bitch, I am broke, too," I laughed right along with her. "We will make Link or Nick give us money. They'll do it for us because they love us, right?"

We laughed for what seemed like an hour, trying to move on from the serious subject. The moment Nick texted me asking if it was okay for him to come back, I hung up with Brie because I knew I had to tell him how I was feeling today, or I would chicken out.

So I did.

Chapter Twenty-Eight

Nick

I gave Callie an hour and a half of privacy. I walked the beach for about an hour, then grabbed us some cheesecake for dessert. When I texted her, she immediately wrote back that it was okay to come up.

When I opened the door, I could tell she had been crying.

I put the dessert on the table and ran up to her. "Hey baby, Are you okay?" I instinctively tried to put my arms around her without thinking. She flinched, and I froze. She was regretting everything. Fuck, this can't be happening.

"I am okay. I just want to talk to you without touching you, if that's okay?"

I stepped back, putting more space between us. "Of course it's okay. I am sorry I touched you without permission. I won't do it again."

I should have been more considerate. She was dealing with a lot, then here comes my dumbass touching her when she didn't want to be touched.

She placed her hand on my forearm and leaned up, hesitantly kissing me on the cheek. "That isn't what I meant. I mean, thank you for saying that, but you don't need permission to touch me. I will work through this." She leaned in a little. "I am yours, Nick. Nothing is going to change that. I just want to talk about it. I know I have been standoffish the past few days, and you are probably longing for attention, and I know I owe it to you. I will do my best to—"

She cut herself off and gave me a concerned look when I stepped even further away from her. I couldn't believe she just said that. She owes me fucking nothing.

"You owe me nothing, Callie. This relationship isn't transactional. Yes, you are mine, and you will be forever, but that doesn't give me the right to *expect* anything from you."

I stepped back toward her but didn't reach out to touch her. "You don't owe anyone your body, Callie. It is yours to do what you please with. That stupid fucking cocksucker of a little boy, and yes, I said little boy, because no real man would ever hurt a woman like that. That little boy took away that choice from you, and you have every right to heal from that however you want or need. You want me just to sit next to you and not touch you? I'll do it all day long, baby. You want me only to hold your hand, I got you. You want me only to kiss your feet, I'll fucking do that, too."

She smiled a little, but I could see tears forming in the corners of her eyes. I kept talking.

"Callie, I will do anything for you. If I could never get anything physical from you again, I'm okay with that. As long as I'm with you, I am happy."

She grabbed my hands and put them against her chest in a fist. "It won't take forever, I promise." Her smile fell a bit. "But I think I do need some time. I don't know why I am fine when you hold my hand, or even put a chaste touch on my arm or face here and there, but the minute

I think about you fully hugging or kissing me, I feel like I'm going to black out." Her voice was starting to break as she continued talking. "I don't understand it. I know you won't hurt me. I know you're my safe space. Literally, the only thing that even feels remotely normal right now is being near you, and yet I can't let you *really* touch me."

I kissed the back of her hand and let go. "We won't do anything more until you're ready, baby. You're the boss."

She looked up at me with wide eyes and kissed my hand. "I love you."

"I love you too, baby girl."

She leaned in and whispered against my lips. "I secretly love it when you call me that."

I smiled and lightly kissed her. "I know."

Over the next few days, we mostly stayed in the room, playing different board games and watching movies. It was sweet. We hadn't gotten very far in the touching department, but she was trying, and I could tell. It wasn't exactly how we planned to spend the last few days of our vacation, but we made it work.

We got back home last night, and surprisingly, I did a lot better on that flight. I think the fact that I was so focused on Callie and trying not to touch her was making me suppress my fears a little.

Last night, I expected her to sleep in her room, and she did at first. I figured she would want privacy. When two o'clock came around, she climbed into bed with me and cuddled into me. I wasn't sure whether it was consciously or unconsciously. The way she was snuggled into me and rubbing me gave me the biggest fucking erection I'd ever had. I guess being home added another layer of comfort because that was the first time she had done that since she was assaulted.

I got up this morning without disturbing her, thank God. I wanted her to get as much sleep as possible. I texted Aubrey while sitting on the couch, waiting for Callie to wake up.

Hey.

Aubrey

Tell me why she is being weird.

Who?

Aubrey

Stop being an idiot. Callie, you ass wipe.

Hostile much? lol

She is fine. Why do you ask?

Aubrey

She wasn't okay last night on the phone, and for some reason you guys won't tell me why.

Did you hurt her?

I am not dignifying that with an actual answer. I can't believe you would even think that.

If you actually think I would hurt her in any fucking way, then I don't know why we are friends.

Aubrey

> **Okay, okay. I know you didn't hurt her, but why is she being weird?**

> Why don't you come over here so you guys can talk?

> I will make myself scarce, and you guys can have girl time or whatever you call it.

Aubrey

> **TELL ME… we don't hide things from each other.**

I huffed out of annoyance and rolled my eyes. I was lucky she couldn't actually see me. She would beat my fucking ass.

> Aubs, there are us things and then there are me and Callie things.

> There are even you and me things that we have talked about without her.

> This is a me and her thing. When she wants to tell you, she will. Come talk to her. She is still sleeping, but she should be up soon.

Aubrey

> **Fine, tell her I'll be there around ten.**

I sent her a thumbs-up emoji. Things were definitely about to be a lot different for all of us.

Callie

"I am so sorry, Callie. I can't... God dammit." Tears ran down Aubrey's cheeks as I finished telling her everything.

"Aubrey, I'm okay. It could have been so much worse, but luckily, Nick was there."

Aubrey looked at me sternly. "Don't fucking do that."

"What?" I asked, confused.

"Don't make it seem like it was no big deal. Just because you weren't actually...you know. That doesn't make it any less important or scary. You were violated. You deserve to feel all the feelings. Don't downplay it for my benefit."

I thought about it for a few minutes as we sat there in silence.

"I told Brielle."

Aubrey's eyes went wide. "You what?"

"I told Brielle about it. I called her and asked her what to do. I have been struggling with letting Nick do anything but hold my hand and kiss me a few times. We haven't been having sex anymore so I ca—"

She had a massive grin on her face, and I realized I had just inadvertently told her Nick and I had sex.

"We will get back to that. Please continue." She waved off the comment and let me finish telling her about Brie.

"Callie, I understand why you called her. I wish it were me, of course, but I get it."

"Okay," I said hesitantly. I knew what was coming next. She hadn't wiped that smirk off her face since I'd said I had sex with him.

"You and Nick?"

I fidgeted with my fingers and the hem of the nightshirt I was still wearing. "Well...we...um...had sex, a few times."

"No. Fucking. Way." She dragged out the Y. "How did you not call me right away and tell me everything?"

"Well, this kind of changes things. I mean, I don't think I should be telling you every detail about it, right? He deserves privacy, and you look at him like a brother, right? So, do you really want to know all that?"

She thought for a moment, and her face contorted into a wince. "Yeah, I guess you're right." Her tone turned a bit more hesitant. "Are you happy? Like, was it good, at least?"

I gripped her hand. "Very." I wagged my eyebrows up and down. She made a barfing noise. We both started laughing to the point of tears. It felt good to be home. It felt even better to laugh again.

Chapter Twenty-Nine

Callie

Nick and I had been home about a week already and things seemed to be going back to normal. Luckily, I had taken a little extra time off. Originally, it was so I had time to recover from the honeymoon, but today would be the first day back at the restaurant with my mom, and piano lessons start up again tomorrow.

Of course, Sara was working, and I overheard her talking. It sounded like she was dating Jake, *again*. I had chosen not to acknowledge her presence, and so far, so good. She had kept her distance. I thought maybe I would get through today without any issues.

I was very wrong. I walked outside to leave, and saw Jake leaning on my car.

"Jake? What are you doing here?"

"You are ignoring me."

He looked...different. His eyes were almost manic, and he looked like he hadn't showered in well over a week.

"I'm not ignoring you. I just have no reason to talk to you." I tried to say it as calmly, but directly, as possible.

He stepped toward me, and I stepped back immediately, my whole body tensing in fear. My heart began to race, but I was trying to stay as calm as possible without showing him he was having an effect on me.

"You didn't speak to me for months, Callie. Then you completely ghost me and go on our honeymoon alone. Then you went as far as lying when you finally picked up the phone."

My eyes went wide. How the hell would he know I went there? I mean, he had called, but I told him I was just out of town. I guess the good thing was he thought I went alone. He heard Nick that day, so I don't know why he hadn't put two and two together yet.

"Callie, please let me talk to you. I just wanna talk." He reached out to touch my arm, and I flinched again.

"What was that? Are you scared of me?"

"No," I said curtly. "I have no reason to be, right?" I stepped away so we had the original amount of space between us. "I just don't want to talk to you right now. Jake, I am really glad you are getting help. I am also glad you are working on yourself, but I want no part of it. Our reasons for talking to each other ended the day I found your dick inside one of my friends."

He was getting agitated and started pacing back and forth. He dragged his fingers through his greasy hair. When he finally looked at me, it was like a switch had gone off, and he practically dove at me.

He gripped both my upper arms and pulled me in so close that I could smell his breath—it smelled like straight bourbon. His eyes were dark, and it was like I was looking at a different person altogether. I closed my eyes because now I was scared.

"Jake," I cried out. "Let me go right n—"

Before I could finish my sentence, Jake was thrown to the ground. I heard him let out a grunt and a swear. When I opened my eyes, I was looking at Nick's back. He put himself between Jake and me.

I started to sob, and it felt like I was thrown back into the dressing room situation. I sank down against the back door of the restaurant. I was starting to gasp for air, remembering every minute detail about that day. That man's hands running up and down my body, and the feeling of his hands gripping me tight.

I watched Nick's mouth move as if he was saying something, but it wasn't processing in my brain because I began having a flashback.

"Nick, I'm scared—"

The next thing I knew, everything went dark.

NICK

I called Callie's mom as soon as we got into the ambulance. They didn't allow me in with her, but when her mom showed up she assured me she would come get me as soon as she could.

They had been in the hospital room for over an hour. Callie had hit her head on the stairs when she fainted. Luckily, she was already sitting down, so she didn't fall hard or far, but it still cut up her head.

Aubrey was teaching a student when I called her, so she was on her way now with Link. Brielle was already here with me, and she hadn't let go of my hand since she got here. I was just about to say something to Brie when Callie's mom walked out.

"She is looking for you, dear," her voice was calm.

I looked at Brie and let her hand go. "Okay, I will be back. Let Aubrey know I'm in there when she gets here."

I started to step away, but Callie's mom grabbed my arm and stopped me. "Not you, Nicky, Brielle."

I looked at her, then at Brie. "Oh, okay." That definitely hurt a little. I just wanted to hold her. I needed to know she was alright. Brielle put her hand on my forearm and waited until I looked at her.

She always looked so sweet. It's crazy how different she looked compared to Aubrey, but so similar at the same time. Her green eyes bore into me, making sure I was hearing her. "You will go in there next. She will be okay. She just wants to talk to me about the blackout. I know what she's going through."

I nodded my head in agreement without saying anything. I sat back down and waited. After another hour, Callie's mom had left to go to the house to gather some stuff for Callie. I guessed she would be here for a few days.

Aubrey and Lincoln had shown up, and just like Brielle, Aubrey fell into my arms in tears. After calming down, Aubrey sat between me and Lincoln, gripping onto one of each of our hands like she was holding on for dear life. We sat there in silence until we saw Brielle coming back down the hall. All three of us stood without letting our hands go free. I held my breath, fully expecting Aubrey to be next to go in.

"You can go in now, Nick," she said softly.

"What about me?" asked Aubrey.

I knew visiting hours were almost over, so I was getting nervous about not being allowed to see her.

"Everyone else will have to come back tomorrow. She said thank you for coming, and she loves you. She did ask for Nick, though."

Aubrey looked at me and kissed my cheek. "Give her a hug and kiss for me."

I pulled her into a hug. "Call you later, okay?"

Aubrey nodded her head. Link hugged me, and then they left.

Before I made my way to the room, Brie grabbed me and looked at me with a serious face.

"Callie has a black eye and a concussion. She also tried pulling the IV out of her arm during her episode, so her arm is all scratched up. She may be a little confused and may not want you to touch her." I nodded my head. "Nick, do not touch her unless she asks you to, even her hands. I know it was okay before, but she is really fragile right now and, like I said, confused."

"Brielle, I got it," I said louder and more forcefully than I had planned. I knew I'd scared her by the look in her eyes. "Sorry, I didn't mean to—"

"I know, Nick. It's okay. Just promise me you won't touch her unless she asks."

"I promise."

I walked down the hallway and stood at Callie's door for a moment. It was cracked open, so I could see partially inside. There she was in her hospital gown with her blanket thrown haphazardly over herself. I could see the scratches on her arm that Brielle told me about, and her eye was a deep purple color and nearly swollen shut. She was somewhat sitting up and had her head leaning back on the pillow.

I thought about turning around, but the second I decided I was going to let her rest, she saw me.

"Hey," her voice sounded raspy, like she was sick.

"Hey, Sweets." I walked into the room and went to shut the door but thought better of it and looked back at her. "Do you want this open?"

She thought about it for a moment, looking at the door and then at me a few times.

"No, it's okay to shut it," she said with confidence.

I shut it, then walked up to her bed and sat in the chair beside it. She moved around to face me.

"Hi," she said with a smile.

"Hi, beautiful." I was trying my best to keep it together and not tear up at the sight of her eye up close.

"Pfft, I am anything but beautiful right now," she joked. She always tried to joke through the hard stuff. It was nice to hear her kind of being herself.

I looked down at my hands and then up at her. "You are always beautiful, Callie."

She stared at me for a moment, and I could see her eyes getting glassy.

"You are too nice to me, Nick. I look like I've been run over and broken into a million pieces. I am surprised you're not running away from how broken I am."

I smirked, still trying to keep from crying, and looked down at my hands again. "I will always love every broken piece of you." I looked up at her. My gaze took on a more serious look as I went to grab her hand, but I hesitated. She saw it and grabbed my hand. My body relaxed on contact. "I will spend every day helping glue you back together for the rest of my life if I have to," I paused, "Forever and always."

Chapter Thirty

Callie

Mid-November

The next few weeks passed without much drama. Jake called once after I got out of the hospital, and I told him to stop contacting me. So far he's listened. Honestly, it felt weird not hearing from him. Even though I only answered those few times over the almost five hundred times he called, it was still weird not to talk to him.

It was almost Thanksgiving. Soon we would be getting together with our friends and my mom. I couldn't wait to be surrounded by all of my favorite people. We hadn't seen much of each other lately since I basically just worked, went to therapy, and then came back home. I was afraid to go out of the house because I feared seeing Jake or other people I knew and having another flashback. My mom had pretty much covered my shifts at the restaurant, but Aubrey took anything she couldn't cover if she wasn't busy.

Nick and I had some intimate moments that didn't involve sex, mostly holding hands or a fleeting touch above our clothing, because it was still hard to be touched without flinching, but it seemed to be getting better over time. I hadn't slept in bed with him since coming back from the hospital because I was still having nightmares and waking up every night. He said he didn't care and came in whenever he heard me screaming. Most nights he slept in the chair in my room after I fell back to sleep. I really didn't deserve him.

Most of my days were filled with my piano lessons. A few days a week, I also had my standing appointments to see my therapist. I was so glad my teaching schedule wasn't affected too much, and I still got to see all the little ones. We still had a ton of time until the May concert, but so much was left to be done.

I sat in my therapist's office, waiting for her to come in. She was just doing some paperwork with her previous client in the foyer. I was wringing my hands together in my lap.

Though I had been here quite a few times over the past month, it still felt weird every time I walked in. The room was very cold-looking. It was a dark tan, almost brown color with a wall full of all of her framed degrees from school and a few small sculptures that I still hadn't figured out what they were supposed to be. There was a weird stone lion in the corner. I swore the eyes followed me when I walked into the room. The smell was surprisingly pleasant. It smelled like we were back on a tropical island. She had one of those air fresheners that sent a puff of fragrance out every so often. That was probably my favorite part about being there.

"Sorry about that, Callie." She smiled and sat across from me in one of the high-back chairs. Unlike the surroundings, my therapist was bright and bubbly. She wore thick-rimmed, brightly colored glasses and always had on some variation of an intricate dress. She looked more like an art teacher than a therapist to me, but who was I to judge? Lately, I have looked like a sloth who has forgotten how to coordinate colors because all I wear is my comfy sweats.

"So, what is new since your last session? Any current nightmares?"

"Only one this time," I said, embarrassed.

"That is great, Callie. That makes," she looked down at her papers. "Only three this week. That's an improvement from the five last week."

"Yeah. I am actually feeling a lot better. I even let Nick hold me while I came out of one of the nightmares. He has been helping me so much."

"That is great. Have you thought any more about bringing him in to do a two-on-one session with us? Or are you still not ready?"

My heart raced, and my skin became clammy at the thought of him attending a session with me.

"I don't think he should have to deal with this. He deals with it enough at home. Know what I mean?"

"I do." She bit the tip of her pen while she stared at me for a second. She wrote something down and looked back up at me. "Why don't we try to think of it as him coming to help? It's basically him gaining the tools he needs to learn to best help you deal with them. Would that change your mind at all?"

"He probably won't want to come," I said curtly.

She leaned in, put her papers onto the table between us, and clasped her hands in her lap. "Callie, if you are not ready, that is okay. But let's not assume we know how Nick feels without asking him. It sounds like he really wants to help you through this."

I swallowed the lump in my throat. "I will think it over. What exactly would be involved?"

"Well, he can come to your next session, or you can have him come in on his own, and he can ask any questions he may have."

I nodded my head. "Okay. I will ask."

"That is great, Callie. This will be beneficial for you both. I promise."

"How do I bring up being intimate again? I know I'm not ready for sex yet. Or maybe I am, but I want him to touch me without clothes on, and I think he's scared to."

She smiled, picked up her papers, and wrote something down. "Callie, that is amazing. Nick sounds like he's completely understanding. I think if you took the initiative and showed him what you wanted, he would follow your lead and do as much or as little as you wanted him to."

I nodded.

"I can't wait to meet him," she added.

When I got home from therapy, Nick was still working, and I didn't feel like sitting all alone in the living room, so I grabbed a glass of water and plopped on the bed, staring up at the ceiling. My eyelids grew super heavy as I reviewed everything the therapist had discussed with me today. I still didn't understand exactly why I couldn't let Nick touch me more.

After all the racing thoughts subsided, I felt myself beginning to drift off to sleep. When I turned toward my side table to get more comfortable, I noticed there was a single Bluebell flower in one of my water cups with a handwritten note next to it.

I FIGURED SINCE YOU KEEP LEAVING THIS WATER IN HERE, WE COULD AT LEAST MAKE IT LOOK PRETTY. I LOVE YOU, CALLIE. I HOPE YOU HAD A GOOD SESSION. SEE YOU WHEN I

GET HOME. LET ME KNOW WHAT YOU WANT ME TO GRAB FOR DINNER, AND I'LL MAKE IT HAPPEN.

LOVE, YOUR FAVORITE PERSON

My heart swelled with love and admiration. I don't think this man could be any more thoughtful. He was the literal epitome of a perfect partner. Now, if only I could get my shit together and be a good partner for him as well, we would be golden.

After lying on my bed for a little while, I texted Brielle and Aubrey to ask if they wanted to have a girls' night after our Thanksgiving dinner next week. I missed them. We needed to just get out and get drunk. They clearly missed me, too, because both of them sent their answers back in all caps.

Aubs

> **FUCK YES BITCH**

Brie

> **YES PLEASE!**

> **PS: I HAVE TEA AND YOU HAVE TO WAIT LOL**

Aubs

> **Spill, Bean. You know I'm too damn nosey to wait that long. lol.**

> Brie, you can't just drop that you have tea and say "oh but I'll tell you next week".

> What if we already know by then?

I waited a few minutes for her response, but it didn't come. Right before I texted again, Aubrey did instead. She took the words right out of my brain. She proves all the time why we are best friends.

Aubs

> BITCH, if you don't tell me, I'm going to come to your dorm and make a scene.

A few more minutes went by before Brie finally responded.

Brie

> Sorry, someone came over to ask me about an assignment. Unless you are me or Dax you wouldn't know.

> Who the fuck is Dax?

Aubs

> WHO IS DAX? Is that the guy you work with? Isn't he old?

Brie

> Talk to you at Thanksgiving dinner. I promise it is worth the wait.

Aubs

> BITCH I HATE YOU.

> You suck.

Brie

> Not yet. :-P

I would try to get it out of her somehow. I needed to know who this Dax person was. From the tone of her text, she seemed excited. If she could be happy about her love life after everything she had gone through, then there was hope for me to do the same.

Chapter Thirty-One

Nick

The smell of jasmine wafted into my nose the moment I opened the front door. My body reacted immediately, sending a shiver down my spine. That jasmine smell has been my favorite scent for as long as I could remember. I put all my work stuff down and knocked on the door with one knuckle.

"Sweets, I'm home." I heard the water slosh. "Sorry. I didn't mean to scare you."

She was quiet for a moment, then I heard her voice come out just above a whisper. "It's okay."

It broke my heart into pieces to hear her like that. I placed my hands and forehead on the door.

"Callie, I'm really sorry. I just wanted you to know I was home. I will be in the kitchen, okay?"

I started walking away, but before I made it to the kitchen, the bathroom door swung open. She was standing there in nothing but a towel.

We both stood still, just staring at each other in silence. I went to speak, but my words were cut off when she motioned with her head toward the bathroom.

"Sit with me?"

I didn't even need to think about it. I would take any inch she gave me. I nodded my head and took a step forward. She walked in with me following close behind. I sat on the toilet and turned my head to give her some privacy to get back into the tub if she wanted it. I felt her hand turning my cheek, and before I could turn it fully, she dropped her towel to the floor. It took everything in me to keep my eyes on hers and my hands to myself. I miss touching her bare skin.

"Nick," Callie whispered.

"Yeah, baby?" I swallowed the lump that was forming.

In one fluid motion, she pulled me up. I still kept my hands to my side. She leaned up on her tiptoes and kissed me. I felt the pleasure roll down my spine, warming my entire body.

When she pulled back, she kept her mouth closed, but her eyes raked over my face. I didn't know what she was doing, but I fucking loved it.

"Take a bath with me," Callie whispered.

I knew my face was showing all my hesitation because her face dropped.

"Oh, it's okay. You don't have to. If you don't want to, you—"

"Yes," I blurted out. I cleared my throat to rein myself in. "Only if you're sure."

She nodded and helped me out of my clothes. I was half embarrassed at how fucking hard I was just from smelling and kissing her.

We got into the bathtub, and I fully expected her to sit across from me, but she just plopped down right in front of me. The top of her perfect ass rubbed up against my erection. I let out an involuntary groan. I saw her tense a little, but she didn't pull away.

After a few quiet seconds, I leaned in. "Can I wash your back?"

She nodded, then handed me the loofah.

I placed it on her back, and she let out a small moan. My dick twitched, and I was hoping to God she hadn't felt it. I washed her back, but before I could finish, she reached forward to grab the shower head that was hanging from the holder and turned it on. She handed it to me, and I rinsed her back off. When I moved her hair to rinse off the last of the soap, I saw her perfect neck. The urge to kiss her there overwhelmed me. Usually, I let her steal the touches and kisses, but I just had to take the lead this time.

My voice came out unsure, almost as if I was whispering, "Can I kiss you here?" I pointed to right above her collarbone. She nodded her head again and leaned her back into me further.

I slowly kissed her warm, wet skin, but kept my mouth still. Once I could tell she was fine with that contact, I moved up her neck, and she gave me more of those beautiful moans.

"I've missed you," she whispered.

"Not as much as I've missed you, baby."

She grabbed my hand and took the loofah away. She put my hand over her breast, and my whole body lit up with excitement.

"Are you sure?" I asked.

She nodded as her head fell back into me.

I slowly began rubbing her nipple between my thumb and index finger.

"Fuck," she panted. "That feels so fucking good."

I added my other hand around her stomach to keep her close.

"I'll make you feel good any way you want, baby." I kissed her neck again, this time licking the side of her neck before latching my lips onto it. "You say the word, baby, and I'll do whatever you fucking want me to."

She was writhing in my hold, moaning my name. Then she said the most beautiful words I'd heard in weeks. "Nick, I want...I want you to make me cum."

"Tell me what to do. What is okay?" I asked way too eagerly.

She moved one of my hands off her breast and put the shower head in it. I knew exactly what she was asking me to do. She wanted me to use it on her sweet clit and make her cum without actually touching her.

Challenge Accepted

I turned her face to mine. "Tell me if I need to stop, okay?"

She nodded.

I turned the pressure to the setting right before the jet setting. It was called power spray. I started at her shoulders, letting her get used to me having control of it. Once the spray reached her stomach, she grabbed my hand and stopped me.

"I'm...I...dammit." She sounded so defeated.

I dropped the shower head immediately, like it was burning me, and removed my hands from her body completely. "Hey. Baby, this was a lot." I kissed her shoulder. "We can get out, and I can hold you on the couch." I kissed her temple.

She turned to look at me head-on. "No. I want this, but can I guide your hand? I will feel like I'm more in control. I think I need to know what's coming before you do it."

I gave her a smile and kissed her lips fleetingly. "I would love for you to tell me what to do."

She gave me a sultry smile that made me think some of her confidence was returning. She turned her back to me once again, grabbed the shower head, and placed it in my hand. She leaned her head back onto my shoulder and closed her eyes before putting her hand over mine.

She let out a soft moan as the water began cascading down her body. Watching her take control over her pleasure was something I would never forget. She ran the sprayer over her budding nipples and breasts in circular motions for a moment.

I nipped at her ear and sucked her earlobe into my mouth. "You are so fucking beautiful." She let out a beautiful moan at the sound of my voice.

When she moved the shower head down to right above her pussy, I spoke again.

"Are you ready to pleasure yourself for me, beautiful girl?"

"Mmm, yes. Very ready."

"Nice and slow. Guide me where you want me, baby."

She put my other hand back on her breast.

As she moved our hands lower, I felt the moment the spray hit her clit. She bowed her back and began squirming.

"Fuck," she whined.

"So fucking beautiful," I whispered before licking her ear.

I felt her back arch as her hand slipped in between us. She grabbed my dick and began pumping me into her hand.

"Fuuuck," I muttered. "Baby, this isn't about me. Enjoy your pleasure."

"I want you to feel good, too."

Through my moans, I managed to form a few coherent sentences. "I feel good just being near you. You make every moment with you the best moment of my life."

Her body tensed, and she moved her hands off me to grip the sides of the tub. I knew she was cumming the moment she leaned into me, rubbing her ass on my cock as she rode out her orgasm with the water flow rhythmically pulsating directly on her clit.

"Nick, I..." Her legs began to shake. "I love you."

"I love you too, baby."

Once she was through her orgasm, she slumped back onto me, and I went to wrap my arms around her but stopped myself.

"Is this okay?"

"Yes." She nuzzled into me, and we sat there for a few minutes before standing to shower off. Before I could get very far, she stepped toward me and grabbed me by the cock.

"I need to finish what I started," she said confidently. I heard her pull the plug to let out the water with her foot.

"No, baby, it's...baby, wait." I tried to protest, but it came out as a groan. My eyes closed, and I tipped my head back, leaning it against the wall.

I had meant what I'd said. This isn't about me. I wanted her to feel good. I could worry about myself later when I was alone.

She pumped her hand faster and faster until I felt the tightening in my balls, and I was getting ready to tell her I was about to cum when she let go. Before I could even open my eyes, I felt her kneel in front of me on the porcelain tub.

"Do you really want me to wait?"

I looked down at what had to be the sexiest thing I had ever seen in my life. I shook my head no. She motioned for me to stand in front of her. I did, and before I was even fully upright, I felt her hot mouth covering the head of my rock-hard erection.

"Callie," I breathed softly. "Baby, I'm about to cum."

She let out a hum around my cock. Instinctively, I wrapped her hair around my hand and began pushing her head further onto me. I pulled my hand away quickly, realizing she probably didn't want that, but without missing a beat, she placed my hand back on her head and pushed my cock further into her mouth, making herself gag a little. The tingling at the base of my spine intensified.

My head fell back against the wall again. "You are so fucking perfect, Callie."

I felt her smile around my cock, and two seconds later, I was cumming. She worked her mouth over me, not missing a drop.

After she finished working me through my orgasm, she looked up at me with a shy smile. I pulled her up and kissed her forehead.

Being this close with Callie after all this time felt like I was finally home again. I pulled away to thank her, but she spoke first. She looked into my eyes, and I saw a flicker of my Callie again. "Thank you, Nick."

I kissed her nose as we held each other. "No, baby, thank *you*."

Callie's head rested on my bare chest while we chatted about our day. I could feel the air leaving her nose and flowing across my abdomen. I think she liked it when my heartbeat lulled her to sleep. I was mindlessly rubbing her hair, trying to help her relax more so she could fall asleep and I could go to my room. My eyes were getting heavy when her voice startled me.

"Do you want to go to therapy with me?"

I looked down at her, but she wasn't looking up at me. "What?"

She sat upright and crossed her legs. Her cheeks were turning a beautiful shade of light pink. "I knew it was stupid. I'm sorry I asked. I knew you wouldn't wan—"

I put my finger over her lips. "Sweets. I didn't hear what you said, but nothing you could ever say is stupid."

I actually had heard her, but I wanted her to say it again to make sure I'd heard her correctly before responding.

She looked down and bit her lip, then looked back at me with glossy eyes. "My therapist thinks I would benefit from you being in a session with me."

"Okay, I'm in. Just let me know when," I said without hesitation.

"You will have to take off work."

She said it like I didn't already realize that would be the case. It was like she couldn't believe I would take time off work for her. I wasn't sure why she even questioned those things anymore, but we'd get there eventually.

"Just let me know when, baby. I will be there with bells on." I moved my hand to her face, and this time she didn't flinch. That was a big step in the right direction.

She laughed, and her smile lit up the room.

"How did I get so lucky to find you?" I rubbed my thumb over her jaw. Her smile fell a little, and she moved my hand to her cheek and placed it over mine. She held it there for a moment, leaning into it, and embracing our touch.

"Thank you again for today," she said softly.

"Forever and always, baby."

Chapter Thirty-Two

Callie

I let Nick sort of touch me in the bathtub about a week ago. Everything went down the drain after that. We both acted as if that day had never even happened.

We were currently midway through my therapy session, and I hadn't said a word. I was literally just listening to them talk back and forth. Nick grabbed my hand the moment we sat down, and thirty minutes later, he was still holding it while he talked.

"So, Nick, what do you think you need from Callie after this appointment? What would you like to see change when you leave here?"

Nick looked at me and then back at my therapist. "I don't want her to change anything. I want her to take this at her own pace. I think she is making great strides in her healing."

I squeezed his hand as a thank you, but stayed silent.

My therapist directed her attention toward me. "And you, Callie? What do you want or hope to change when you leave here today?"

"Nothing," I said curtly.

She closed her notebook and pushed her glasses up onto her head. "Callie, if we want this to be productive, we definitely need to be honest with ourselves and each other. Do you want to try again?"

I looked at Nick, and he was all smiles. His face immediately turned a beautiful reddish pink from the next words that left my mouth.

"I want him to fuck me without treating me like a broken doll, but I can't let him. My brain won't let me. My brain tells me he doesn't want to or doesn't find me attractive anymore."

His mouth opened in complete awe. He was staring blankly at me, then swallowed hard before looking at my therapist.

"Nick, do you have a response to that?" she asked.

"I...well...I...I don't know what to say here without getting in trouble or making anything worse."

"Say whatever is on your mind," I muttered.

He turned toward me fully in order to give me his full attention.

"First, nothing that has or will ever happen will change the fact that you are the most beautiful woman I have ever met. Don't let anything *ever* make you think any different. Second, I'm scared to touch you because I'm scared that I will push you too fast and you won't be ready. You don't talk to me about anything anymore, so I just never know what you are feeling."

"You never ask," I quickly responded.

"Callie. You can't say that. I ask you every day and you ignore the question like you didn't even hear me."

I pulled my hand away and felt a tingling bit of blush run up my neck. I just kept staring between the both of them looking at me.

"Callie, is that true? Does he ask, and maybe you just don't hear him, or you block it out? Because that can be something we—"

I cut her off because I didn't want to talk about it anymore. "Okay. Maybe you do ask, but I just don't wanna talk about it."

Nick looked toward my therapist for what to say next, but she spoke to me.

"Callie, he's telling you what he needs, and you are dismissing him. That is exactly what he is saying. He would like you to share what you are feeling. You told me in one of our first sessions that Nick was the person you are closest to." Nick side-eyed me with a big smile. I blushed even more than I already was. "If you start by sharing everything with him, then you will be able to share with other people."

"Callie, I love you. Just trust me a little, okay?"

I nodded my head in agreement. "Okay."

I honestly didn't need to think about it anymore. I just wanted to make love to my man without flinching. I knew that I was the one holding us back, but that was all changing tonight.

I was about to say more, but the red light in her office flickered, indicating her next appointment was here.

"We will save the rest for next time, okay?"

I looked at Nick and smiled. I reached for his hand and leaned in to kiss him. Without looking away from each other, Nick and I nodded. I looked back at the therapist, "Yes, next time, we will definitely have more to talk about."

The moment we got in the car, Nick began nervously babbling. "Is that what every session is like? That was a bit intense." I looked over and shrugged as he backed out of the parking lot.

"Yeah, a little."

"I liked her. She seemed like someone who takes no shit but in a nice way." He laughed. "It felt really good to get some of that off my chest." He grabbed my hand and squeezed it lightly. "And it felt really good to hear how you were feeling and connect a little more than we have been."

"Yeah, it did. Thank you for coming with me. I am really glad you did." I looked down and let his hand go. I began twisting my fingers in my lap. "And I'm really sorry it took that for me to really talk to you about this."

Nick reached his hand back over to grab mine again. "Never apologize for protecting yourself or your feelings. It doesn't matter how long it took. It matters that we talked about it a little, and now, hopefully, we will have more of an open dialogue, right?

"Yes, I hope so."

He kissed my hand. "I love you, Callie." He let go only to put on some music, then held my hand the entire ride home.

When we got home, Nick went to his room and took a shower, and I went into the back of the house, where my piano was. It was sweet that he knew I needed some thinking space.

I began playing and did my best to get lost in the music, but I couldn't find my focus. I closed my eyes and just let the music guide me. When I opened them again, Nick was leaning on the door frame with his arms crossed, biting his bottom lip.

"You play so beautifully, Sweets. I could listen to you play all day."

"Thank you. Any requests?" I joked.

He playfully tapped his chin like he was thinking as he walked into the room and sat down in the chair that I normally used during my lessons.

"Play something that reminds you of me."

He brushed a lock of my hair off my forehead and tucked it behind my ear. The gesture sent shivers down my spine, but I didn't say anything back. I smiled, closed my eyes, and started playing Make You Feel My Love by Adele.

One minute into the song, I assumed he stood when I heard the chair scratch the floor. He squatted down behind me, and I felt his torso press into my back. He leaned in and whispered in my ear. "I can't wait to feel your love again, Callie."

An intense warmth traveled through my body. Goosebumps erupted over my arms.

"I can't play with you doing that," I giggled.

I was trying my best not to mess up the song since I was playing from memory. I felt his warm lips on my neck, followed by his tongue. I stopped playing for a moment and tried to turn around, but he put a hand on each side of my face and turned me back to keep me playing.

"Try," he whispered.

I let out a low hum and began to play again. I tilted my head to give him more access. He kissed my neck over and over again as his lips slowly traveled down to my collarbone.

"Can I touch you here?" he whispered as he pointed to my chest.

I nodded. I had taken off my sweatshirt and only had on my sports bra and tank top.

The moment he touched my breast, I shuddered and missed a few notes, making both of us chuckle lightly.

"Do you know how fucking perfect you are?" he whispered. "Do you know what you do to me? I think about you all damn day and dream about touching you again. I love you so much, baby."

I hummed at his words, and he continued to massage my breasts. I was just hitting random keys until I stopped completely so he could pull the straps of my top and bra down. I turned, baring my naked chest to him.

He bit his lower lip. "You are so fucking perfect." He stepped back to give me room to get up, but I quickly crowded him.

"I love you too."

His lips found mine, and we were lost in a heated kiss. He lifted my body up, gripping my thighs right under my ass, and set me on top of the piano.

I broke the kiss, thinking about my weight on top of my piano.

"I can't be up here, Nick. I am too heavy."

He gripped my chin. "Shh, baby. Just go with the flow. I am living a fantasy here."

I smirked. "A fantasy?"

He rubbed his thumb over my lips, and his tone became a little more serious. "You stop me when it's too much, okay?"

I nodded in agreement.

He pulled my leggings down and groaned at the sight of me. He started tracing every stretch mark I had on my hips and thighs with his pointer finger.

"Can I kiss you here?"

"You don't have to. Just ignore them."

He bent down and kissed and licked a few of the marks on my hip before speaking again. "I could never ignore them. I want to worship them, and every inch of you, if you will let me."

His words took mine away. I had never felt such a sensual act toward something I felt was so ugly. I had always been self-conscious about my stretch marks, and Jake used to ask if there was anything I could do to remove them, so I always just hated them.

"I love every single one of these beautiful marks. If they are part of you, I love them.

I whimpered as he got closer to my center. His nose nudged my clit, and I flinched out of pleasure.

"I want to taste you."

I gripped his hair. "Please," I begged.

He lifted his head a little to look at me. "Please, what?"

"Taste me. Please."

"Do you want me to tell you before I do things?" He asked softly before kissing my right thigh.

"No, just do it," I moaned.

He kissed closer to my center, and he groaned when his nose brushed my entrance once again. He was nuzzling into me, enjoying every small moment. "Are you sure?"

"Yes!" I screamed in an impatient tone.

He chuckled and licked me fast and lapped up every drop of me. I don't think I was even able to have one single thought before my orgasm hit, and I was moaning his name.

Before I could catch my breath, he lifted me into his arms and walked toward my room.

"Yours," I breathed out between kisses.

He looked at me and raised a brow. "Are you sure?"

I nodded, and he continued walking. We stopped a few times to make out against the walls. I would never understand how this man could hold my thick body up so easily, but he did it without even breaking a sweat. He held me up as if I weighed next to nothing.

He kept stopping against the wall to take my nipples into his mouth, giving them each their own attention. I could feel his erection growing thicker in his pants.

We finally reached the bed, and he delicately placed me down like I was a feather.

"You tell me to stop, I stop. No questions asked, no hesitation."

"Okay," I said confidently.

He spent a moment looking over my body.

"How do you get even more beautiful every time I see you?"

My skin flushed, and I began to cover myself with the blanket when he grabbed it and tossed it across the room. I laughed with a huge grin on my face.

He moved closer, and I reached out to take off his pants and pulled his boxers down with them.

"Fuck."

Nick chuckled, and I realized I had said that audibly, not just in my head. I tried to look down out of embarrassment, but before I could look away, he grabbed my jaw and looked into my eyes.

"You say no or stop, and we stop, got it?"

I nodded.

"Use your words, baby."

Hearing him say that made wetness immediately pool between my thighs, remembering our vacation and the first time we made love.

"Yes, I got it."

"Good girl."

A wave of excitement ran through me when he called me a good girl. I loved when he talked to me like that. He started by kissing the inside of my thighs, and I flinched. Not from fear, but because my skin was still buzzing from my orgasm on the piano. He was rubbing his rough five-o'clock shadow against me, making the buzz intensify.

God, I've missed him.

I let out a low moan, and he hummed in response, sending a vibration through my core that made my back bow off the bed.

Within minutes, another orgasm overtook me. Nick worked me through it. He slowly and expertly kissed up my body when the orgasm was subsiding. Before he kissed me, he whispered in my ear, "You are perfect."

We kissed for a moment as he played with my nipple again, making me squirm. "Let's go shower and get you cleaned up. We both need a good night's sleep before work tomorrow."

"And you need an orgasm," I added.

He got up with a smile and put out his hand. "If I have to suffer through one, I will," he pulled me in and kissed my forehead. "Anything for you, my Sweets." He smiled down at me.

I looked up at him. "I love you, Nick."

"Not as much as I love you."

Chapter Thirty-Three

Nick

Work was hard to focus on with all my thoughts of Callie and how happy I was for things to be progressing as they were. It was the worst time to be distracted since I had a play to run. My co-teacher and I chose to do Babes in Toyland for the winter play. The kids were so excited, and tryouts happened while I was on vacation with Callie, so everything was pretty much just practice when I got back.

We did some staging of the finale, and I had Aubrey helping me with some music. She wouldn't be able to help me like she had been the past few years because Lincoln needed her.

"Are you sure I can't steal you away from Lincoln's show? We need you more. We have more acoustic songs than he does."

She knew I was joking, but I had to try. She chuckled and looked me in the eye with all the seriousness in the world.

"Lincoln told me no more orgasms for me if I chose to help you over him, so he wins. Sorry, the orgasms are just too good."

"Shit, Aubrey," I laughed. "We are around kids. You can't talk like that." I looked around, realizing we were the only two left.

She laughed as she walked up to me after packing away her guitar. "Come on, Nick, you know me better than that." She tapped my shoulder. "Get up and hug me so I can go."

I stood to hug her. "You're so lucky I love you, weirdo."

"No, Nicholas. You are lucky I love you."

I put my hands up in defeat. "Okay, you win."

I had a little time to get some paperwork done before I headed home, so I stayed in my office because it was quiet. Unfortunately, that didn't last long.

There was a knock at my door. It was one of my students.

"Hey, Mr. Clark, I was on my way out after debate club and saw that you have a flat tire. Do you want me to call for some help?"

Fuck, that's just what I didn't need right now. "Thank you, Jen. No, I can handle it. I appreciate the warning, though."

"No problem," she said in a chipper tone as she went on her way.

After going outside and checking the trunk, I remembered I had used the spare not even a week ago. I called Callie to let her know I was going to be late coming home tonight. Unfortunately, she was stuck in lessons and couldn't pick me up. I called Link, and thank God he was able to help me out.

Callie already gave me shit for not getting the spare fixed after needing it last week. She harped on me all of last week about how I needed to get it fixed as soon as possible. She even joked about how the only time you ever need the spare is when you don't have it. I hate that she was right.

I stood there, leaning against my car, scrolling on my phone for about five minutes when I saw a familiar car pull up in my peripheral. I couldn't place it at first, but then I saw Jake getting out and coming toward me rather quickly. I didn't move toward him, but my instincts kicked in, and I hit the record button on my phone.

"Are you fucking my bitch?" Jake yelled. He looked like he was on a mission. His face was a deep red, and as he spoke, spit went flying out of his mouth. He looked like a rabid dog.

I raised my eyebrows in surprise. "Excuse me?"

"Are. You. Fucking. My. Girl." He was a few feet away and enunciated his words slowly like he was speaking to a damn child.

I laughed, and that made his face flush a darker shade of crimson, if that was even possible. He stepped toward me, leaving only a few inches between us.

"No, I am not fucking your girl."

He seemed to back up, and just as his anger subsided a little, I added, "I'm fucking *my* girl." I smiled.

His breathing quickened, and he took another step toward me, but again, I remained unmoved.

"I knew she was cheating on me with your skinny ass. That's why I started sleeping with other people an—"

I held up my hand to stop him. "Woah, okay, stop right there. We are not going to try to blame you not being able to keep your dick in your pants on Callie. She was faithful to you to the bitter end. Believe me, I wish she'd left sooner. Callie and I never, and I mean never, got together when she was with you." I paused for a second and decided to break his balls a little more and gestured to my ass. "And thank you for noticing my nice ass."

"Fuck you and fuck her. You were probably fucking her every time I was out of town."

I shrugged. "You can believe whatever you want to, dude. I never touched her while you were together. I would never be the other person. No matter how much I loved her and knew that you were wrong for her, I never made a move."

He clenched his fists by his sides. He seemed to think about something and then thought better of it because he smiled an evil kind of grin, mumbled something I couldn't hear, and then walked away.

As he was getting into his car, it dawned on me that he had impeccable timing. He somehow knew I was here. *Did he pop my tire on purpose?*

Before he left, he rolled his window down and yelled, "Enjoy it while it lasts. That girl loves me, and I will get her back one way or another."

I saluted him. I didn't have time for childish games. "Can't wait to see it."

He huffed and rolled up his window.

I knew it shouldn't bother me at all because I knew Callie was mine, and she would remain mine, but that look on his face gave me an uneasy feeling. Jake was sneaky. I was afraid he'd try to jeopardize what Callie and I had. She wouldn't let that happen...*right?*

On the ride home, I gave Link the rundown of what had happened with Jake and let him listen to my recording. He seemed just as concerned as I was.

"Do we need to do something, like call the cops? I only met the guy a few times since I came around when their relationship was toward the end, but he sounds kinda crazy to me."

I didn't respond right away. I was asking myself the same question. "Honestly, I don't know what we could say. He didn't technically do anything. I mean, I think he popped my tires, but I have no proof of that. I had no reason to even think of it until he pulled up today. I kind of assumed he knew Callie and I were together. He is still dating that chick he cheated on Callie with who works at the restaurant. Callie hasn't really worked there since we got back, but I know that girl has seen us together."

"Damn. Should I tell Aubrey? Do you think he will try to hurt them? I will fucking go to jail, Nick. If he comes ne—"

"Chill. He has no reason to want to hurt anyone but me, really. He won't hurt Callie; at least, I assume he won't. He seems to know he fucked this up, and he's doing everything he can to get her back."

"He better pray he just lets it go. I'll send his ass back to Nevada or wherever the fuck he's from."

I laughed as we pulled into the driveway. "California, dude."

"Whatever. I will kill him if he touches any of you."

I slapped my hand on his shoulder. "I appreciate it."

I walked in right as Callie was finishing up making dinner. She had plates waiting for Link.

"Here, I made you dinner as a thank you for picking up the man-child. I already called Aubs and let her know."

Link laughed, and I rolled my eyes.

He gave her a side hug before walking out the door. "Thanks Cal."

I kissed her cheek and went to change out of my work clothes. She was glaring at me before I was even fully in the room. I stopped short in the hallway.

"Why did Link tell me to have you call him if anything else happens?" She leaned against the counter and pointed the spatula in her hand at me

I walked up to her and put my arms around her waist. *No flinching. That's a good sign.* "Would you let it go if I told you it was nothing?" She gave me a stern look. I laughed uncomfortably. "Didn't think so."

We sat down to eat, and I told Callie about my encounter with Jake and asked her to be careful. She was becoming angrier by the minute as

I gave her more details. Even though she looked mad, her eyes were filled with tears.

"Baby, what is it?"

She sniffled. "This is all my damn fault." She put her face in her hands.

I walked around the table, knelt down in front of her, and moved her hair out of her face. "Baby, look at me. How could this possibly be your fault?"

She gripped my hand, which was in her lap. "I went to tell my mom I could start picking up more shifts, and she asked how you were. I thought we were alone in the office, so I told Mom that we were dating."

"You did?" I asked excitedly. She chuckled through her tears and nodded.

"I realized, after I said it, that Sara was standing at the door. I was hoping she didn't hear me, but I guess she did."

"Callie, I want everyone in the world to know you are mine. I will tell everyone we know right now." I took my phone out. "I was just waiting for you to be okay with telling people."

She put her hand on the phone to stop me.

"Let's tell our friends and family next week. I think we have told everyone separately, but I want to make sure we tell them all that it's official."

"I can't fucking wait," I whispered. I leaned in and captured her lips with mine. Callie deepened the kiss. I picked her up and placed her on the couch to get more comfortable. As soon as her perfect ass hit the couch, Callie's phone rang. She let it go to voicemail, but then it started ringing again. She hesitantly pulled away from the kiss.

"I have to get that."

"Have to? Or want to?"

She chuckled. "Get up ya horn dog. I will only be a minute."

I went back to my food as she picked up the call.

"Hey Aubs. What's up?" she paused, seeming to listen to a very long-winded Aubrey. "Um, let me ask him." She looked at me. "Link has been trying to call you. He said Elijah is passing through on his way to Boston and wants to grab beers with the two of you."

I started talking with my mouth full. "He just left twenty minutes ago. When did he want to go?" I hadn't checked my phone since I got home. I looked around and realized it wasn't there. I must have left it in my room in my school bag.

"Tonight. He said he could pick you up at eight if you want."

"I don't know how I feel about leaving you alone after what happened today."

She rolled her eyes, and I heard Aubrey yell into the phone, "What happened today?".

She shushed me and then went back to her conversation. "Come over so I'm not alone, and he will go."

"I never said—"

She held up her hand and said a few yeahs and yups with a few nods thrown in. Then she hung up. "Link and Aubrey will be here at eight. We are having a girl's night, and you are not allowed, so you have to go."

"I don't know, Cal," I said hesitantly.

"I will be fine. Now go shower and make yourself look hot for all the thirsty women."

I looked at her in shock. "What? Why would I want to look hot for other women?"

She walked up to me and grabbed my ass—or lack thereof—and gripped it tight. "Make them want what they can't have, baby."

I chuckled and kissed her nose. "You are the weirdest woman I know."

"I just trust my man." She leaned back, giving me a look. "You would think, after what happened, I would be worried, but I guess I just know I don't need to worry about you."

I looked at her with admiration and love. I pushed my fingers into the hair at the base of her neck. "Never, Sweets. You will never have to worry about me even glancing in their direction."

She stood up on her tiptoes and kissed me and pinched my ass. "I know."

CHAPTER THIRTY-FOUR

Callie

Aubrey came over, and we immediately started talking about our students and how their programs were going. She asked a little about therapy but understood and didn't push when I didn't want to elaborate on certain things. I don't really tell her much about Nick and I sleeping together because we have already established it's like her hearing about her brother having sex, but I did want to tell her I let him at least touch me.

"After the last session, we had a very sensual moment at the piano, and I have honestly been flinching a lot less since. I think therapy is really helping."

She looked at me with a homemade margarita in her hand and queso on her lip. "That's good, babe. I love that for you."

I giggled and wiped her mouth. "Me too. I think things are really going to work out with us. It feels...perfect."

She grabbed my hand. "It is perfect. It has been a long time coming."

We chatted and watched a few chick flicks until it was two in the morning. I didn't realize how much I had missed her. Our lives had changed so much in such a short time. We were both successful music teachers, and we were both in happy, loving relationships. It's exactly what we both always dreamed of. I think things were finally going to be good for both of us.

❧

NICK

We went to our favorite bar, Spectators. The name made it sound like a strip club, but it wasn't. It was just a dive bar with really good wings. It's old but well-kept. They had a small corner stage for karaoke night and two pool tables with two dartboards on the wall. There was a rooftop bar, but it closed in October for the winter.

When I got to the bar, the whole band was with Elijah. Elijah was the lead vocalist for the band Reckless Riders. All the guys seemed pretty nice. I only met them once before when we went to their concert back in June. Elijah was the exception since we had met a few times when he and Link got together and I tagged along.

Owen, Elijah's brother, played guitar. Connor was their bassist, Hunter was on drums, and Beck was their keyboard player. Hunter was a bit standoffish the last time I saw him, but he seemed fine this time, probably because of the alcohol.

There were a few women who recognized them, but they told them they would find them later and went with us to a booth in the back. Hunter told me about their last gig while we waited for some beers.

"It was wild. We had bras being thrown at us left and right."

I looked at Elijah in question, and he shrugged. "Happens more than you think, honestly. I slept with a girl last night who had the biggest tits

I've ever seen. They were fake as shit, though, so it wasn't even attractive. I want an all-natural girl that I can throw around." He looked over at Link. "How is my girl, Brielle? Is she burning for me yet?"

I snorted, coughing up the water I was sipping.

Link's voice was firm but friendly, "Elijah, she wouldn't burn for you if you were the last person on this earth."

I laughed again.

"I will keep trying, bro," Elijah stated. He slapped Link on the shoulder, "Dude, if I can get her to want me, then we can be brothers."

Link's eyes went wide. "So what you are saying is you want to get married."

Elijah's eyes went wide. "That's not what I meant."

Link pointed at him. "But you said it." Link chuckled.

The waitress arrived and dropped off our drinks, and the entire band was checking her out. Beck, Connor, and Hunter took off to flirt with some women near the pool tables.

Elijah leaned back in the booth to look at us. Then his attention fell on me.

"You fuck her yet?"

"Who?" I asked.

He looked at me like I was stupid. "Callie, dumbass. Last time I saw you guys together, you were fucking each other with your eyes."

"Fuck you," I said with a chuckle. "And yes, we are together."

He laughed loudly, making a few people look over and notice us. "I fucking knew it. Congrats, my guy. When's the wedding?"

"Tomorrow, if she would let me," I joked. I took a sip of my beer. "But really, I think I will propose sometime next year. We can settle into our life together and then get married."

Link cleared his throat, eyeing the both of us strangely. I was about to take a little offense, thinking he didn't want me to propose to Callie or something, but then his words cut off my thoughts.

"I am proposing the day after New Year's, on the second. Two is Aubrey's favorite number."

Elijah and I looked at each other and smiled. Elijah looked away to motion to the bartender.

"Hey, love, can we get a round of shots over here?"

"What kind, handsome?" The waitress leaned one hip on the side of the booth, giving Elijah sex eyes.

Elijah looked at both of us and asked, "Whiskey?"

Link and I nodded. She motioned for Elijah to follow her, which I thought was weird since we just ordered drinks, but he got up.

"Gentleman, if you will excuse me, I'll be right back with those shots."

I looked at Link, and he rolled his eyes.

"Elijah likes to fuck in bathrooms everywhere he goes," Link stated.

I looked over to see Elijah shutting the bathroom door. "Got it." I looked back at Link. "So, you are going to tie my girl down, huh?"

Link smiled. "*My* girl."

I put my hands up in defeat. "Touché. Are you going to involve Callie? They will both cut your balls off if you don't."

"Of course. I would never think of doing it without her or Brie. I kinda like my balls." We both laughed.

Moments later, Elijah came back holding our shots with a big ass grin plastered on his face.

"That was quick," I said with a grin.

He shot back one of the six whisky shots. "Doesn't take long to make them scream when you know what you're doing."

Link was giving Elijah a funny look. "I thought you don't drink when you are on tour?"

Elijah took another shot. "Usually I don't, but I thought this time was an exception. We get to celebrate you proposing soon, and I also have some news for you guys."

We both looked at him, eyes wide.

"Reckless Riders officially got a headline tour for next year."

"Dude, that's fucking awesome," Link said.

"Yeah, that's great! I will have to buy some tickets for all of us." I grinned, knowing he wouldn't ever let us pay for them.

"Fuck you, Nick. You know you aren't paying for shit," Elijah said.

"You really should let us pay for general admission tickets at least. There are a lot of us," I chuckled.

"Never. My friends are always free." Elijah seemed to be slurring his words a little.

"I am glad we have stuff to celebrate, but are you sure you're good? I'm talking about the drinking thing." Link asked.

"Dude, I'm good. I promise."

I couldn't figure out why Link was so focused on Elijah's drinking, but it was probably none of my business, so I didn't ask.

We caught up on all the things happening in our lives, and Elijah told us a little about the tour and some of the stops. I honestly wasn't listening much because I couldn't stop thinking about the girls being home alone. I was getting a bit anxious, so I gave in and texted Callie to check in. on them.

Callie

> No. I'm missing you, but I'm okay. We are probably going to pass out soon. Aubrey is going to sleep in my bed with me so Link can stay on the couch if he doesn't want to go home.

> Why don't you sleep in my bed and they can have yours?

The text back was a little delayed. I almost texted again to tell her to forget about it, but then one came through.

Callie

> Okay.

> Don't feel pressured, but the offer is there. You can also sleep in yours alone, and they can have mine. Totally up to you. I love you Sweets.

Callie

> I love you too.

Link and I headed home around two thirty after saying our goodbyes to the band. When I opened my bedroom door, my perfect girl was in my bed waiting for me. I changed my clothes quietly before making my way to the bed. I put my hand on her shoulder before getting into bed just in case I scared her. Once she opened her eyes a little to see it was me, I got in the bed next to her. She turned, kissed me, and then spoke in the cutest, groggy tone.

"You're back," she said as she kissed me again. "How was Elijah?"

"He's good, baby. Get some rest. We can talk when we wake up."

She hummed. "Okay. Goodnight." She turned, putting her back to me and snuggling in close.

I put my nose in her hair, taking in that jasmine scent I love so much. "I love you, Callie."

Talking to Link about proposing to Aubrey really put some ideas in my head about Callie and me. I think I want to talk with Callie about it. I just assumed we would eventually get engaged and then get married someday, but I never actually mentioned it to her. It had only been a few weeks of us technically being together, even though I've been hers forever. Like I told Elijah and Link, I would marry her tomorrow if she would let me, but I wanted to give her some time. I wanted to mention to her and let her know that I did see that in the future so I could gauge her thoughts on it. I shook off the thought and kissed her head as I drifted off to sleep.

CHAPTER THIRTY-FIVE

Callie

It was finally Thanksgiving, my favorite time of the year. Nick and I were planning to tell our family that we're really doing this. Technically, they all know already, so I guess we're just making it official today.

My mom came over to do all the cooking for us like she usually did for holidays. Aubrey, Lincoln, Nick, and I all watched the Macy's Thanksgiving Day Parade on T.V., just like Aubrey and I did as children. I always wrote down the different floats and balloons that we saw just to feel some nostalgia. It was probably something I would continue to do forever, especially if I ever had kids.

This was my way of remembering the good things about my dad. He was the one who used to help me write it all down. That only lasted until I was about seven years old because he was too high to help me after that. Luckily, when he left three years later, it didn't really phase me because I had already given up on him years prior.

"Calliebug, check the popper in the turkey to see if we are all set, please."

"It's popped!" I exclaimed after opening the oven. "That's too early, right? It's only noon."

She waved me off. "Oh, that's totally fine. It needs to rest for a bit. Just turn the oven off for me and go get the girls from the sunroom and have them help you set the table. Nick and Lincoln should be back any minute with the drinks, and Aubrey's parents are on their way. They just texted me. We should be ready to eat in less than an hour.

I loved seeing my family all together for holidays, and yes, I consider all of them my family. We will get to see even more of them for Christmas at Aubrey's house when her biological dad and his wife also come up. It will be her first time hosting in her and Lincoln's home for a holiday. She was planning to host Thanksgiving, but her biological dad couldn't make it to Connecticut. A friend of theirs needed help after surgery, so they are staying in Tennessee.

We made our official announcement once everyone finished their meal. Just as I had expected, no one was surprised—except Aubrey's dad, apparently. He told us to make it last and that he couldn't wait to have some grandchildren. He gave Aubrey and Lincoln a look.

"Don't look at me," Aubrey stated. "Until there is a ring on this finger, no babies are coming out of this body."

Lincoln leaned in and said, "We can arrange that."

Aubrey playfully smacked him and then kissed him deeply. I loved seeing my best friend so happy. My thoughts from the other day came flooding back, and I was instantly grateful once again that Aubrey and I were finally in healthy, happy relationships.

We all crowded into the living room to watch some football. I had zero interest in who was playing, but Nick cared, so I watched it for him. I sat on the floor directly in front of him. He'd been much more touchy today. I didn't know if it was because we made our announcement, so he was more comfortable now, or if it was because he was just a little sad that his family wasn't here. Honestly, it's probably a little bit of everything. I know sometimes these days when we all get together are really difficult for him, so I planned to ask him about it as soon as we had a moment alone.

After everyone left and the house was clean, Nick and I went for a walk since it was surprisingly warm for November, especially for Thanksgiving. It was fun to just catch up and talk with him. We may have been living together, but we had barely seen each other lately since we had both been so busy.

When we were almost back home, my phone buzzed in my hand. I looked down, and my heart dropped. It was a number I didn't have saved, but I knew who it was from the moment I opened the message. It was an old picture of me. I was lying on my old bed with my head hanging over the side, and Jake's puny excuse for a dick was down my throat while my hand was between my legs, and I was pleasuring myself. Another text immediately followed.

Unknown

> **Leave Nick, or the whole world will see what kind of slut you really are.**

Surprised, I stopped short and let out a loud gasp. I held the phone to my chest so Nick wouldn't see it.

"What? What is it?" Nick looked around for something he obviously wasn't going to find. I coughed to hide the scared look I knew I had on my face.

"Nothing. I thought I was going to fall. Just tripped a little, that's all. I will be fine. It was just a—"

"Callie, you are rambling, which means you are lying. Did you get that trait from Aubrey?" He chuckled, trying to make light of the situation.

I stayed quiet and just shrugged it off until he spoke again. "Wanna try again, Sweets?"

I got defensive, and my tone was a little rough and harsh. "I just tripped, okay? I don't wanna talk about it. It was embarrassing. Get over it."

Nick stopped walking and let go of my hand. "Woah. Wanna try *that* again? What is the attitude for?"

I began walking inside since we were at the steps already. "It's nothing. Forget it, please."

Nick shut the door behind us and turned to me. "No, I won't forget it. What the fuck happened in the last ten minutes for you to do a damn one-eighty like that? Are you okay?

"I am fine," I tried to say, a little calmer.

Nick gave me a curious look. I realized he saw me clutching my phone. I could see in his eyes he was thinking about what to say or maybe just thinking about how to say it. I knew what he was going to say before he even uttered a word.

"Let me see what he said." He put his open hand out in front of me.

"Who?" I gave him my best dumb-look impression.

"Callie." His eyes were narrowing in size and darkening in color with every moment that passed. I looked down in order to spare myself a moment to think.

"I don't have to show you my phone, Nick. You don't fucking own me."

He took a step forward, and his lips were mere inches from mine. His eyes met mine when I finally looked back up. "You are right. I don't own you, but you are mine. If someone is bothering you, or hurting what is mine, I have the right to know, and I have a right—as your boyfriend—to help you." He took a long, heavy breath. "Let. Me. See. It."

The next words just flew out of my mouth, even though I didn't mean a single one of them. "I don't need you to worry about me, Nick. Especially if you are going to act like a damn caveman. Maybe I don't need you as a boyfriend, either. Maybe I just need some goddamn space for once."

He stepped away from me. I could tell he was trying hard to hide the hurt. "What?"

"You heard me," I said curtly.

His eyes went wide with shock. He started to scratch his head and was looking around. It pissed me off for some reason.

"What the fuck are you looking around for?" I asked.

"Cameras or someone to tell me I'm being pranked."

"Why would someone be pranking you?"

"Callie, what the hell just fucking happened? Did you get body snatched or something? How did we go from taking a nice walk together to you saying that bullshit to me?"

"I—" I started to speak, but then he turned to me.

"You know what...when you are ready to tell me, go for it. Until then, I'm going to give you the space you *need* all of a sudden." He kissed my forehead. "Have a nice night, Callie." Without another look back at me, he stormed down the hallway and into his room.

"Now what?" I said out loud, wishing like hell someone would give me the answer.

The next day, Nick left for work earlier than normal. He was probably trying to avoid me. I heard him getting ready and the front door closed around seven this morning. I got up and had some coffee while I reread the messages Jake had sent over and over. I never answered him, but I knew I had to.

> **Why are you doing this?**

I waited a few minutes and got no response, so I took a shower and got ready for my students to arrive. Luckily, today was a more laid-back day since it was a last-minute session with only one student. It's technically a holiday for school, and I normally don't teach lessons on those days, but when she reached out asking me if I had some spare time, I couldn't say no. I needed the extra money anyway since it looked like I was going to have to find a new place to live. I had to work a shift at the restaurant today, as well. Thankfully that wasn't until later.

This session was becoming one of my favorites of all time. Carly was doing amazing. Hearing her play was a complete joy. It was helping me get out of my head a little. She's sixteen and is trying out for Julliard next year, so we were working on building on her skills. She has come up with two audition pieces so far that she plays to perfection. One she wrote herself with Aubrey's guidance, and the other was Bach's Prelude & Figure BWV 851 in D Minor.

I kept catching Carly staring at me while she was playing, but I assumed it was just because she was a little nervous since she was showing me the music she and Aubrey had recently finalized.

After we finished, she packed up her bags and turned toward me. "Miss Diaz, are you okay?"

Her question caught me off guard, but I tried to recover quickly. "Carly, how many times have I asked you just to call me Callie?"

She blushed a little and laughed. "Sorry. It just feels weird since you're my teacher."

"It's okay. Either is fine, really. Though I am more comfortable with just Callie," I laughed. "The answer to your question is yes, I am fine. I just had a rough night. Why do you ask?"

"I don't know, you just look...different. Maybe even a little bit sad. You don't look like your normal happy self."

"Thank you, Carly. I appreciate your concern, but I am okay. I just need more sleep."

"Okay," she said with a shy smile.

"You are doing great, you know."

She looked up at me again. "Thanks, I am trying really hard."

I gave her a smile back. "I can tell."

Once she left, I checked my phone again, and there was a response. The timing scared me a little. It was like he was watching me since the message came the moment she was gone. I checked outside to make sure she got into her car okay and to see if I could see anyone lurking or anything, but luckily, I didn't

Unknown

> I am not joking, Callie.

> You leave him and that house or I will let everyone see this and all the others I have collected over the years.

> Please don't do this. Just go be happy with someone else. Why can't you let this go?

Unknown

> Callie, I can't let you go. I wanted to keep you forever and you left.

I don't know why he bothered using a private number if he wasn't even going to try to hide who he was. I knew if this was ever going to stop; I needed some sort of proof that it was him.

> I had to leave. We weren't happy.

Unknown

Callie, you know I love you. That is why I proposed.

Got him.

> Jake, please don't do this.

Unknown

I have no choice. You won't let me talk to you to fix this. I don't want anyone but you.

> There is nothing to fix.

Unknown

If I can't have you, then neither can he. If you ask for help or go to the cops, I will start sending these to everyone you know.

I could see the conversation was going nowhere, so I stopped texting and thought through the situation. I didn't really think Jake would hurt me like this. He was jealous as hell and never wanted anyone even looking at me, but then again, I never knew I was being recorded, and I would have never fucking guessed he was doing that.

I didn't know how the hell I was going to fix this, but I did know that Nick couldn't be involved. One of them would likely end up getting hurt, and I would absolutely die if it was Nick. Seeing Nick hurt would kill me. If Jake was capable of something like this, as well as already messing with Nick's car, what else could he possibly do?

As much as Nick claims to love me, seeing these photos would most definitely change that. Plus, I still don't know the extent of what Jake actually has. It's one thing to know someone else had other relationships, but it's another thing to *see* it. I can't subject him to dealing with this. This is something that will have to be solved by me, and me alone.

Chapter Thirty-Six

Nick

C allie and I hadn't spoken more than ten words to each other in the past two weeks. She hasn't apologized or told me what happened Thanksgiving night, but whatever it was, it affected her enough she has become a completely different person.

I've been trying to get Aubrey to tell me what was wrong with Callie, but she didn't seem to know what I was talking about. She hadn't seen Callie since Thanksgiving, but she said she had talked to her a few times on the phone, and Callie seemed fine. So, apparently, she was just mad at me.

I knew something had happened on her phone, something that she didn't want me to see, but I still couldn't figure out what it might have been. My immediate thought was that she was cheating, and I almost caught her doing it. That thought only lasted two seconds. I knew her better than that. Plus, with how her relationship with Jake ended, I honestly couldn't see her being a cheater.

Of course, my second thought was Jake. Was she talking to him? Trying to fix shit with him? I honestly didn't know what it could be outside of that.

I heard Callie's bedroom door open, and goddamn, she looked fucking cute. Her hair was down and curly. I could tell she spent time getting ready this morning. Her curls only look like that when she takes the time to do it. Her black jeans were tight, and she was wearing a white long-sleeved crop-top sweater and carrying a few other articles of clothing in her hands. Clearly, she was going somewhere. I felt jealousy coil inside me.

She placed her belongings on the kitchen island and went to the fridge to get her energy drink. I could tell she was trying her best to keep her eyes off me. I loved watching her when she was all awkward. I knew I was not in the wrong here, and I would not apologize, so her cute, stubborn ass was going to have to.

I was leaning against the counter, sipping my coffee. I didn't take my eyes off her the entire time.

She finally snapped and glared at me. "What are you looking at?"

"You," I said simply.

She gathered everything and mumbled something I didn't hear.

"What was that?" I leaned toward her a little.

"I said stop. It's making me uncomfortable."

I turned and put my cup in the sink. "Well, I'm sorry if my presence makes you uncomfortable, but this situation was your doing."

"Don't worry about it. I won't be here for long."

I spun around, propelled by all the anger that just flooded my body. "Excuse me?"

She looked down at her feet. "I got an apartment. It won't be available until the end of January, but I can afford it and—"

"No."

"No? What do you mean, no? I have some money that Aubrey gave me, and I—"

"I gave you that damn money," I bitterly replied.

Fuck. I didn't mean to say that out loud.

"What?" she asked.

"Never mind." I rubbed my hands over my stubble and looked at her, trying to calm myself down. "You are not moving out."

I saw her sassy demeanor fall into place. "Says who? Last I knew, I was a single woman and could do whatever the hell I wanted."

Single?

"Oh, so this is just over? Are you single now without any explanation? Are you serious?"

"Nick, this is the most we have spoken to each other in two weeks."

"Yeah, and whose fault is that?" I snapped. I took a step forward toward the island, and she stepped back toward the door.

"Don't." She held up her hand.

I ran my fingers through my hair, letting out a frustrated huff. "Callie, what the fuck is happening to us? Why are you doing this?"

She looked down at her feet again as she turned toward the door. I thought she was going to leave without answering me. She stopped right before the door and whispered, "I don't have a choice. Plus, you just made my mind up for me. Apparently, I can't trust you. I can't believe you had our best friend lie to me about money. Well, I didn't need the money, and I don't need you."

I took a step closer to her. "You don't mean that, Callie. Tell me right now that you didn't fucking mean that."

"I'll pay you back as soon as I settle into my new place."

Before I could respond, the door shut behind her.

She doesn't have a choice?

CHAPTER THIRTY-SEVEN

Callie

I let the tears flow the moment I closed my car door. I'd been waiting to tell Nick that I was moving out for a few days now. My therapist told me I needed to get it over with or it would eat away at me. I felt like every time I worked through one issue with her, I just created another.

My therapist kept asking questions about why I would be leaving. I always answer as vaguely as possible with, "It just isn't what I want anymore. I would rather be his friend. Nothing more." I doubt she believed a single word of it. She assured me each time that we wouldn't get very far into my healing journey if I was not honest with her. I shrugged her off every time.

Jake sent me a total of five photos and videos. I hadn't told anyone yet because he made it clear that he would release them if anyone found out or if I got back with Nick. He has tried to get me to move out, but the soonest I could find in my price range was the end of January. I started picking up more shifts at my mom's restaurant, and I'd taken on two additional students. I needed to save up as much money as I could.

I honestly didn't know what was going to happen. Jake wouldn't tell me what he wanted other than me leaving Nick. I didn't know how to solve this without being utterly and completely humiliated by those pictures becoming available to the public. Once I am out, then what? Would he use it to make me do something else? Would he just delete them? He didn't say anything when I asked.

I pulled into the parking lot at the restaurant just as Sara was getting out of Jake's car. My defenses and anger immediately rose. I pretended to rummage in the back seat, trying to buy time. Luckily, he left without acknowledging me.

When I got out of the car, I realized Sara was in tears. Her makeup was running down her face. My anger dissipated the moment I saw her legs were about to give out. I caught her just before she fell to the ground.

"Sara, what happened? Are you okay?"

She sniffled before speaking. She looked up at me with scared eyes. She almost looked like she was about to apologize.

"Callie…I'm pregnant."

"Woah!" I didn't mean to say it out loud, but I had.

My mom came out the back door, probably looking for me since I had told her I was on my way. I looked up at her.

"We are going to need a minute."

Mom looked down at Sara and nodded. "Take your time. We are slow right now. Just wanted to let you know I put the work shirt on the table."

I nodded back as a thank you. I had texted her to ask her for an extra. I forgot to put mine in the dryer last night.

Sara righted herself and ran her hands over her apron and then under her eyes to clean her face a little. She grabbed my hand and I helped her up the stairs and into the bathroom. I stepped back to give her some space. I was still deciding if I wanted to pry. After a few minutes of silence, I did. I felt weird just staring at her.

"Are you happy? Like, is this something you want?"

She looked at me without saying anything, so I continued. "You don't look very happy, Sara. You know you don't have to—"

"I want it," she blurted.

I let out a breath. "Good."

I waited for her to finish cleaning her face, and then she looked at me in the mirror. "Then why are you crying like that? Those aren't happy tears."

She ignored my question and surprised me with the one she asked me, "Why are you helping me?"

I was a bit taken aback, but I answered as honestly as I could. "I've been on the other side of those tears. I wanted to make sure he didn't—"

"He doesn't hit me. At least not yet," she added.

"Good."

"Did he hit you?" she asked.

"No, but he tried. He made me cry a lot toward the end of our relationship. When I finally thought about it, I think I knew he was cheating. I just didn't want to admit that I had wasted so much time on someone."

We both sat in silence for a minute before she spoke again. "I am crying because he wants me to end the pregnancy. He said if I didn't, I would lose him."

My stomach dropped. "He wants you to have an abortion?"

She nodded her head in confirmation. "He said it's the baby or him. I told him I needed time to think. He told me not to come back until I chose him. I don't know what I'm going to do. My mom moved in with her boyfriend when I moved into Jake's. If I leave him, I will have nowhere to go. I literally have no one."

I pulled her into a hug. It felt very weird, honestly. "Sara, I'm so sorry you are dealing with this."

"Don't be sorry. I don't deserve your sympathy. I ruined your life."

I thought for a moment, looking away. She was technically right, but I didn't think of it like that anymore. "Honestly, Sara, I wouldn't say you ruined it. You upended it, for sure." We both let out a hesitant chuckle. "But I would say what you did drove me to where I should have been all along."

She looked at me with questions in her eyes. "Really?"

I nodded and grabbed her hand in mine. "Really," I said softly. "I realized quickly after leaving that Jake was just comfortable. I wasn't actually happy being with him."

She looked down at her hands. Then she whispered, "Lucky."

I pulled her hand to get her attention on me again. "You don't have to stay with him. You could totally do this on your own. I am sure your mom would help you, too."

"I know. I just don't want this child growing up without a dad. I had to, and it always made me wonder why I wasn't good enough for my dad to stick around."

"Do you really want a man like him around your child? Don't you think it's better to get out while you can?"

She shrugged.

"That isn't a reason not to have the baby, Sara. Think about the here and now. Do you want to have this baby?"

"I do."

"Then let's get you the hell out of there."

I started to get up, but she pulled on my hand, which made me look down at her.

"Callie," she said cautiously.

"Yeah?"

"He has pictures and videos of you on his computer."

My body froze. "You saw them?"

She nodded. "Is he using them to hurt you, Callie?"

I got on her level and gave her a curious look. "Why would you ask that?"

She looked at her hands. "I figured there was a reason you were trying to help me. You want me to help you get them back?" It was a question. Not a statement.

"Actually, no. I hadn't even thought of that. To answer your question though, yes, he's been blackmailing me, forcing me to leave Nick and move out."

She looked appalled. That look honestly surprised me. I just assumed she was in on it. "Really?"

"Really."

Could Sara really help me? Was there a way both our problems could be solved?

"So, how are you going to handle it?" she asked.

"I told Nick we couldn't be together. I have an apartment ready in January so he doesn't have to be involved in my mess."

"Callie, he loves you. You can't leave him. He is so perfect for you. You just admitted that a few seconds ago"

Tears began to sting the back of my eyes. I looked up to try to stop them from falling down my face. Sara saw this and put her hand on my forearm. "You haven't told him? I am sure he could help you."

"I've been trying to figure it out myself. I don't want him to get in trouble because of me. I am not worth it."

"Nick thinks you are."

Her words made butterflies erupt in my stomach. I nodded to acknowledge her since I didn't really know how to respond.

She looked around for a moment. I think she was looking to make sure we were alone. Then she stood up and looked at me with a devious smile.

"It doesn't solve my problem, but," she put her hand out to help me up, "I have a house key."

I smiled back and grabbed her hand. "You have a house key."

CHAPTER THIRTY-EIGHT

Callie

When it came time for Christmas at Aubrey's house, Nick and I drove together so we didn't get asked too many questions. I thought we were doing a good job of just steering clear of each other all night so we didn't have to really talk. He grabbed my hand at the dinner table and kissed my forehead when he excused himself to the bathroom, but all I could do was smile. I didn't know if it was him trying to make us seem normal or just instinct. After dinner, I was supposed to be helping Aubrey clean up, but I was stuck in thought, wondering if Nick would ever forgive me for this whole mess.

I was leaning against the counter while Aubrey cleaned the last of the dishes after everyone but Nick and I had left. I was looking into the living room, and I could see Aubrey next to me out of the corner of my eye, trying to decide if she was going to talk to me or not. I knew she noticed Nick and I acting weird. Honestly, I had been waiting for her to ask me about it all night. I still didn't know what answer I was going to give her.

She put the dishrag down and leaned in, nudging my shoulder to get me to look at her. "You gonna tell me what's up willingly, or are you going to make me pull it out of you?"

I gave a weak smile. "What do you mean?"

She dropped her voice so no one else would hear us. "Cal, you look sad. And you look especially sad while looking at Nick. What happened? You guys barely spoke today. The last time I saw you guys, you were announcing your relationship to everyone. I mean, I already knew something was going on from the conversations we've had, but this is a complete one-eighty from that."

"I'm not sad, Aubs; I just wish things were a bit different. We are going through some stuff, and I don't know if it will ever get better."

"Wanna talk about it?"

I turned and smiled at her, wishing I had the balls to tell her what was happening, but I didn't. "Not today, no. This is your night."

I loved my best friend and didn't want to ruin her first hosting of the holidays with my drama, so I changed the subject. I leaned in and whispered to her. "I am so happy for you, Aubrey. If anyone deserves this amazing life, it's you, babe. You guys are so happy and put together in such a short amount of time."

She hugged me and laughed. "We are the furthest thing from put together."

That made me laugh with her. Our loud laughter attracted the attention of the boys in the living room.

"I love you, Cal. It will all work out. You can tell me anything. Never forget that, okay?"

"Of course. Now let's get this cleaned up." I finished cleaning the counter, and then Nick and I said our goodbyes and left.

The silence that fell over the car the moment we got in was deafening. I heard that ringing you get in your head when it's just too silent. Nick didn't even put music on. I was fine with that because I had a lot on my mind, but it made me a little uncomfortable the longer it lasted. Sara and I had been doing our best to figure out if Jake had any hard copies of the photos and videos. Sara was pretending to stay with Jake, and she told him she got rid of the pregnancy so he would let her come back. That way, she could do some hands-on searching.

She would tell him the truth about the baby, of course, after she left his sorry ass for good. She just had to get to a safe place for her and the baby. We found a one-bedroom apartment she would be able to afford with some help from her mom. The last thing to figure out was those damn files. We could ruin the computer and phone by smashing them, but I hadn't been able to figure out if he had saved them somewhere else, and I had to be sure they were destroyed entirely.

I hadn't dared to go near his house in case he had any cameras set up that I didn't know about...obviously, that was his thing. In doing some research, Sara found some videos of herself, too. Sadly, we had already expected that. Luckily, there was no sign of those on his phone, so it looked like she would be safe unless there were hard copies.

I knew I needed to handle this soon...I think I was stalling because of fear. If there are no hard copies, it's over...if there are...well, I'm screwed. I honestly wasn't one hundred percent sure I was ready to find out the truth yet.

As I got out of the car, my phone rang. My heart dropped when I saw it was Sara. We agreed on no calls, so I thought it was weird.

"Sara, what's—"

"I need you to come get me. Now." Her voice sounded scared, like she was whispering, so I didn't ask questions.

"On my way."

I took the keys from Nick, got in the car, and left without even saying anything. I didn't know why I had to go get her, but she sounded scared, and that was all I needed to kick my ass into high gear.

When I arrived at my old house, Sara was waiting outside with a few bags in her hands. I got out and helped her put them in the trunk. I noticed one of her eyes was red, and she had fresh bruises on her arm and neck. When I reached out to touch the side of her face, she pushed me away.

"Just get me out of here." She looked at me with tired eyes. "Please."

I nodded and helped her into the car. When we pulled away from the house, I noticed a cop car sitting a few houses down. The moment I pulled away, so did they, but they were going in the opposite direction.

I drove her back to Nick's house. She still hadn't looked at me once by the time we got there. Her gaze was fixed on looking out the window. When we pulled up, she began to sob uncontrollably. The moment she tried to step out of the car, her legs gave out. I tried to help her, but she was pushing me away.

Nick was waiting at the door. He had worry written all over his face. He came running out the door when he saw me struggling to help Sara.

"I got her. Can you grab all her bags, please?"

He nodded, making sure I really had her before fully letting go of her arm. Once he brought all the bags inside, I made her some tea before hesitantly sitting beside her on the couch. Nick kept his distance by sitting at the kitchen island.

"He is in jail for tonight, so I had to get out." She looked up at me from her cup.

"What happened?" I asked.

"It happened last night, but I didn't have the balls to call the cops until today when he left to check on a job site," Sara said, looking back into her cup like she was searching for the answers to all her problems. She let out a big sigh. "I never thought he would actually do it."

I saw Nick's body straighten from the corner of my eye, but he stayed put.

"Sara, did he—"

"He hit me." She looked at me with tear-filled eyes. "We were watching a show on T.V., and he was looking at something on his computer. He started swearing and then threw it across the room at me. He was yelling and asking what the fuck I did to his stuff. He said some other things I can't remember because he came at me fast. The computer missed me," she reached up to touch her eye, "but his fist didn't."

"Sara, I am so sorry. You didn't have to do anything yet. I told you to wait and—"

She sat up a little straighter. "Wait, Callie, I didn't do anything." She gave me an unsettled look. "I thought you did. He said all the files were removed from the computer. He checked his phone right after, too, and he kept asking how I did it. I obviously had no idea what he was talking about, so I told him the truth. He grabbed my phone and read our texts. Before I could explain, he started wailing on me. Once he left, I called the cops, gave them my statement down at the station, and then went home and packed what I could. Then I called you when the cop who escorted me home told me his bail had already been paid and he would be let out in the morning. I knew I had to get the hell out of there."

"Fuck," I heard Nick whisper. He took out his phone and started dialing.

I stood up and tilted my head at him in question. "Are you okay?"

He waved me off. "Hold on a sec."

He held the phone to his ear. And before he could speak, I heard a loud, billowing voice coming from the phone. I couldn't exactly hear who it was, but the voice wasn't very familiar.

"You didn't do it yet, right? I told you to wait."

I obviously couldn't hear what was being said on the other end, but Nick looked aggravated.

"Dude... I mean, thanks, but I told you to fucking wait till the girls were safe and I gave you the green light. He...he fucking hurt her."

That piqued my interest more than a little bit.

"What the fuck is going on?" I asked, louder than before.

Nick put up his pointer finger, asking me to hold on for a minute, but I was in no mood. "Point that damn finger at me again, and I will fucking break it, Nicholas."

He rolled his eyes and continued listening to the call. Sara grabbed my arm and pulled me down to sit again. "Give him a minute."

Nick hung up the phone, walked over slowly, and bent in front of Sara, silently asking if it was okay to touch her face. I knew it was innocent, and he was probably just trying to make sure she was okay, but it still kicked up quite a bit of jealousy.

"Sara, I am so fucking sorry. This is all my fault."

She placed her hand on his. "Nick, you couldn't have known he was going to hurt me. You are probably so confused. You don't even know what is happening."

"Sara, don't," I blurted.

Nick sat back on his feet, still kneeling, and looked between the both of us. "Actually, I do."

NICK

How the hell was I going to explain this to her? I wasn't planning on telling her I knew everything until after Christmas was over. Now I have no choice.

Once I realized a full month had passed since Callie had not talked to me, I finally got sick of wondering why. I wasn't proud to admit it, but I snooped on her phone one day when she was in the shower. I had to see if I could find something to help me make sense of everything. She was being so secretive. I just couldn't take it anymore.

When I grabbed her phone, I was momentarily grateful for her usual stubbornness. She didn't listen to me when I told her to use a different number for her passcode. She always used her birthday.

After taking a few minutes and searching all the conversations with the usual people who would know what was going on with her, I realized there was nothing out of the ordinary in any of them—until I saw a message with the notifications silenced. There was no name because it wasn't saved in her contacts. I immediately got jealous and sick to my stomach. My only thought was that she actually *was* cheating on me.

I was weirdly relieved, then quickly disgusted with what I saw. Jake had been messaging her photos and videos that literally turned my stomach. I knew what it looked like when she was enjoying herself, and that wasn't even close. There were videos of him taking her from every position possible. She was saying no to some things, but he was making her do it anyway. There was even a picture of what I can only assume is Callie after he was done with her, and she was crying or having to pleasure herself while he was watching.

When I saw Jake touching *my* girl, I wanted to find him and kill him. My blood was boiling. I don't think I had ever been filled with so much fucking rage in my life.

Only one thing kept me from going after him right then—her text messages with Sara, of all people. At first, I got angry that she wouldn't ask me for help, but as I kept reading the X messages, I saw all the threats to her, her mom, her mom's restaurant, Aubrey, and me.

From the quick look I got at the messages, it seemed like Sara and Callie were devising a plan to find Sara a place to live and ruin the files. Their biggest worry seemed to be that it would be done correctly and at the right time so no one would get hurt.

I wondered why she wouldn't just go to the cops. The obvious reason, of course, is that the pictures and videos get out, but other than that, why did she not ask for help?

I began doing my own research to help and try to find out what type of recourse could be taken against him for what he was doing to her. When I looked up what happens with revenge porn cases, the results were disheartening. Basically, nothing happens the first time someone is caught doing it, maybe a restraining order and some community service in the more severe cases, but if they ever got caught doing it again, then the authorities would do something about it.

Knowing Callie and how impatient she always was, I understood why she was trying to handle it herself and be done with it. I wasn't happy about it, but again, I understood.

After doing more research, I realized this wasn't something I was going to be able to help her with on my own. In all my thinking, I remembered Elijah mentioning one of his bandmates being super tech-savvy, like he wasn't allowed to own a computer because of his past crimes kinda savvy.

I messaged Elijah, trying to get a feel for whether his friend would be a creeper about the situation, but from everything Elijah told me, he wouldn't pry. I gave the vaguest reasons possible that I needed his friend's info, and luckily, Elijah being the go-with-the-flow guy I knew he would be, didn't even ask me why.

Once his bandmate, Beck, messaged me, I told him I needed help getting rid of some files without someone knowing. He, like Elijah, didn't ask questions, and I was grateful. After a few hours of sleuthing, Beck was able to help walk me through a site that told us where the files originated, were saved to, and where they were sent. From what we could find, the files were only on Jake's computer and his phone, which he wasn't even backing up to any cloud or anything.

Beck explained that if we got rid of the files on the phone and computer, there would be nothing left unless Jake had made an external copy of them, and according to the messages I saw between the girls, they hadn't found any yet.

I did my due diligence and had some luck moving the plan forward. I was just waiting to tell Callie and make sure Sara was safe from that fucker before Beck removed everything.

I wasn't sure how I was going to tell Callie that I betrayed her trust and looked at her phone, but I also didn't want Callie to deal with the situation any longer than she needed to.

I guess the time to tell her is now.

CHAPTER THIRTY-NINE

Nick

Callie and Sara were both staring down at me. My heart started racing uncontrollably. I stood, pacing the floor a few times. I started rubbing the back of my neck, unsure of how to even start the conversation. When I finally turned back to face them, Callie looked up at me worried, almost defeated, like she just realized I did something wrong.

"How do you know what's going on?" she asked calmly.

I looked at Sara and back to Callie. I stepped toward Callie and gripped her arms with both my hands so she couldn't pull away or slap me. "I looked at your phone without you knowing. I knew what was going on. Please don't hate me. I really did this to help. I texted Elijah and told him I needed his bandmate's help. After we figured out what to do, I told him to wait. I know that you guys were trying to get Sara somewhere safe and I—"

Callie's lips were on mine. I pushed my hands into her hair, holding her face to mine. Emotion overtook me, and I felt myself getting choked up. I have missed those lips so much. I didn't know what possessed her to kiss me, but I didn't give two fucks in that moment. I was just glad she was doing it.

"I love you," I whispered.

I heard Sara clear her throat. "I can get out of here if you need me to."

I pulled away from the kiss and looked over at her. "No. You can have my room as long as you need. This was my fault."

She smiled. "No, it wasn't. It sounds like all you did was protect your girl. I wouldn't expect anything less from a good guy like you but thank you. I can go to my mom's until my apartment is ready once she's back in town. I just need a few days. I'll give you guys some time to talk."

Before Sara could get far, Callie pulled her into a hug. "This isn't over. I will help you through this. He fucked us both over. It's our turn to hurt him."

Sara smiled and nodded. Then she whispered, "I brought my head-phones. Take your time and come get me when you are done."

Callie smirked and came back up to me, wrapping her arms around my waist. "What did you do?" she asked, shaking her head.

After stealing a few more kisses, I sat her down and explained every-thing.

"From your texts with Sara, I knew you were just waiting to see if he had a hard copy. I have been following him for a few days. Yesterday, I was looking through the window when I saw him stand on a chair and open the air duct in the ceiling. I saw the camera and watched him put a new memory card in it. Then saw where he put the one he took out."

Callie smiled. I rubbed my thumb over her full lips, taking in the beauty of it.

"Did you know he didn't change the locks after you left? You gave me a key for emergencies, so I used it. When he left a few minutes after I saw him, I went to the box he had them in, and I found about ten memory cards. I...I am sorry to say, but I watched them all. Luckily, it looked like everything he had been blackmailing you with, and everything he seemed to have over Sara, was in there. Even a few other women I don't know."

I shrugged, knowing I didn't really need to continue, but I did anyway. "I got them all, Callie. I messaged Beck to let him know I found everything, and I would need his help as soon as I could tell you everything and get Sara somewhere safe. I guess he misunderstood and just did it. The good news is there are now no hard copies and nothing on his phone or computer. You are both safe now."

She straddled me and leaned in for a kiss. I just about lost my breath when her tongue touched mine. Her mouth moving down my neck and biting lightly on my collar bone sent all the blood in my body rushing to my cock. She pulled away for a moment and placed her hands on either side of my face.

"I love you, Nicholas James Clark." She gave me another peck on the lips. "Thank you. Thank you so fucking much. I was so scared that I would never—" She cut herself off, and tears began to fall. "I thought I would never be able to kiss you again. I thought you would move on after being mad long enough. You just waited all this time, and then I went and fucked it all up. I thought for sure you would just finally give up on me. Instead, you helped me without me even knowing."

She sat back a little and gripped my chin harshly. She got really close and looked me in the eyes. "If you ever invade my privacy again, I will hurt you in unspeakable ways." She laughed against my lips, but I knew she wasn't joking.

"I will agree to that on one condition."

"Name it."

I removed the smile from my face so she wouldn't think I was joking in any way. I ran my fingers through her hair on one side, and she leaned into my touch.

"If anyone ever, and I mean ever, tries to hurt you again, you will tell me, immediately. You are not allowed to run away like that again." Her smile dropped a little, "Callie, I told you, this is forever. I meant it when I said you were mine. You are not going anywhere. You sure as hell aren't moving anywhere in January. I don't know what we will have to do to get—"

She placed her finger over my lips to shut me up. She leaned down to whisper in my ear. "Sara is taking my apartment. I wasn't going anywhere." She leaned back. "Once I realized there would eventually be a fix for the Jake issue, I knew I wasn't going to leave. It is the perfect little two bedroom for Sara and her baby. She can afford it, so we transferred the lease into her name. Mom knows the landlord, that's how I got it so cheap in the first place."

I stood up excitedly, and she gripped onto me for dear life. "Thank fucking God." I took her lips in mine and walked Callie to her room, stopping a few times to kiss her against the wall and then the door.

I pulled my face away. "I have one more secret," I admitted. She looked worried. "I dyed my hair for you. I overheard you say you didn't like blonds to Aubs, and I wasn't able to get it out of my head, so I just dyed it, and I've been secretly doing it every few weeks since the day we went out for your birthday. I wanted to do everything I could to make you mine."

She ran her fingers through my hair and smirked. "I know, baby. You can't hide that smell." She let out a chuckle. "I love you, blond or not."

Callie leaned in and whispered against my lips with a smile. "Are you going to punish me now?"

I growled and squeezed her ass before pushing her bedroom door open and throwing her onto the bed. "You have no fucking idea what I am going to do to you, baby. My hand hasn't been nearly good enough."

"I might have some idea," she joked.

I kissed her so deeply I felt like we were becoming one. I couldn't hold her tight enough. I didn't know why, but my eyes were stinging with tears. Callie noticed and held me at arm's length.

"What is it? What's wrong?"

I kissed her softly on the lips and continued kissing down her neck, trying anything to make the tears go away, but nothing worked. I finally looked her in the eyes. "I thought I lost you, Callie."

"Baby, I am so sorry." She kissed one tear away as it fell. "So fucking sorry."

"I know."

She pushed me back and stood up. I realized quickly that she was switching places with me and getting on top. She spoke as she started kissing down my body.

"I love you, and not just with my heart. I love you with my entire soul. You are my forever. I don't know what possessed me to think I could fix this without you." She made her way down to my sternum, removed my shirt, and continued on. I let out an involuntary "fuck" at the feeling of her tongue tracing over my abs.

"Nick, I want to be consumed by you, every moment of every day. I need to know that I am yours." She bit my hip bone, making me moan again. My cock was straining against my jeans, it was almost painful.

"Callie," I groaned.

"I know, baby. I am getting there."

"Hurry up," I begged with a laugh.

She laughed, too, and then whispered, "Don't be so impatient, sir. I am trying to apologize for my mistakes."

"Fuck," I groaned, dragging out the U sound when she palmed my cock through my jeans.

"Apologize faster, baby. We can make love later. I need to fuck you right now. My cock has missed your pussy so bad."

She unbuttoned my pants and pulled them down my legs, flinging them across the room. Her tongue darted out, licking the tip of my cock. She blew air across the wetness her tongue had left. I was about to yell at her for teasing me but lost my breath when her hot, warm mouth wrapped around me.

"Fuck, baby, you feel so good."

I was still treading a little cautiously with her. I wanted to drive my cock down her throat, but I didn't want to lose any of the progress she'd made by being too forceful. I wrapped her hair around my hand, making her moan in pleasure. She began sucking even harder, and I felt my arousal heightening at the base of my spine, then traveling to my balls.

Callie took her mouth off me, and I whined in protest at the loss of her heat. "Are you going to shove your dick down my throat or what? I thought you didn't want to make love?"

I let out a low growl and smiled. I shoved her mouth down onto me. I let out a low "Fuck," and she giggled and tried to pull away to say something.

"Baby, you really shouldn't try to talk with your mouth full."

I shoved my cock down her throat, making her gag. Her eyes filled with tears, and she hummed around me. I thrust into her mouth two more times before I saw stars. I moaned, letting out words of praise as I let go of everything I had, and she took it all like the perfect good girl she was.

Callie removed her mouth from me once I was finished. She was the most beautiful sight I had ever seen, running her thumb across her lips and licking it clean to make sure she got it all.

She smirked, then bit her lip. "Apology accepted?" she asked innocently. She made a halo over her head with her fingers.

I sat up and took her shirt off, tweaking her nipple through her bra, making her let out a yelp. "You think that was enough to apologize for the hell you've put me through?"

She nodded with a smirk.

"I think it was almost enough," I agreed.

"What else can I do to make it up to you?"

She slid her hand behind her back, unclasping her bra, then handed it to me.

I threw it across the room and laid her back down on the bed. I pulled off her pants and lowered my face to her pussy. I ran my nose over her thong right between her slit. "You are going to let me worship this pussy until you have nothing left. Then maybe I can forgive you."

"You have a lot to make up for too, you know," she mewled.

I let out a hum and took her thong between my teeth, dragging it down her legs. I began kissing up her leg from her ankle. I waited until I reached the inside of her thighs before I spoke again. "Baby, I will make this up to you every day of my fucking life." I finally reached her entrance, and the moment my tongue touched her, she gasped.

Her hand went into my hair, gripping whatever she could grab. "God, I've fucking missed you."

"Not as much as I missed you." I ran my tongue over her, sucking her clit into my mouth. I sure had missed all the sounds that she made. My memories didn't do them justice, that was for sure.

She let out another intense moan as she pulled me into her with one hand and began playing with her breast and pinching her nipples with the other. I lifted her legs over my shoulders to get a different, deeper angle.

I began tongue fucking her as she was still grinding herself on me.

"Nick. Yes... Yes, baby. Fuck, I mis—" She cut herself off with a scream when her orgasm overtook her. I kept going until she had nothing left, making sure I didn't waste a single drop of her before pulling away.

She didn't let me get far. She pulled me up and kissed me like it was the last time she ever would.

After we both caught our breath, I felt her reach down and rub my cock over her entrance. Lifting her hips so the head of my cock was pushing into her. She let out a low moan. I let my arms relax so I slid deeper inside her. Through her moan, she said, "Now, fuck me like a good boy so we can get to the lovemaking I wanted."

I kissed her and pushed my cock slowly to the hilt, making her lift off the bed a little. "As you wish, baby. I hope you're ready because we are making love all fucking night long."

She whispered, "Forever and always."

CHAPTER FORTY

Callie

Jake made bail the next day. He called Sara a total of twenty-six times, and the last time I checked my phone had thirty-one missed notifications from him. Every message kept getting worse and worse. We brought the evidence of him harassing us to the police and both got a restraining order. He was still out on bail for the domestic dispute with Sara, but he would go to court in the beginning of January. I was hoping they would do something. Sara asked that she be given all the videos of her that Beck removed. She was hoping it would help her case by showing that she was filmed without her consent. She didn't want him getting anywhere near her and her baby.

Nick asked me if I wanted my videos and photos or if I wanted Beck to destroy them. I took a few days to think about it. I honestly just wanted to cut any ties I had with Jake. I didn't have the connection Sara did, so I could just be done if I wanted to, and ultimately that was what I chose. I knew it was the right decision.

New Year's Eve had snuck up on me with everything going on, and everyone was over our house to celebrate. I had to explain a few things when Aubrey and Lincoln realized Sara was still here a few days after Christmas. She only stayed for four days. In the meantime, she was able to move in with her mom until the apartment was available.

Aubrey was still not speaking to me for not telling her what was going on with Jake. She was mad that I went through it without her, but I knew she would get over it. She was just being a little petty. Lincoln was still talking to me, which meant she would be soon because she couldn't stand to have FOMO—fear of missing out. She couldn't be mad at me for too long. I was, after all, her only best friend, besides Nick.

Lincoln was giving me a weird look, and every time I glanced at him, he looked away. I was about to call him out when I felt a finger move my hair to one side and a warm breath traveled up the back of my neck. I leaned into Nick's touch as he whispered in my ear. "Don't make a scene, you will ruin everything."

I turned to look at him, and he motioned with his eyes over to Lincoln, who was leaving the room.

"Follow him," he added.

"Yes, sir," I joked. I was walking by each room, looking in because I had no idea where he'd gone. Lincoln's arm came out of nowhere and pulled me into Nick's room. Logically, I knew it was Link, but my fight or flight kicked in a little bit.

"What the...what are you doing?"

He was giving me a stern look. "When are you two going to get your shit together and talk?"

I laughed, covering my mouth when he shushed me. "Tell your girlfriend to get over it, and we will talk." I laughed again.

"I need you to fix it today, Callie." He ran his fingers through his hair. He had that James Dean look, but his hair was a little too long most of the time. Aubrey was the only person he would let near his hair. It was weird if you asked me. She doesn't even know how to make it look nice.

"It has to be today," he added.

There were beads of sweat lining his brow. He looked nervous, almost like he was going to puke. He even began pacing a little. I hadn't seen him like this since he made a grand gesture at one of Elijah's concerts this past summer when he basically confessed his love for Aubrey. Then it dawned on me.

"You're going to propose. Aren't you?" I said, rather loudly.

He cupped his hand over my mouth. "Tell the whole fucking house, why don't you? God, Cal. You suck at secrets."

He said it with a smile, so I knew he was joking...at least a little bit.

"Oh. My Gosh, Link!" I went to pull him into a hug, but then I froze. "Wait, she will kill you if you propose on a holiday. She hates that cliché shit"

"I know. I am doing it on the second. Two is her favorite number."

I rolled my eyes. Sometimes he talked to me like she wasn't my soul-mate first. "I know two is her favorite, Link." I smacked his shoulder. "Why didn't you tell me sooner? What the fuck? I could have helped with everything."

"I thought Nick would have told you. He has known for a while that I was going to do it."

"Nick fucking knows, and I didn't?" I slapped him again. "What the fuck! How could you guys not tell me?"

"Well, you weren't talking to anyone, Callie. What did you expect me to do?"

I looked down at my feet. "Shit, you're right. Sorry." I looked back up at him. "I'm really sorry."

He pulled me into a hug. "I know you are, and I'm sorry you didn't feel you could come to any of us for help." Then he pulled back to look at me. "Don't do that shit again."

I was about to speak, but the door opened. Aubrey leaned on the doorframe and crossed her arms.

"Am I interrupting something?"

I knew she wasn't the least bit concerned about catching us in a hug. She knew better than to think I would ever do something like that to her. But I knew how to make her blood boil a little. I looked her dead in the face and smirked. "Yeah, actually, you are. I was just about to take his pants off and suck his dick."

Lincoln's face drained of all its color.

"No.. no.. it's not—"

Aubrey put her hand up. "Stop stammering, Link. She was just trying to make me mad." She looked back at me while still talking to him, "It didn't work."

She and I remained staring at each other for a moment. I needed to get her to forgive me if I was going to be able to celebrate with her in a few days. Joking about sucking her boyfriend's dick probably wasn't the best way to break the ice.

"Link, give us the room, please?" I asked.

He looked at Aubrey for confirmation.

"Don't worry, I'm not going to fuck her or anything," I joked.

Aubrey gestured for him to leave. He kissed her head and then widened his eyes at me. I got the silent hint to fix it as he'd demanded a few minutes prior. Once the door shut, she sat on the edge of the bed and looked at me, waiting for me to talk.

"Did you need something?" I asked.

"Nope," she said curtly, popping the p.

"Then why did you interrupt us? We were just getting to the good part." I smiled, knowing my smile would make hers appear.

She smiled but tried to hide it by looking down at her hands. "Shut the fuck up." She paused, then looked back up at me. "I am so fucking mad at you."

"I know."

"Callie, you can't do shit like that. We don't keep secrets. I hate that you didn't—"

"I know." I grabbed her hand.

"Callie, you almost lost everything."

"I know."

She stood up. "Stop saying you know. I hate that."

We both laughed.

"I know," I said one more time with a big smile.

Her smile matched mine. "God, I fucking hate you sometimes." She let out another laugh.

I sat next to her and pulled her into a big hug. Then I looked her right in the eyes, knowing she might try to choke me out, and said for the final time, "I know."

We sat and chatted a little more so I could share Sara's whole story with her in more detail now that she wasn't seething with anger.

We started to walk out the door, but she stopped me.

"Wait, why were you and Link in here?"

I smiled, trying to keep it normal and not an 'Oh my god, you are going to be engaged smile.'

"He just wanted to see if I was okay. He knew that not talking to each other was bothering me."

She looked at me, narrowing her eyes, trying to gauge if I was lying. She clearly saw something because her eyes went wide. She began jumping up and down, covering her mouth as she excitedly chanted, "Yes, yes, yes."

"When?" She looked at me expectantly.

"When what?" I asked, keeping my face as neutral as possible.

"Bitch, tell me, or I'll stay mad. We don't keep secrets. We just went over this."

I opened the door, then whispered in her ear. "This one I take to the grave."

Chapter Forty-One

Nick

Lincoln explained himself when he walked out of the bedroom. He didn't have to. I assumed he was finally talking to her about the engagement.

"Dude, why didn't you tell her? She was so damn mad. She is going to seriously hurt you for not telling her."

I smiled. "I can't fucking wait."

"I hope they make up. I don't think I can wait. I need her to be able to be excited with her best friend."

"Callie will fix it. She will make sure everything is good. Those girls in there are true soulmates. They will always love each other more than they even love us. Nothing will come between them."

"I know. I'm just nervous."

"I get it, man. Come on, let's have a beer while we wait for them to kiss and make up."

Brie, Amani, and Beck were all sitting on my couch, and Link sat down in the chair. Elijah was sitting in front of Brie on the floor. The band was on a two-week break until their next show in New York. They parked their tour bus in Lincoln's driveway. We knew Elijah would tag along for the night with Link and Aubrey. He was always welcome, but we also invited Beck over as a thank-you. Elijah had also mentioned Beck would be alone since he was coming, so it was a no-brainer.

The rest of the guys flew to Tennessee to spend the holidays with their families. From what I had heard through Link, Elijah didn't speak to his family—only his brother, Owen, who was in the band with him. I had no idea about Beck's situation, but I was glad he came and we could get to know him a little better.

Callie hadn't seen them yet since she was in the room with Link when they arrived. She didn't know Beck was coming, so I hoped she wouldn't cry when she thanked him. I didn't want her to get all nervous.

The girls came walking out of the room, smiling arm in arm.

"There are my girls," I murmured. I realized I said it out loud when Link's head turned toward them, and he stood up.

"Thank God. That was the worst time of my life."

Aubrey looked up at him. "Oh, so the time we spent apart after breaking up wasn't bad for you?" she asked slyly.

He pulled her into a passionate kiss. "We didn't break up. You took a vacation without me. But you're right, that was absolute torture."

She laughed and kissed him again. "Whatever you say, Grumpy Butt." She patted his chest and walked back into the living room. Link followed right behind her and sat down first to pull her onto his lap.

Callie hugged me and whispered in my ear, "Everything is fine. Oh, and I am going to kill you for not telling me about the engagement."

I whispered back with a smile. "I can't wait, baby."

We walked further into the room when Callie became rigid. She saw Beck joking with Amani and Brielle and looked straight at me. I knew she was silently thanking me for inviting him, so I nodded.

"Hey," Callie said, walking into the room. Elijah got up and hugged her.

"Damn girl, you smell good."

"Watch yourself," I murmured with a smile. Elijah and Callie both let out a laugh.

"Don't listen to him. You can compliment me anytime you want," Callie joked and slapped his chest.

Beck stood up and put out his hand to shake Callie's. "Nice to see you again."

Callie's demeanor dropped a little. "Can I hug you?" she whispered.

He smiled, "Of course you can."

He looked a bit awkward and uncomfortable, but she pulled him into a hug and just kept saying thank you over and over again. He got a little more comfortable after she let go. I got the impression he wasn't used to being praised or thanked for anything.

Once they pulled away, he put both hands in his pockets. "Don't sweat it." He shrugged. "It really was nothing. It didn't take long at all." He looked over at me. "I am just glad I was able to help when Nick reached out."

I walked up beside Callie and put my arm around her. "We are both very thankful for you."

He nodded and went back to his conversation with Amani.

Brielle was making her way into the kitchen, so I followed her. She was looking a little down.

"What's with the long face, pip?"

She rolled her eyes. "I hate when you call me that. I am not a little pipsqueak anymore."

"You are to me," I laughed. "The girls both have a nickname, and you needed one too."

She looked at me with a sad smile and changed the subject. "I'm just worried is all."

Concern filled my stomach. "Worried about what?" I was pretty sure it wasn't my business, but I knew if she didn't want to talk about it she would tell me to fuck off.

"Eli. He seems so," she paused. "I don't know, different. Like he is acting like himself but... different somehow, and a lot more drunk."

"At least he is a happy drunk, right?"

She gave me a half smile and nodded. "Sure."

We chatted for a few more minutes until there were about thirty seconds until the new year. I gave Brie a quick hug and headed toward my girl. I saw her standing across the room at the entrance to the hallway, staring at me with a smile on her face. She curled a finger, beckoning me, so of course I obliged. When I reached her, she leaped into my arms and brought her legs around my waist.

"I am glad this new year is starting off with a bang."

I gave her a sly look and pressed her against the wall, my hardening cock pushing against her. "I'll give you a good bang."

I took her lips into mine as our friends' voices faded in the background.

"...Three. Two. One."

After everyone finished screaming and hugging each other, we sat with our friends and shared our resolutions and what we wanted to gain from the year. Most of the answers were similar. A few people talked about weight loss. Brielle was hoping for a new internship. She didn't say why, but she made it seem like she wasn't very happy with her current one. Of course, Elijah said the dumbest thing he possibly could have.

"My resolution is to get in Brielle's pants."

She scoffed and rolled her eyes at him as a slight blush covered her cheeks. "Eli, you're hot, but I wouldn't even let you in my pants if you were the last man on earth." She and Aubrey broke out into a laugh.

Brielle was the only one who ever called him Eli. He corrected anyone else who did.

"I would," Amani butted in.

Brielle gave her a surprised look. "Hey, what about solidarity? What about girl code?"

"Girl code only exists if you dated him. I mean, just look at him. He is a fucking sex god. If he weren't head over heels for you and wouldn't leave me for you in a heartbeat, I would have already had that dick inside me."

Brielle spit out her water, and she and Elijah both looked at Amani and then at each other.

"I'm not... I mean, Brie is great, but I was...fuck. That backfired on me, huh?" Elijah laughed nervously, rubbing the back of his reddening neck.

"You walked right into that, bro," Beck added before sipping his beer.

Brie patted his shoulder. "It's okay, Eli. We both know you could never handle my amazingness anyway. You will have to obsess from a distance, Mr. Rockstar."

Everyone laughed except for Lincoln, who was, for whatever reason, still staring Elijah down like he knew something we all didn't.

Everyone was spending the night. Elijah and Beck took the couch and chair. Brielle and Amani brought their own blow-up mattress, and Link and Aubrey took Callie's room.

As I was lying in my bed with my perfect girl snoring lightly beside me, I couldn't help but think about how my life had changed so much over the years. I was really excited to see where this new year would take us.

I loved having a house full of people. For a long while, it had been me and my grandma alone. Of course, I always had my friends around, but this felt different. This felt like the perfect start to a new time in my life—a new life with Callie, a life where we'll become a family of our own.

Chapter Forty-Two

Callie

My best friend's life was about to be changed forever. Lincoln planned everything. Even down to what I needed to have Aubrey wear. He thought it was still a surprise, and I didn't want to ruin that. Aubrey was very observant and far from stupid. She knew that something was up when I wouldn't tell her why Link was talking to me. She made it clear to him that he was to make sure that four people knew beforehand when he was going to propose. He needed to include Brielle and me. He was told to ask both her dads, which one of them is his dad, too...technically. It's weird to think about, but they aren't blood-related, so it's all fine.

She and Lincoln have the craziest story, and they owe it all to fate. She knew from the moment she met him that they were fated to be together. They just had a few hiccups along the way.

When I first met Lincoln, I knew he was her person. I could just tell. That was honestly what made me start questioning my relationship with Jake. So I guess you could say fate played a part in my journey, too. If I hadn't questioned my relationship in the way I had been, I never would have gone home that night instead of staying at Aubrey's, and I never would have caught him cheating. I wouldn't be with Nick right now. I would probably be miserably married to Jake.

I would never know what could have been, and I am completely okay with that. I am excited to see where this life will take us.

I told Aubrey I wanted to have some best friend pictures done of us to start the new year. Brielle, of course, was taking them for us because she was a photographer as well as an artist. Luckily, it snowed, so the ground was covered in fluffy white beauty. Perfect for a winter engagement shoot, which was obviously what the real photo shoot would be.

Aubrey asked me if she needed to get her nails done, which meant she totally knew because she wasn't normally the type to get her nails done. Like I said, she's observant. I told her no to try to throw her off, but she made both of us an appointment anyway.

I tried to make the photoshoot seem very nonchalant, and Lincoln had planned to do it at our house in the backyard since there was a cute little gazebo.

Our house.

I am still getting used to that. It had only been a few days since I had actually started thinking of it as our house and not just Nick's. I totally should have felt that way for a long time now, since it's been months since I moved in, but thinking of this being our house now feels...good. It feels safe. I have always felt safe with Nick. I am glad I finally realized it.

We had Aubrey's parents, both sets, hidden in Nick's room with Link, my mom, Elijah, and Amani. Everyone who was close to us is here. I wanted this to be the best moment of her life.

When Link professed his love to her back in June, we joked that Link's proposal better be fucking perfect. He had a lot to live up to with how perfect his speech was at the concert.

Hearing that people might assume she means extravagant and big, but not for Aubrey. She liked things simple and quiet with just the important people around, which was why I was so proud of Link for planning all this. It was going to be exactly what she always hoped for.

We walked in the house, and I think she expected to see some clues of more people, but she didn't. Like I said, Link had planned this completely. He knew she shared her location with her parents, Brielle and himself, so he had everyone but Brielle leave their phones at home so all the locations would not show here. I told him she wouldn't think of that, but she was currently pulling it up, so I guess I was wrong.

I saw her face fall at the realization that no one was here but us, and Brielle's location showed she was on her way to us.

She looked at me with sad eyes. "This is really just a bestie shoot, huh?"

I shrugged, "I told you it was."

"Damn. I really had myself thinking he was proposing today. He has been so weird lately. I guess he's just been busy."

Then it was like a lightbulb went off in her head.

"You don't think he is ch—"

"Don't even finish that sentence." I cut her off because I didn't want her to have that thought for one minute. Plus, what if he heard her? He would be devastated.

"You never thought Jake would do it to you," she stated.

"Aubrey, really? This is Link we are talking about. He worships the ground you fucking walk on."

She shook off the thought. "Wow, you're right. Sorry, I lost myself for a second. He would never. Damn, I just really thought…Never mind. You told me it was just a photoshoot for us, and you meant it."

She linked her arm to mine, and I put my head on her shoulder. "I just wanted to do something nice for you as an apology for not looping you in on the Jake drama." She smiled at me. "It will happen when he's ready. You guys were fated to be together forever. No one has a more perfect story than you."

She nudged me with her hip to get me to look at her and raised her eyebrows. "Except for my two best friends, their story is one for books."

"Me and Nick?" I asked with wide eyes.

"No, Beavis and Butt-head," she rolled her eyes. "Who else would I be talking about?"

I smiled. "Shut up."

She laughed, "What? You and Nick are the perfect best friends to lovers." She paused, "or is it enemies to lovers, since you guys hated each other?"

I scoffed. "I never hated him."

"I know, I'm just kidding." She pulled me into a hug. "You guys have the perfect story and it isn't even done being written yet."

"Thanks, Aubs."

The doorbell rang, and we both looked over and saw Brielle through the glass on the door. Then we heard something from my room, and I had to avert Aubrey's attention back to me.

I smacked her butt and twirled her toward the backyard. "Let's go take some hot ass pictures."

NICK

Lincoln was pacing back and forth when we heard the doorbell and he jumped. Callie's mom made an excited sound, and I put my finger over my mouth to quiet her.

"Sorry," she whispered.

"It's okay, it's exciting. We are almost there," I whispered back.

Once we heard the back door shut, we waited for a text from Brielle. When they were set, we made our way to the side of the house. Lincoln was waiting inside by the back door. He let them take a few pics, and then I walked out back, acting like I had just gotten home.

"Hey beautiful ladies." All three of them turned toward me. Callie came over and kissed me.

"Hey, you."

I pulled her into a deeper kiss and I heard Brielle make a gagging noise. Callie and I laughed against each other's mouths.

"Go take your damn pictures so I can finish this kiss."

Brielle instructed them to take a photo with Aubrey's back to the door and Callie beside her. She called it an "I got your back picture". I thought that was brilliant. It gave Lincoln time to come out and kneel behind her.

A moment later, Brielle asked them to turn around and caught the picture of Aubrey's face, seeing Link down on one knee and everyone else behind him. She looked over at Callie and me in a silent thank you. She looked back at Link with so much love and appreciation.

"Lincoln," she whispered.

"Hey, Songbird. You look beautiful."

I think I heard a small sniffle from Lincoln. Callie came up beside me and hugged me around my waist. I looked down at her and kissed her nose. "I love you."

She leaned up and kissed mine. "I love you more."

We both watched our best friends' dreams come true. If anyone deserved this, it was Aubrey.

"Songbird, this past year has been a whirlwind. It has been full of excitement and pain and I wouldn't change a single moment of it for anything," he paused. "Except maybe the nickname you gave me."

Everyone laughed.

It was a pretty weird nickname. She calls him Grumpy Butt. They really were perfect for each other. Their weirdness just fits.

"Aubrey, I love you with all my heart. You have completed my life in a way I never thought possible."

Callie squeezed me tight with every word Lincoln said. I could tell she was trying not to cry, and honestly, my eyes were stinging a little, too.

We all watched Lincoln as he continued one of the most beautiful speeches I think I'd ever heard.

"Fate brought you home to me and made me a believer in what is meant for you will always find a way. Aubrey Lynn Miller, will you make me the happiest and luckiest man in the world and be my forever?"

Aubrey let out a cry and fell to the ground covering herself in snow. She wrapped her arms around his neck, kissing him all over his face. Everyone smiled and let out a few laughs.

"Yes. Yes. Yes." She was ending each kiss on his face with a yes.

After everyone gave their congratulations, we made our way inside since it was so cold out. We sat around chatting, and the girls were already making plans and talking about wedding colors.

I couldn't help but smile across the room at Callie. She looked so happy and carefree. She had been through hell and back in such a short amount of time, and I hoped the universe got it out of its system for now.

Callie must have heard my thoughts because she looked over at me and smiled even bigger. She mouthed, "I love you so much," before blowing me a kiss. I made a show of catching it and fell backward into the counter dramatically. I heard her beautiful giggle from across the room.

"You guys are sickening," Elijah joked.

I patted his arm. "Thanks. I will take that as a compliment."

Before he could say anything else, I went into the hallway, motioning with my head to get Callie to follow me.

I shut the door behind us, and before I could fully turn toward her, she had me up against the door. I was hoping the loudness of my friends and family chatting hid the thump of my body. I ran my hands in her hair, cupping her face. I never wanted to let her go. I was praying I never had to again.

"I miss you," Callie said as she pulled away.

I smiled and let out a laugh. "I am right here, baby." I ran my thumb over her bottom lip.

She nuzzled her face into my hand. "I know, but I just missed kissing you."

I smirked, placing a light kiss on her forehead. "You kiss me anywhere, anytime you are missing me. I don't care who's around. You get anything you want from me. All you have to do is take it, baby."

Her playful look changed into a much more serious one. "I want to spend forever with you."

Her admission surprised me, and I let my hands fall. I knew I felt that way, and would marry her tomorrow if she let me. I knew she loved me, but didn't in a million years think about bringing up marriage so soon after her relationship with Jake.

"I didn't mean right now," she stammered. "I...damn...I scared you. Sorry, I didn't mean to drop that on you. I just—"

I cut her off with a kiss. A kiss so deep neither one of us would ever forget it. I pulled away, and she was smiling again.

"Sweets, I didn't have that look because I don't want to spend forever with you. That's literally the only thing I want in this life is for you to be mine forever. I just didn't expect you to say it first."

She began to blush. "What do you mean, say it first?"

I stepped in even closer to her and held both her hands in mine. "Callie, I would marry you tomorrow if you let me. I didn't want to rush you. I didn't want to overwhelm you with everything that's been going on."

She looked up at me. "Can we? Tomorrow?"

My stomach filled with excitement, but I knew she deserved more than that. "What? Callie, we can't elope. Our friends and your mom would kill us." I stated.

"We don't have to elope. Let's just tell everyone we're going to city hall. I don't want to spend one more day not being yours."

I picked her up, and she wrapped her legs around me. "Baby, I don't need a piece of paper to know that you are mine. Let them have their wedding time. I want to give you the wedding you deserve. I want to have fun planning it and give you everything you wanted."

She looked at me in disbelief. "I don't want anything but you, Nick."

I gave her a serious look. "Baby, let me do this for you. Please."

She looked at me, seeming to consider something. Then she spoke against my lips. "I will love you forever, whether we are married or not." She gave me another passionate kiss.

When we pulled away, I looked her in the eyes, and we said it at the same time... "Forever and Always."

Callie

EPILOGUE

May

I just called Brielle to make sure she was on her way to help me set up for Aubrey's engagement party at the restaurant. Luckily, the weather held out, and we could have the party on the roof deck just like we were hoping.

She was talking to me through her car's Bluetooth since she was driving, so I could barely hear her.

"I will be there in twenty minutes. I had to pick up Eli."

"Hey Calster, what's up, girl?"

Calster? His speech was very slurred, and alarm bells went off in my head. There was no way this man was going to show up to a party where his best friend is celebrating and be sloshed. He was the best man for crying out loud.

"Elijah, are you drunk? It is ten in the morning."

"It's five o'clock somewhere, babyyy," he said, dragging out the "E" sound.

I slapped my hand to my face in disgust. "You better not be too drunk. I will kick your ass out. Do you hear me? This is an important day for Aubs and Link."

"I will be fine I—"

Brielle cut him off. "I will watch him. He is fine."

"No, I will have Nick watch him. You are the maid of honor. You have more than enough to do."

"Callie, I got it, okay?" She sounded very mad and I didn't see that side of her often, so I let it go.

"Fine. See you in twenty."

She hung up, and I immediately notified Nick and Link. I didn't want anyone ruining this for Aubrey.

A few hours later, everything was going off without a hitch. Aubrey was surprised. We told her we were going to do it in the summer, and then moved it up because her dad, August, and his wife, Liza, were going to be up here for a few days. I loved surprising her because she hated surprises so much. She literally had to know everything, all the time.

Nick was doing a good job of keeping an eye on Elijah, so it made my life a lot easier. Brielle made a speech and had everyone crying. Including myself. I still believed she should be a writer since she was so damn creative, but she's always stuck to art and photography.

I saw Amani flirting with Beck and one of the other guys. It almost looked like both guys had their hands on her, but I couldn't see that well now that it was getting dark and the fairy lights were the only light source.

Nick asked me to dance, and when I went to protest that he needed to stay with Elijah, he motioned over to Elijah who was having a heated conversation with Brielle. I knew that conversation would take a few minutes, so we danced.

As the song was ending, I saw Brielle excuse herself and go into the bathroom, so I walked over to talk to Elijah.

I stared out onto the dance floor where Nick was now dancing with Aubrey's mom. Her mom saw me staring and pretended to grab his ass, so I dragged my hand across my neck in a cutting motion. I was joking, of course. I didn't plan on saying anything to him. I just wanted to sit with him. I tried my best to look forward and watch the man of my dreams smiling and laughing. Elijah's voice cut me off.

"You really love him, huh?"

I looked over at him and could tell he was still two sheets to the wind. Luckily, he was a nice drunk for the most part. His eyes looked sad.

"Are you okay?" I asked. I completely ignored his question, but I knew he didn't need an answer.

"I will be. I just need to get my shit together."

I gave him a surprised look.

"What?" he asked.

"Nothing. I just thought I was going to have to say it." I smiled, trying to ease the tension.

"Thanks, friend," he said sarcastically.

I nudged his arm with mine. "You know if you need help, all you have to do is ask, right? We are all here for you."

I looked around the room to find Brielle who was dancing with Link, then looked back at Elijah, motioning over toward Brie with a nod. "Especially that one over there."

He looked me in the eye this time. "Brielle? She basically hates me now. She pretty much wrote me off when I told her I didn't need rehab. She told me to get it together or never talk to her again."

"So, what are you going to do?"

He was quiet for a moment and smirked, looking down at his feet. "I looked up a few rehabs before the party."

My eyebrows went up in surprise. That is definitely not what I thought was going to come out of his mouth.

"It's kind of funny. I have heard that line a thousand times, and I've always chosen to just not talk to whoever said it. My entire family, for example. But with her...I just...I don't think I can choose not to talk to her. It's different. It's like the thought of not seeing or talking to her is more important than getting rid of this pain with alcohol. No one has ever cared enough to offer me help and kindness like she has."

He looked over at me; I thought for validation, but I was speechless at his rawness. He was about to say something else, but Nick interrupted us.

"Can I steal my girl for a minute?"

"Steal away, my guy," Elijah stated.

I leaned in to kiss Elijah's cheek before getting up. "She cares about you more than you think."

Before I could pull away completely, Elijah grabbed my wrist. "This stays between us, okay?"

I made the zipper motion across my lips before smiling and walking away to dance with my man again.

Nick twirled me around, pulling me in with his arm around my hip with my back to him. He whispered in my ear. "Do I need to fight Elijah?

I turned in his arm and kissed him. "Calm it down, caveman. I only have eyes for you."

"You better."

I couldn't help but look over to Elijah while I was dancing. I know he would make the right decision for himself, but it really hurt to see him hurting like that. We had been getting a little closer with each other since Brielle, Nick, him and I were all in the bridal party. We had a group chat, and we basically bullshit or throw ideas for wedding stuff out. It helped me learn a lot more about him.

"What's on your mind, Sweets?" Nick's voice pulled me from my thoughts.

"Hmm?"

"What are you thinking about? You just went to another world for a second."

"I'm fine." I smiled at him, "I'm just thinking about how lucky we are to have the friends we do. I am grateful for every single one of them."

Nick chuckled. "Me too, baby."

After we got home that night, I changed and went into the kitchen to find a note from Nick.

Meet me at your favorite place.

My piano.

I walked into the sunroom where my piano sat. Nick was there, smiling at me with sheet music in his hand.

"What's this?" I asked, taking it from him.

My stomach dropped when I saw it was the music for Make You Feel My Love by Adele. I stared at it for a moment then looked back at him.

"I don't need this. I know how to play it."

His smile was sweet, and it almost looked like he was blushing, "But I don't."

"What?" It came out choked. The tears were stinging my eyes. My heart began to melt. Was he asking what I thought he was?

"Teach me to play our song."

I couldn't help myself. I was so overcome with emotion that I straddled him and kissed him. We kissed for a few minutes when he pulled back a little and laughed. "Is that a yes?"

I nodded. "It's a yes."

He looked really nervous like he still had something to say. "Turn it over."

I gave him a questioning look but did as he asked.

His grip on me tightened. "Is that a yes, too?"

Will You Marry Me?

I looked at him; the tears flowing freely now. Before he could speak again, I grabbed his face in my hands. "I thought we were waiting."

"I told you I wanted you to have everything you ever wanted. You and Aubrey have always wanted a double wedding. Now we can plan one. Plus, I didn't want to wait anymore."

"What about Aub–"

"She is the one who suggested it," Nick assured me. "I was telling her how I was going to propose, and she practically begged me not to wait. She said you guys have pages and pages of information about putting together a double wedding dating back to when you were young. I knew as soon as I saw it, this would be exactly what you wanted."

I kissed him passionately, "Yes. Yes. One hundred times, yes."

He pulled a beautiful princess-cut diamond ring out of his pocket. It was perfect. He was perfect.

He slipped it on my finger and looked into my eyes. "This is going to be my favorite moment forever."

I kissed him softly. "Forever and Always."

I kissed him softly. "Forever and Always."

Acknowledgements

Dave, once again, thank you for being my rock. Thank you for taking on the brunt of parenting when needed. The boys and I are so lucky to have an amazing man like you in our lives. I love you more than words.

Cooper and Carson, I love you more than the air I breathe. Thank you for letting mommy continue chasing her dreams. You are the best kids a girl could ask for. I can't wait to see what hopes and dreams you boys have, and I can't wait to help you achieve them.

I want to thank my parents for always instilling in my sister and me that we can do anything we set our minds to. I love you both so much.

Jahaira, thank you for being my best friend. Thank you for never letting me give up on myself. Thank you for enriching not only my book but also my life in more ways than one. I am so blessed to have you in my life as my sista from another mister. Thank you for helping me make this book what it is.

Jenn (AKA Bean), I love you so much. I am so grateful to have had you cheering me on and helping me edit this book. It couldn't have come to fruition without you.

Arthur and Lora- Thank you for being my sounding boards. I couldn't have gotten this book to where it is without you both. Thank you for dealing with my crazy voice notes and calls at anytime I needed you.

To my amazing editor Emarie, I AM OBSESSED WITH YOU. Thank you so much for helping me navigate this book. Thank you for helping me become a better writer. I don't know what I would do without you.

To my amazing cover designer Kristin- Thank you so much for this beautiful cover. You made magic happen with the mess of ideas in my brain. I can't wait to see how the rest of the series turns out.

Thank you to every family member, friend, and stranger who has supported me throughout this journey. I couldn't have done it without the help of all of you cheering me on.

To my readers, thank you for taking a chance on me and this debut series. I hope you all enjoyed Callie and Nick's story as much as I do. I hope you stick around to see where everyone's lives go in book three.

Content Warnings

Cheating (Not between MCs)

Loss of Parent/Grandparent

Revenge Porn

Blackmail

Domestic Violence

Sexual Assault

Therapy

Talk of abortion(Not MCs)

Talk of addiction(Not MCs)

About the Author

Danielle Lynn spends most of her time with her husband, Dave, and two amazing boys, Cooper and Carson. She gave up her career in data entry to take care of those perfect boys over seven years ago (totally willingly and happily) but lost who she was in the process. She was never a reader or writer until she needed something to help with her post-partum depression and anxiety. That is when she found books and writing. She currently lives in Connecticut. She can always be found writing, reading, or listening to music. She is so excited for all the amazing stories to come.

Where to follow Danielle for updates on future projects.

Also by Danielle Lynn

Danielle Lynn is also the author of the first novel in this fate series,

<u>Fate Will Bring You Home</u>

Fate Will Bring You Home is a story of Family, Love, and a little bit of
Fate. This story follows Aubrey and Lincoln and how their story began.
Catch the sneak peek on the next page.

Don't miss out on the next part of the story. Follow Danielle's socials
to discover what happens with Brielle and Elijah.

Preview of Fate Will Bring You Home

PROLOGUE

AUBREY

"Guys...I...I can't...breathe."

I'm unsure if what I just tried to say was said aloud or only in my head. I don't know what is happening to me. We are on our way to Nashville and have just made our last stop for gas in a town called White Mountain just. I was getting into the music and enjoying the view out the back window of Nick's car when my chest felt tight. It feels like someone is sucking the air out of my lungs. My heart feels like it will pound out of my chest, and my skin is feeling flushed.

I must have said it out loud because when I opened my eyes, I saw my friends and boyfriend looking at me with concern. My boyfriend Max seemed to realize what I said first, and he moved closer to me.

"Guys, something is wrong with Aubrey. Nick, pull over...Now!"

"What? What's wrong?" Callie asked turning toward the backseat.

"Aubs, do you need me to pull over?" Nick asked.

"Babe, are you okay?" Max asked.

All of their voices at the same time overwhelmed me even more. Max tried to put his hands around my shoulders to pull me into a hug, but the last thing I wanted right now was to be touched, so I pushed him away.

I started talking even louder. "Don't...touch...me," I said between gasps for air. "I... I can't—"

My eyes were filled with tears, and despite my best efforts to hold them in, they began falling down my face. I could hear my friends talking, but nothing was registering in my brain until Callie opened the back door and pulled me out of the car and the fresh air hit my face.

She placed a cold bottle of water on the back of my neck and pushed me down into a sitting position on the curb. Max must be holding the bottle because now she is squatting in front of me with both hands on my cheeks.

"Aubrey...Aubs, Look around and tell me five things you can see."

"What—"

"Aubrey, just do it," Callie said sternly.

"Sky...you...Max...ground...car," I said, still gasping.

"Okay, good. Name four things you can touch."

I put my hands down and then touched her hands on my cheeks. I was reaching out to feel anything within my immediate surroundings. "Grass...pavement...your hand, and my jeans." Speaking was a little easier, and there was less gasping.

"Good, you're doing great. Okay, now tell me three things you can hear."

I sat for a moment and closed my eyes.

"Um.. cars...your voice and Nick chewing."

I opened my eyes and gave Nick a look. He was constantly chewing with his mouth open. His face went a little pink. It made me smile because I realized I was starting to calm down.

Callie laughed and gave Nick the stink eye. "Of course you can hear his dumbass chewing," she scoffed. "So gross. Okay, now name two things you smell."

I stared at her, realizing I was almost completely calmed down, but I kept going. "My perfume and the Smarties on your breath." I almost laughed because this girl is forever eating those stupid candies.

"Fuck," she said as she laughed and covered her mouth. "Sorry. Okay, last one. Name one thing you can taste."

I took a deep breath before answering. "I can taste the chips Max and I were sharing."

She smiled at me. "Perfect." She removed her hands from my cheeks. "How are you feeling now?"

I looked around for a moment, and Nick and Callie were focused on me while Max was texting someone. That man is always so focused on his phone. I looked back at Callie and said, "Yes, I think so."

Callie helped me to my feet. I could feel the embarrassment flooding my cheeks. "Sorry guys. I don't know what that was. It came out of nowhere."

"It was a panic attack," Callie said confidently.

"A panic attack? I don't have a panic problem." It came out sounding more defensive than I intended. I really just meant I don't have anything like that wrong with me.

"Sometimes shit like that just happens. It was probably a one-and-done thing. Maybe you're just nervous about being away from your family. It's the first time, right?" Nick asked.

I nodded my head yes. This is the first time out of state for all of us except for Max and of course Nick who lived in a different state before moving to Connecticut.

This trip is the first college spring break for most of us, and we are meeting up with a few more classmates in Nashville, where we rented a huge house and are room-sharing to save money. The plan is to explore the music scene because most of us are music nerds in some way or another. Callie is a piano major, Nick majors in musical theater, and I plan to major in songwriting and voice. I want to be a singer-songwriter one day. Writing songs has always been my passion, but I could definitely improve my voice a little.

Max is a few years older and is on a hockey scholarship. He has hopes of getting drafted to play professionally. He supports my music obsession for the most part, but it has been half-hearted lately. Max finally got his face out of his phone and came over.

"Baby, I'm glad you are okay." He wrapped his arms around me. "I'm glad Cal knew how to do that weird breathing thing. I was clueless on how to help."

I rolled my eyes and pushed him off me.

"Let's just go; the others are probably waiting for us," I seethed. "I'm fine now."

As much as I was trying to be okay, I wasn't.

I took my phone out and started Googling panic attacks. I'm known for having no chill or patience; some might even call me neurotic. Some of these answers are just outrageous. I'm getting more and more uncomfortable as I read.

Callie reached back and grabbed my phone. "No Googling."

I tried to protest, but she turned back toward the front and turned my favorite song on loud enough so she couldn't hear me. As much as I wanted to grab it from her, I knew it was the right thing. I'm just praying it won't happen again and I can move past this.

I was so anxious and in my head the first few days that I could not bring myself to leave the house. I was rude to everyone whenever they tried to entice me to go with them. I'm surprised no one tried to off me with how irritable I've been. I haven't been able to get out of my head long enough to enjoy doing anything with my friends, so I keep making them go out without me.

Max and I have been doing exactly what we do at home: staying in, watching movies, and having mediocre sex. He doesn't ever plan anything outside of our dorms. He never wants to do anything new. Technically, he is on his phone when we're watching the movies. I always catch him smiling when he's talking to his friends, but he tells me not to worry about it when I ask who he's talking to. He's been so busy lately. He has canceled our last three date nights because of schoolwork and hockey practices to prepare the new guys for the games. He told me I couldn't attend his practice games anymore since looking at me was so distracting. I thought it was sweet, I guess.

I honestly didn't care much since I knew we were going on this trip together. I thought we would spend some time together and connect on this trip, and he might give the phone a rest, but I guess I was wrong.

Logically, I knew not going out and seeing Nashville was ridiculous, so this morning, I was able to muster up some courage and go out. It's been a long day of music, fun, and food. We also took Callie to the airport before returning to the rental house. She is flying home to spend time with her boyfriend, Jake, for the remainder of the break. Tomorrow is our last day here, but Nick, Max, and I have a few stops planned for the way home.

The Next Day

We were driving to our next stop today, and Nick said it was a surprise as to where. We had the windows down, and I heard some fantastic music that drew me in. I looked around to find the source, and then I spotted it.

"Nick, stop!" I shouted as I reached out and grabbed his arm. "Look at that coffee shop, it's music-themed. It's so stinking cute." I gave my best attempt at puppy dog eyes. I know I'm acting pathetic, but they love me and won't judge. "Can we go?"

"Aubs, everything here is music-themed," he said with a chuckle.

"Nick, please. There is something about it that's calling me."

Nick looked at Max, and he shrugged. I got weirdly sad that his response was so uncaring, but I'm learning I shouldn't be surprised by his lack of enthusiasm. His interest in anything related to spending time with me has been going downhill for months.

As we walked up to the shop, the music stopped, and one of the men who had been playing welcomed us.

"Welcome to Brew Beats."

"Thank you!" I said in an excited voice. "This is such a cute shop; I just had to stop. Is it yours?"

"Oh no, no. Just one of the many places we meet up when we're all free." He gestured to the three other men sitting with him. They were eccentric-looking, and I loved it.

We all grabbed a coffee and settled at one of the tables outside to continue talking to the band. They were all so welcoming and sweet. The one who had greeted us initially was a hippy-dippy type who talked about auras, fate, and the planets aligning. I ignored most of that stuff because I don't believe in it, but I would never stop someone from talking about what they love.

We started telling them about ourselves. Nick was chatting with one of the guys sitting a little farther away from the door while I chatted with our hippy friend.

"I love playing guitar and—" He cut me off and tried handing me his guitar.

"Here, play me something." He tilted it toward me.

"Oh no, I couldn't. That guitar looks special," I said nervously.

"Please, it would be a pleasure to hear you play it," he insisted.

I was hesitant, but I obliged. The guitar was a vibrant shade of green, almost like the color of fresh grass in the summer, with darker green striations throughout. The sleek and glossy finish of the body made it even more enchanting to look at. The fretboard was adorned with intricate inlays that added a touch of elegance to it. The sound that emanated from this guitar was just as beautiful as its appearance, producing clear and crisp notes that seemed to resonate with my soul. It was a truly breathtaking instrument that any musician would be lucky to own. It's not something you see every day. The moment I played it, I felt a release of stress.

After playing a few songs, I handed it back to him. "Thank you, I needed that. I'm saving up to buy a new one. Someone stole mine from my dorm a few weeks ago, so it felt really good to play again."

"No problem; it was a pleasure to hear you play."

He started telling us about his touring days and how his band had opened for some of the greats like Journey, Def Leppard, and even Rascal Flatts. I was blown away by how many pictures he had. He shared that he stopped touring because his health was declining.

"Oh, I'm so sorry to hear that."

"Oh, sweetheart, I'm not. I have a beautiful wife and people who miss me when I'm on the road. Spending time with them is more important than being a rock star. My wife is my once-in-a-lifetime love, and I will take advantage of the time I have left with her." He seemed a little sad at that admission, but he continued. "She and I both help out at my best friend's shop a few towns over so were playing and listening to music all day which is good enough for me. As long as she is there, that is all I need."

His story was breaking my heart. I didn't ask exactly what was wrong with him because it was none of my business, and he was a stranger, but my heart goes out to him.

Max was bored, so he went off and found an arcade down the road. Nick and I ended up talking to them for three hours. We got up to leave, and my hippy friend pulled me aside.

"Here, I want you to have this."

My eyes went wide. I was so surprised that I blushed and laughed. Blushing is my telltale sign that I'm uncomfortable.

"What?" I asked.

He stood there with his arm outstretched, holding the guitar towards me. I put my hands up in protest. "Oh no, I can't. Thank you so much for the offer. It's very kind."

He continued looking at me but pulled the guitar back and set it down. "Please, I insist. It sounds like you have an amazing music career ahead of you, plus it's filled with good juju. I got it from my best friend. You actually remind me of him."

This man. This is the sweetest thing someone has ever offered me. I don't know how else to decline politely. I could never take something so precious. I insisted again, and he dropped the subject.

I walked around and said goodbye to everyone else we had met. Finally, I said goodbye to my new hippie friend. He told us to look him up if we ever returned to Nashville.

I couldn't shut up about them after we left. They were so cool. They almost felt like old friends; it was weirdly calming.

We stopped at our first gas station about two hours into the trip home. Max ran inside to pay for the gas, and Nick and I got out to stretch quickly.

"Hey, Aubs," Nick grabbed my arm. He looked a bit nervous. "There's...um, something for you in the trunk." I gave him a weird look and followed him to the back of the car as he popped open the trunk.

"What...I can't...How?" I was almost speechless; I couldn't believe what I was seeing. There, lying in the trunk, was the beautiful green guitar. I looked at Nick with tears in my eyes.

He shrugged. "He told me not to tell you until we were far enough away so you wouldn't make me turn back," Nick said hesitantly. "Maybe it was just one of those serendipitous things, and you were meant to meet. He said to contact him if we ever return, so maybe we can do that."

I looked back at the guitar as the tears wet my cheeks. Then I looked at Nick as regret struck me. "Nick...we didn't get his name."

FWBYH Chapter One

NOVEMBER FIVE YEARS LATER

AUBREY

I stood in the attic silently for what felt like forever. It was as if time was standing still or I was having an out-of-body experience. I wasn't quite sure what I was looking at, but I got the feeling that this paper was about to change everything.

I've seen this document a few times throughout my life. I needed it for important things such as obtaining my license or signing up for college. I would remember if it looked like this. Now that I think about it, I'm pretty sure I packed it already. Even if this is a duplicate, why would they be different? I definitely would've noticed...*right?*

My name on this birth certificate was different. I had my mom's maiden name. But the weirdest part is where my father's name should be...is blank.

I had to sit down because I was starting to have a panic attack. The walls felt like they were caving around me, and I couldn't steady my breath. I don't know the cause of these panic attacks, but I do remember when they started.

Lately, I've been panicking more often whenever I think about moving out. I'm leaving my parents' house to move in with my best friend Callie and her boyfriend Jake. She and I have been discussing and planning this day since we were ten. We have scrapbooks full of ideas. We have always said we were each other's soulmates, although we are opposite in every way. It seems to be a theme in my life because no one is ever like me.

Callie and I have always been close. We were roomies during college and planned to live together, or at least very close to each other, forever, no matter what. Even though she was in a relationship, she made it clear to her boyfriend that we would come as a package deal from the moment they met.

I insisted she and Jake take the house without me and start their life together. I was fine living at home with my family for now, while I'm still getting my music classes up and going. She was offended, saying she would never leave me high and dry. Luckily, he and I can tolerate each other. However, I always felt as if something was off with him, but if she was happy, I was happy.

Now, here we are, planning our move for next week. The move is the reason I'm even up here in my parent's attic. I was looking for Christmas decorations to decorate the new place because it's only a few weeks away. I want to be prepared, but nothing could have prepared me for this.

When I realized how badly I was panicking, I didn't know what else to do other than pick up the phone and call my sister.

My younger sister Brielle is my opposite in every way imaginable, but we are closer than any sisters I know. I've always been known as the girl with the hot, skinny younger sister. She's thin, like our parents, never having to watch what she eats. She's got dark hair and piercing green eyes that have some gold specks in them. She also has the cutest freckles across her cheeks, just like our dad. People are always drawn to her beauty. She also wears glasses that add to the hotness factor.

Besides looks, we're also opposite in personalities. I'm extroverted, and she's introverted. I'm loud, and she's soft spoken. Unless, of course, she's defending friends or family, then she is not someone you want to mess with. We have so many differences I can't even name them all.

I pressed her contact on my phone. It rang once and went to voice-mail, so I knew she was avoiding me on purpose. She's in the backyard, probably ignoring me to get me to go out there, but I tried again.

"What do you want?" She picked up on the second ring this time. I know she was trying to be funny because she laughed a little. She probably thought I was just being lazy.

I didn't speak right away. She got the hint and said, "I'm on my way."

I heard a thud before she hung up. I imagine she threw her book. Seconds later I heard the back door open and slam shut and her bare footsteps in the kitchen. She knew immediately that something was wrong and came running. This is one of the reasons she's my favorite person in the world. She just knows me. Luckily, she flew to the attic in just a few seconds.

"What's wrong?" She bent down and grabbed my shoulders to get me to look at her. I dropped the paper and stared at her. I couldn't get any words out. Tears were running down my face. I tried to hug her, but she had me at arm's length, checking for injuries to ensure I had no blood or anything on me. I tried pushing her off, but she grabbed me harder and asked again, saying the words slower and louder this time.

"What. Is. Wrong. Are you hurt?"

She finally let me go. All I could do was reach down to where I had dropped the paper and hand it to her. She stared at it for a few seconds, then leaned back off her knees and sat cross-legged with confusion on her face. She looked back up at me. "Okay, what am I looking at? This looks like your birth certificate."

I nodded. "It is. Look at the names on it," I said through my tears.

She took another look, and I knew the moment she saw it. Her mouth dropped open and she covered it with her hand.

"What the...Why the hell is your name different?" Her brows went up in surprise. When she looked back at me, I just shrugged. "Did you know you were born with a different last name?" Now that she was with me and I had calmed slightly, I could finally speak more than a few words.

"Do you think I'd be freaking out like this, giving myself a panic attack, if I did?" I rolled my eyes at her.

I reached into the box where I found the birth certificate. The next thing I pulled out was a certificate of the name change for me, changing my last name from Maturo to Miller. After I finished gawking at it, I handed it to Brielle.

"What am I going to do? What does this mean?" I hung my head.

She put her hands on my cheeks and glared at me with her green eyes.

"We're going to go confront them," she said calmly. "We will figure this out. I'm not leaving your side until we get answers. There has to be an explanation for this."

I found what I was initially looking for, and then Brie helped me grab all the papers in the box I found in case they could help us figure this out. I frantically searched the entire attic for clues about what this could mean, but I found nothing.

There were a few other things, like pictures from the day I was born, a little bracelet they put on my ankle, and a damn picture of me in a god-awful dress at my parents' wedding. I stopped and stared at a picture of my dad holding me in the hospital; he was crying. Looking at this only made me more confused. How could he be there the day I was born but not be on the birth certificate?

My parents and I have always had open lines of communication between us. From a young age I knew that no matter my situation, where I was or how I got there, I could call my parents for help with no questions asked. God knows I've used and abused that. You could say their parenting style helped me grow the confidence I have today. I never questioned being able to trust them, but this paper...this paper could change everything.

Authors Note

Thank YOU!

You are what makes this journey so incredible. Thank you for taking the chance on an indie author like me. I hope you know you are an integral part of not only my journey but every author out there. Writing these books has changed my life. I hope one day something I write will inspire or change one of yours.

With love,

Danielle Lynn